Advance praise for *Sudden Death Overtime*

"... *A fascinating international legal thriller* ... *penetrating the world of a foreign legal system and fashioning a tale that only a legal expert could tell.*"

— Gary Taylor
   Pulitzer Prize Nominee Journalist
   Author of true-crime bestseller *Luggage by Kroger*

"Sudden Death Overtime ... *demonstrates that a great lawyer is a skilled storyteller. David Crump makes it real, through lessons learned in the school of hard knocks—which may be the best law school in the country.*"

— Lynne Liberato
   Past President, State Bar of Texas

"*David Crump* ... *knows his courtroom procedure and trial tactics. I like reading his legal fiction, which has the authentic ring of truth, but [in his job as a law professor] he would scare the hell out of me in class.*"

— Michael A. Olivas
   Professor of Law and Former President,
   American Association of Law Schools

"*David Crump describes the reality of a trial better than anyone! After 30 years as a trial lawyer and 14 years as a trial judge, I have had the same experiences.*"

— R. Terence Ney
   Past President, Virginia Bar Association

SUDDEN
DEATH
OVERTIME

SUDDEN DEATH OVERTIME

A Courtroom Novel

David Crump

QP BOOKS
New Orleans, Louisiana

Published in 2015 by QP Books, an imprint of Quid Pro Books.

ISBN 978-1-61027-303-9 (paperback)
ISBN 978-1-61027-309-1 (ebook)

QP BOOKS
Quid Pro, LLC
5860 Citrus Blvd., suite D-101
New Orleans, Louisiana 70123
www.qpbooks.com

qp

Cataloging-in-Publication Data

Crump, David.
    Sudden death overtime : a courtroom novel / David Crump.
        p. cm.
    ISBN 978-1-61027-303-9 (pbk.)
  1. Trials—United States—Fiction. 2. Law Firms—United States—Fiction. I. Title.

PS3549.R3842C2 2015

831' .22.4—dc21
2015342197
CIP

Also by David Crump, in the
Robert Herrick Courtroom Series

Conflict of Interest

The Holding Company

Murder in Sugar Land

The Target Defendant

Author's Preface

Fiction about lawyers usually distorts. It almost never shows the law the way it is. Most writers seem to think that actual legal procedures are too complicated for their readers to follow, and the lawyers they write about don't do what real lawyers do. In a democracy, that's bad, because most people get most of their exposure to the law through fiction.

Well, the story in this book is different. It's based on the American system of justice, accurately described. In a good novel, the plot grows out of the characters, and in this one, it grows out of the character of American justice—with all of its conflicts, contradictions, and flaws.

But real lawsuits are built on tedious work, and nobody wants a tedious story. A good novel about lawyers needs a certain amount of what writers call "dramatic compression." There has to be more action and less work than would really make up a lawsuit, and this story is no exception.

Even so, this is a novel that shows the law accurately. The critics say that my books describe courtrooms the way they really are. And just to be sure, at the end, I've added a Postscript that will tell you what is true and what is fiction.

. . . But now, it's time to move on. To get into our story. Imagine that you're a new associate at the law firm of Robert Herrick and Associates. You'll be representing ordinary folks who've been injured by huge businesses, or by government, or by other big evildoers. And if you turn the page, you'll see what you're up against.

SUDDEN
DEATH
OVERTIME

1

Three clumsy figures spilled out of an eighteen-wheeled truck. All of them were dressed strangely, in Islamic-style burqas. Women's clothing, all black, and covering their whole bodies, with only their eyes showing. They opened the back gates of the trailer and strained to pull out a large object, which was laced with folded ropes.

Their vehicle was parked on Mangum Road near 18th Street, just outside Delmar Stadium. The high school football game had progressed to sudden death overtime, and even from out here, the crowd noise boomed. Working fast, they positioned the balloon. Then, these three men in women's clothes ignited the torch that would fill the balloon's canopy.

"Careful," said the tall man, whose name was al Ibrahim. "Watch out for that stuff in the basket, because we don't want to martyr ourselves. That is . . . not now, at least!" He laughed.

"There it goes!" exulted the bigger of the two followers, who was called Mansouri. The balloon staggered, carrying its heavy cargo. It stood upright, then hesitated, and finally lifted. "Praise Allah!"

"Praise Allah," repeated Hamadi, the third man in black. "Allah, who always is merciful!"

"Let's lower the speed a little," al Ibrahim ordered. Hamadi dialed numbers on an electronic remote. The balloon steadied, and its rise slowed.

The three disguised men got back into the truck.

"Drive normally," the tall man told Mansouri. "Don't attract attention." Al Ibrahim was a towering figure, six feet seven inches tall, and it was obvious that he was the boss. His face was angular, his hair black, and his eyes dark, signaling his middle eastern lineage.

Mansouri drove the big trailer to the far side of the stadium. There, on 18th Street, the three black figures abandoned the stolen vehicle. Al Ibrahim looked up at the balloon, which was sailing majestically toward the stadium.

"Hamadi, give me the controls."

Ibrahim maneuvered the balloon up a hundred more feet, then kept its altitude steady, as he guided it toward the center of the stadium. "Let's hope the assembled multitude will think it's just part of the show."

"No difference, really, if they don't," Mansouri said. "There's nothing they can do anyway. A little panic will help."

"There'll be panic enough when that explosive hits the oxygen," the tall man answered. "And now, we need to get out of here."

They looked like three women in black burqas scurrying awkwardly down 18th Street. They headed toward their pickup point. Ibrahim continued maneuvering the balloon toward the middle of the stadium. And then, he began lowering it inside.

* * *

A thousand miles away in northern Virginia, two men sat in front of a computer inside the CIA building. The traditional eagle-shield-and-star seal of the CIA faced them.

"Look at this," said the man directly in front of the monitor, as he changed the screen. "Here's the voice of that tall guy, al Ibrahim, talking about . . . giving 'presents' to the neighborhood."

"Right." The second man nodded. "It's got to be code."

"Let's see what else we get from the ninth floor in Maryland. That is, what we get from the CIA brass. But we need surveillance on this six-foot-seven guy, this Ibrahim, soon as possible."

"There's something in the conversation that looks like a date. Or something. Maybe it's the date when they intend to carry out their plan."

"But it's not the kind of code we can break. We can recognize the words as improbable in a real message, and that tells us it's code, but that's as far as we can go."

"Who is this guy?"

"Al Ibrahim? Born in Pittsburgh. His parents came here from Pakistan, and they went there originally from Kuwait. He bounced back to the old country several times a year, from when he was a baby. Went to school there, too. Lived there as a grownup. Fluent in Arabic and Pashto as well as English. At the University of Pennsylvania, he was a standout basketball player. Really tall, even if he was a little bit clumsy. Sharp nose and face, the perfect middle eastern stereotype, and he's definitely gotten radicalized."

"Sounds like he could be the archangel of darkness."

"Yes. He's an electronics wizard, probably knows something about bombs. He's an angry, angry type, and always impatient. Ran a blog for a while that denounced America even during the time he lived here. Then he gave up writing. Maybe he quit so he could go underground and carry out the plans he's making now."

"I don't like it. We should have been watching this Ibrahim, already. He's a whacko bird, and he scares me."

"The listening post in Pennsylvania had Ibrahim located for a long time. They were processing it in Maryland, at the CIA ninth floor. Took forever to get their warrant to listen to him in the United States. There are several other guys he's talking to, around him. Especially this other raghead named Hamadi."

"I just don't want something to happen and find out we're too late to do anything about it," the second man said.

The first man nodded. "That would be just plain agonizing."

* * *

"Almost there," said al Ibrahim, the tall man. He was the most disciplined of the three, but now he was getting excited too.

"What's 'butadiene'? And whatever it is, why are we using it inside this balloon?" Hamadi asked.

"BU-ta-DI-een," Ibrahim said, correcting his pronunciation.

"And so, what's BU-ta-DI-een?"

"When the balloon is in place, we can break the container open, using the remote. And we've got butadiene cylinders inside, and we'll open those, too. And a detonator, with sparks. Butadiene is a petroleum product, a carbon compound. It's like some of the hydrocarbons in gasoline, but it's tied up tighter than most of those chemicals, and it can let loose in a bigger way."

"So why's butadiene inside the balloon, instead of some other real cool explosive?"

"Whenever pure butadiene reacts with oxygen in the air, it explodes and burns, especially with a spark. But it doesn't just explode in a simple way. It's spectacular. In these canisters, it will set off all kinds of secondary bursts, like fireworks, over several long minutes. It's a highly exothermic reaction, meaning it produces a huge amount of heat. There will be video cameras all over that stadium, and our butadiene will put on a show that people can see later, everywhere. And marvel at. On television."

The tall man in the black burqa guided the balloon into the stadium. "Almost ready to drop it."

* * *

Inside the stadium, just across the walls from where the three terrorists were, a lawyer named Robert Herrick turned to his wife. "I feel like I'm playing hooky here, watching Robert Junior play high school football. I ought to be working on that contract case where I've got to question the main witness in a couple of days."

Robert Herrick had built a law firm that represented injured plaintiffs and small businesses, usually against huge corporations. He was known as "the lawyer for the little guy." He had made his reputation by putting in more hours on his cases than anyone else, and by having the ability to make his time successful. It was unusual for him to be away from the office in the late afternoon, but here he was, watching a football game. And having a good time, but feeling guilty about it.

"No. It's about time you did something besides work," answered Maria Melendes. "It's about time you spent some quality time with me, your wife." Maria was an assistant district attorney, and she had a heavy-duty job too, but she was usually the one who decided when the two of them would get away for some sort of leisure activity.

"I'm in an uphill battle on that contract case," he said. She just shook her head.

He turned to watch the football game. Then: "O-o-o-o-f. Look at that. The other team's offense ran it right up the middle against us, behind that double team they set up with their center and guard. And they've gained fifteen yards on this play."

"They've been doing that the whole game, and our guys can't stop it. But listen, Robert. You'll do fine on that contract case, the way you always do."

It probably would turn out to be true. With the shock of black hair that came over his forehead and his bright blue eyes, and with his six-foot-two-inch height, Robert Herrick always appealed to the women jurors. The men on the jury were impressed when he could give a hard-hitting argument without any notes at the end of the trial—and when he was able to concede the weak points in his case, without showing any weakness. Other lawyers called him "The Baby-Faced Assassin" for his youthful good looks, together with his ability to beat them in trial. A newspaper reporter had published a story quoting a woman juror who admiringly said, "Mr. Herrick sure does have pretty teeth," and people still teased him about it.

After graduating from college at Harvard and from law school at the University of Houston, Robert had turned down all the high salaries offered by big law firms, because he wanted to go it alone. Today, his firm was called Robert Herrick and Associates, and the big firm lawyers treated him with respect when they paid millions to his clients in settlements. His partners always told him he did too much pro bono work and didn't watch the finances enough, but he had built an immensely profitable firm in spite of that. He did it not only by raw ability but also with hard work: the kind of work he knew he needed to do on the contract case he was thinking about, now.

"So, here we are, watching a football game," said his wife. Maria Melendes was a red-headed Cuban whose father, the Director-General of the largest hospital in Havana, had gotten crosswise of Fidel Castro and ended up in prison. As soon as he could bribe his way to freedom, Papa Melendes had gotten his family out of Cuba on a contraption not much more sophisticated than connected inner tubes. And that was how Maria, while still a child, had come to southern Florida.

She laughed at Robert. "Here we are," she said again, "and you might as well have a good time."

Maria had an unusual job. At the district attorney's office, she held the position that everyone referred to as "the DA's official killer." When a convict got the death sentence, it was Maria's responsibility to follow the case, through repetitive loops of appeals and habeas corpus petitions, to the end. Sometimes it was her job to agree with a defense attorney to set a convict's sentence aside. To let the death penalty go, against the findings of a jury. And sometimes she had to oppose creative technical arguments in cases about stomach-churning murders. It was a job that often required uncomfortable judgments in circumstances that didn't allow time for deep consideration. Maria was a paradox: she loved stuffed animals, she wore feminine dresses, and she traveled to the Walls Unit of the Texas prison system to do her job.

Robert stared at her for the hundredth time today. Maria was beautiful, with pale Hispanic skin, dark eyes, and hair in copper-colored ringlets. And he felt lucky, once again, to have her.

"Okay. Let's have a good time." He nodded. "But did we have to come to a game where Robert Junior's team, the Lamar High School team, is playing North Shore High School? North Shore is whupping up on us now, and here they are, about to score and win in overtime. Can't we go to a game where we can see Robbie's team win?"

"I can't help it. This is the one game that's on a day when both of us can come." She paused. "Hey!" She pointed upward at a gray falling object: tall, with ropes, and round at the top. "What's that?"

Robert had spent four years in the army, a lot of it in combat. "It's probably . . . harmless. Looks like a weather balloon. But it's pretty far away from where it's supposed to be."

The balloon swayed in the wind. A thousand or so people inside the stadium stared at it, and so did three terrorists outside.

"It's coming down." Maria's eyes narrowed. "It looks like it's about to land behind the end zone. Those people better get out of the way."

"I don't think they can! It's just plain dropping, now. Too fast."

Suddenly the earth and sky exploded near the north end zone. The orange fireball ranged outward to the twenty-yard line and swallowed the first tier of seats, then the second, so fast that its expansion barely could be distinguished. It was brighter than daylight, as bright as a splinter ripped out of the sun. The noise was enormous, and everyone in the stadium was shouting.

But the awesome power and the burning of the deaths of so many people was not all of the horror. Seconds later, there was a ripple. And a secondary fireball. Then another, pinwheeling to the opposite side of the holocaust. Then another, drifting toward the north side seats. Then another, then another.

The people who saw it but didn't die were frozen in place. They could only stand and gape at the spinning balls of orange.

* * *

Outside the stadium, three black figures watched the rolling, fiery explosions light up the sky. They were now nestled in a nondescript Ford van, stolen for the occasion and driven by a fourth black-dressed man, who had just picked them up. They still heard and saw remnants of the sound and light. They heard the crowd noise: unnatural, supernatural, a wailing, ranging, horrifying sound.

The three terrorists drove carefully to the northwest while pulling off their costumes. Their burqas had served to disguise them, but disguises were no longer needed.

"Praise Allah!" said Mansouri.

"Praise Allah! echoed Hamadi, the youngster of the three. "Allah the magnificent; Allah the majestic. Allah, who always is merciful."

"Praise Allah. It is done." Ibrahim's voice was matter-of-fact.

Then, incongruously, the tall man laughed. "It's kind of like what football teams call 'sudden death overtime.' But it sure wasn't the kind of sudden death overtime that those devil infidels were expecting."

2

Mr. President, it's going to be rough." The pilot's voice spread through Air Force One. "Because of that terrorist incident, we're going to climb to 30,000 feet in about four minutes. There's gonna be a lot of bumps."

"That's all right, Bob. After that stadium explosion, who knows what kinds of crazy people are out there? Or what kind of hand-held missiles they have? Let's get up there high. And fast."

The President sat at a polished oak conference table amidships of the aircraft. The rest of the table was empty except for his Chief of Staff. "I've got to replace the cream leather on these chairs," he said under his breath, for the hundredth time. He didn't like pastels, as the Chief of Staff knew.

The President's own most striking feature was a way-too-big nose that stretched under brown eyes so dark that they looked almost black. Eyes that drilled into a person who faced him so deeply that anyone talking to him felt that he had the President's full, sole attention. It was a helpful attribute in a politician, because everyone he talked to felt hugely important. The President also had a facility for seeming upbeat even in adverse circumstances, and he seemed that way even now.

The President turned back to the secure telephone. "So, Mr. Vice President, you're saying that it was three *women* who put that balloon bomb into the stadium? And three women have you and me both running way from the world under orders from the Secret Service?"

"Not necessarily three women, no." The Vice President was already in the air, flying to a different unannounced destination, and his voice came through the same smooth sound system as the pilot's. "All we know was that they were dressed like women. Maybe three women. . . ."

"Or . . . maybe. . . ."

". . . Or maybe, they were really three men, but dressed as women. The spooks at CIA haven't figured it out yet."

"Why would three men dress up like that?" The President's big nose flared in disbelief.

"They might have thought people who saw them wouldn't interfere. Or that it would generate more publicity. Or they might even have thought it would have us guessing about who they were. Not only would we not know which individuals they were, but we wouldn't even know whether they were men or women."

"I guess it worked." The big nose exhaled.

"Well . . . that's right. They knew what they were doing. We don't."

"Bob, speaking of knowing what we're doing, do you know where we're going?" the President asked the pilot.

"Just found out from the Secret Service guys. We're flying to Schilling Air Force Base, which is in Salina, Kansas. By the way, we're the only ones flying this kind of equipment. Every commercial flight in the country is grounded, of course."

"Great. A national crisis, and I'll be in the middle of nowhere."

"Schilling AFB was used during the Cold War by the Strategic Air Command," said the pilot. "Great big B-52 bombers, so there's room to land Air Force One."

The pilot paused. Then: "Schilling was mostly decommissioned by the Air Force. But it's still maintained to be used by the President in an emergency, for exactly what we're going to use it for."

"You mean, it's for hiding the President from an unidentified national threat," said the President ruefully. "Such as a terrorist action, when we don't know where they're going to strike next."

"Yes, sir. In the middle of nowhere, as you correctly described it, so you're away from where the bad guys might be going."

The landing gear went up, and the aircraft pointed toward the clouds at an unnatural angle, with unaccustomed speed.

* * *

Meanwhile, a few miles east of the burned stadium, Robert Herrick and Maria Melendes sat in their living room in their home in River Oaks, both wearing unseeing stares that focused upon an imaginary distance. The television set was on, but no one was watching.

"A day after sitting that stadium, and seeing all of those poor people . . ." Robert started to say.

"I know. I can't get that scene, that horror, out of my mind either."

The sunlight drifted in through plantation shutters to brighten the room. The hardwood floors gleamed here, partly covered by an enormous carpet in a Tabriz pattern, with multicolored diamond shapes. The caramel leather couches were nearly as shiny as the floors, and the walls were a medium sandstone color. Boxer, as a dachshund, knew that he had the right to park himself anywhere, and so he curled next to Robert on the smaller couch. The little dog was happily unaware of the thoughts that troubled his humans.

"Everything's shut down," Robert said. "Everywhere. Everything."

"Yes. The Galleria is shut down. Every store in every strip mall. Every airport. Every train station. Every university . . . ."

"The refineries along the ship channel can't shut down. Something about how they have to keep flowing or they'll get damaged internally. So the Governor has the National Guard watching every few feet."

He looked at her. "What a huge criminal case this will be. That's the only way we'll ever know what happened."

Maria answered with the pragmatism of an assistant DA. "But who's going to be the defendants? Nobody has any idea."

She looked at the ceiling. "You know what I was thinking? I was thinking, what a huge civil case this will be. For wrongful death. And that's how we'll know what happened."

Now it was his turn to shake his head. "But who can anyone sue in the civil courts? Nobody has any idea who did this. And when they're caught, they'll just be individual terrorists, who can't pay a judgment against them."

Suddenly, Maria pointed at the television. "Look at that."

The television screen showed images of the football stadium, with the north end charred and blackened. A background voice spoke. " . . . The death toll has risen to over one hundred. And experts tell us it almost certainly will go still higher. The number of injured is unknown, because they were taken to so many hospitals."

Robert stared at the screen. When he finally spoke, it was as if he were a distance away.

"You know, Maria, because of what we saw in that stadium . . . , and it was so close . . . , I've started . . . to have . . . dreams, again. Bad . . . dreams. About the worst of what happened back then . . . , dreams about when I was in the army. Dreams about having to lead search-and-destroy missions, and getting ambushed, and stuff. I'm back in combat again. It comes on without warning, and I dream I'm still in the War, and then . . . everything dissolves . . . into a huge orange fireball, like the one we saw at the football game, . . . and suddenly, the scene changes in my dream, and instead of the War, I'm in Delmar Stadium. I see that explosion in the stadium with hundreds of . . . burning people."

"Oh, Baby, I'm . . . ."

"I feel such a close kinship to those people."

"Me, too. And . . . I have a feeling we're all going to see that scene over and over again," Maria answered unhappily.

* * *

Robert had the dream again that night, the dream he dreaded. He was back in the War, back decades ago. Miserably, the men in his company walked single file through skin-ripping jungle, watching first for leeches and second for the enemy. Suddenly they fell into a firefight that started as an ambush and ended in an explosion. But then, the explosion changed, like the changing of a scene in a movie, the way that stories in a dream can change. And now, in this dream, the nonstop, deafening chatter of automatic rifle fire blossomed into a growing wall of fire that spread and spread and spread; and next, the explosion morphed into a holocaust under a balloon in a stadium, and the growing orange fire landed on hundreds of burning, screaming people who had been watching a football game.

When Robert suddenly woke and found himself groggy and covered with sweat, the clock told him it was past time to rejoin a semblance of normal life. To re-enter the world of the living.

Moving like an automaton, he dressed, ate a practically nonexistent breakfast because he wasn't hungry, drank coffee, and found himself finally at his office.

* * *

"We've got to get ready for this deposition we're going to have this afternoon, in our contract case," Robert said to Tom Kennedy, his favorite partner. The one he worked with most often and talked with the way Sherlock Holmes talked to Dr. Watson. "I can tell you, Tom, I don't feel up to doing anything, after that . . . that football game." He almost said, "After that dream."

"Of course." Tom nodded. "But Robert, what's all that stuff spread out on your desk? I'm just curious."

Robert's desk was a huge block of mahogany, facing three desk chairs. Tom sat in one of them, holding a big Redrope file pocket. Around them, the sunlight shimmered on a beautiful Oriental carpet—a carpet interlocked with crescents, circles, squares and diamonds in every color. Beneath the windows and beside the carpet, a hundred geraniums bloomed in red, pink, and white. The walls were adorned with paintings by Mondrian, Picasso, and Wyeth. The Law Offices of Robert Herrick had been phenomenally successful, with three floors of associates, now; and in spite of Robert's cautionary attitude toward finances, decorators finally had prevailed upon the boss to spend some of what he earned on his surroundings.

The law firm's office was at the top of the Chase Bank Tower. Tallest building in town. Beside Robert's desk, past the tall windows, the rest of downtown stretched to the south in brown, white, and gray spires. Far below, cars struggled like bugs to crawl across the city streets and onto the tiny, faraway spaghetti bowl of freeways. Off to the west, the green banks of Buffalo Bayou blended into Memorial Park and disappeared into the horizon.

"So, what are all those papers on the desk?" Tom asked. "They're not about our contract case today."

Robert looked sheepish, like a little boy who hadn't gone to bed and had been caught by his parents. "Well, Tom . . . , I asked the investigators to get me three or four autopsy reports from the Delmar Stadium explosion."

"What?"

"Well, I . . . feel a bond with these people. Because I was there at the stadium when it happened. I know . . . I know, it's . . . probably foolish, but I needed to find out what happened to them. I mean, these are innocent victims who are identifiable only by dental records, the people in the middle of the holocaust. I feel awful for them. I know, Tom, you think I worry too much about people we don't know, but I want to know this. I need to find out how these people died."

He reached toward the picture of Patricia Herrick on his desk. Patricia had passed away from ovarian cancer six years ago, but before that, she had been Robert's wife of seventeen years. Her photograph sat next to Maria's, now.

Recently, he noticed that he had formed an odd new habit. In uneasy situations, he would touch the picture of Patricia, in its heavy gold frame. For steadiness, perhaps. . . .

"Robert," Tom said sternly, "we have a deposition this afternoon in a completely different case. You have to question the main witness on the other side."

"I know. But I'm through. I've finished reading these autopsy reports. You and I know how to read an autopsy report, and it doesn't freak us out, because we've had wrongful death cases where autopsies were part of the proof. It bothers me here, because I saw it, but not so that I'll be affected in this other case. Our contract case, today."

"Well, I guess that's just . . . you, Robert Herrick. It's what you would do. At least, Robert, you can say that your clients always love you. You feel their cases. They know their damages aren't just technical stuff, to you. You feel the way they do."

"Yes. And Tom, you're always telling me to be more analytical. And you want us to take on more cases where we represent banks and insurance companies. The kinds of clients who can pay big fees up front. And you're probably right."

Tom Kennedy was wearing his trademark: a brown suit, a tan button-down shirt, and a solid brown tie. It was well known that he had a closet full of brown suits in glen plaids, herringbones, houndstooths, and every other pattern. His clothes signaled that he was a busy man, too busy to select what to wear every day. Even his hair and eyes were shades of brown. At six feet one, he was almost as tall as Robert, but heavier. He had played football for the University of Tulsa, as a tight end, before going to law school.

"So." Tom spoke, now. "What do the autopsy results say?"

"These people in the stadium died of asphyxiation and cardiac arrest. I was surprised by that, asphyxiation and cardiac arrest."

"Maybe you shouldn't have been surprised. I imagine their lungs were desiccated and internally burned."

"Yes. I thought maybe they died quickly. That's what we always hope. But an autopsy report never says anything about that, or usually it doesn't. Even though lawyers need to know about the length of a person's death, or whether they felt pain, and most people want to know it. Did my brother/sister/wife/husband suffer? It's the . . . hardest question, and the medical examiners don't tell us."

"Usually, the autopsy is more violent than the death itself. An autopsy is awful. But not in this explosion. This explosion was more awful than most deaths."

"Tom, have you seen an autopsy? Because yes, they're violent."

"Not all the way through. I was there when the doc made what they call 'the usual Y-shaped incision' that starts at the abdomen, and I was struggling not to lose my breakfast when he chopped out the organs and weighed them. Then, it was time to 'reflect the head.' I didn't know what that meant, to 'reflect' the head, so the doc explained it. He was going to take this little high-speed saw and cut all around the skull and remove the cap, then the brain. And that was when I was out of there."

"Unpleasant, right? That's what an autopsy is like. But okay, enough of this. Let's get ready to question the witness this afternoon. Let's get ready for today's deposition."

Suddenly Tom realized that he was craning his neck to see around a pile of file folders on the desk. All the files came from a single pro bono case. It was a case of age discrimination against an oilfield pipe manufacturer, and Robert had insisted on taking it as a pro bono case because he thought what the company had done was terribly wrong, even though the case was almost impossible to prove and the damages were smaller than a reasonable fee would have been.

"That's Robert Herrick," Tom said under his breath.

"Let me go see Janice and get her outline of suggested questions for today," Robert said finally. "That's the first step."

* * *

"Hi, kids!" Robert said as he entered Janice's office, speaking to the twins in their playpen. The floor was littered with blocks, big plastic letters, and shapes pulled from a jigsaw map of the United States.

"Hi, Uncle Robert," the twins answered, together.

"How are they doing? They learning algebra and calculus about now?"

Janice laughed. "Not quite. But hey, James and John! Can you count, guys?"

"Woone . . . , Twooo . . . , Sreeee!" said the boys proudly.

"That's great! Keep up the good work, guys."

"Here's an outline for the deposition today, Robert." Janice smiled. "It's going to be a tough case. I expect this defendant to evade every question, so be ready to ask and re-ask."

"I know. I know. I'd better get with Tom and go over this outline in detail. Thanks."

"Hey, Robert. I'm the one who has to say Thanks—to you. Because of these boys, I can't go and fight in the courtroom these days. And it's not every law firm that would find me a way to have these two monsters and all of their toys in a partner's office."

"Well, Janice, it's in my own interest. You're a valuable member of this law firm. You've been there, in trial, even though these little guys won't let you do that now, and you know what I need. And I'm glad to have you."

He headed for his own office, as he saw Janice with a big smile and the two boys starting to push each other around inside their playpen.

3

Two hours later, after Tom had pronounced Robert ready to question this afternoon's witness, they still sat at the mahogany desk, above the shining Oriental carpet. But now, there were three of them. Their client had joined them, sitting next to Tom in one of the desk chairs. The client wore an inexpensive gray suit with an ornate yellow tie. His complexion was a medium tan color, under a receding gray hairline.

Outside the huge windows, the day was a beautiful china blue, with puffy clouds. The green grass surrounding Buffalo Bayou was unnaturally bright, with the sun at the top of the sky. At least temporarily, Robert had put the Delmar Stadium explosion out of his mind.

"You'll be there during this deposition," he said to Ashok Chadha, his client. "And I want you to know what's going to happen."

The client, then, asked the obvious question. "Robert, what is a . . . 'deposition'? You said you're going to 'take a deposition.' I've heard that word now a dozen times and I still don't understand what a deposition is." The man's lilting, singsong speech marked him as a native of India.

Robert smiled. "Don't worry, Mr. Chadha. I mean, Ashok, because you asked me to call you Ashok. Most people would ask the same question. A 'deposition' just means that we ask witnesses questions. Witnesses from the other side. In this case, it's Markham Shockley that we're going to question. You know, the same Markham Shockley who is president of Shockley Industries, which is the company we've sued on your behalf."

"It's just asking them questions?" Ashok Chadha looked like he thought it would be easier just to call Markham Shockley on the telephone, and to ask the questions that way.

"Well, yes, but there are Rules for this kind of questioning, under the law. The witness—this guy, Markham Shockley—has to answer the questions. We've summoned him here by using what's called a 'deposition

14

notice,' and that makes him have to be here. He will answer under oath, subject to the penalty for perjury. A court reporter will swear him in and take down my questions and his answers."

"Okay." Ashok Chadha understood only halfway.

"And that's why Tom and I are here today. With you. To get ready to ask the best questions possible. Oh, and I should add this. Markham Shockley's lawyer—the lawyer for Shockley Industries—will be there too."

"Oh." Ashok looked vaguely unenthusiastic about that.

"And that's one of the things we want to tell you about. The other lawyer is named Jimmy Coleman. He's been on the other side from our firm in a lot of cases. When he's on the other side, we always know it's going to be difficult. . . . Or . . . well, how would you put it, Tom, about Jimmy Coleman?"

Tom's answer was immediate. "Jimmy Coleman's a jerk."

Ashok Chadha looked unhappy at that, probably because he knew he was going to be deposed later, himself, by this jerk on the other side. The tables would turn, and the jerk was going to act like a jerk, by making poor old Ashok answer mean questions.

Robert intervened. "I wouldn't put it that way, exactly." He had long since figured out that it doesn't pay for your client to think the opposing lawyer is a sleazebag. The time comes, in most lawsuits, when you have to seek the other lawyer's agreement to a postponement or a substitution of witnesses. Or, you have to give something up to get something, in settlement negotiations.

"I think what Tom is saying," Robert went on, "is that Jimmy Coleman is going to make us work hard. We'll have to do a lot of things by complicated procedures, by the book. Procedures that would be done more smoothly with most other lawyers, through informal agreements. Just by being polite, with professional courtesy, but that's hard to do with Jimmy Coleman. And with Jimmy, we'll have to slow down and do everything step by step."

"And it will cost me more." Ashok was miserable, now. "And I'll have to spend more of my blood, more of my life, on this lawsuit. Instead of my business. Or my family."

Robert laughed, sympathetically, and reached out a hand toward his client. "Possibly. But not necessarily. We're doing our best to prevent that."

In fact, he and Tom had talked about Jimmy Coleman while preparing. And they had discussed just this morning the costs to clients of litigation, including what was sometimes the greatest cost: the loss imposed by the time and worry taken from a client's personal life.

* * *

Jimmy Coleman was the head of litigation at the mega-firm of Booker and Bayne. He appeared for this deposition with his usual unnecessary accompaniment: a posse of four other Booker and Bayne lawyers, costing their client multiple thousands of dollars per hour, even though none of them would say anything all day long. Jimmy wore a charcoal suit of shantung silk, almost like dark silver, with a gold tie, a gold-and-white striped shirt, and an enormous gold tie clip. His white hair was tinged with enough brown to color it beige, and his teeth were dirty when he smiled, probably because of the cigar he chewed constantly. He was short, about five feet seven or eight, but magnetic.

Before he sat at the conference table, Jimmy cleared his throat for a long moment and spoke in his rasping, grating voice. "Herrick, you got a piece of shit lawsuit here. I can't believe you've filed this dog case at the courthouse. Embarrassing. Anyway, go ahead and take this deposition, even if it's not going to get anyone anywhere."

Jimmy waved his arms before going on. "So anyway, Herrick, how long you think you gonna take with my client? I got important stuff back at the office."

Robert was used to this. "If the witness answers directly, maybe three hours. Four at the most. If this witness is evasive, then it may take the full six hours that the rules allow."

From experience, Robert knew the advice Jimmy was sure to have given to his client, Markham Shockley. "Answer the question with as little information as you can. Don't help the other side. As often as possible, say that you don't understand the question. Make that lawyer work. Make him pry it out of you."

"We won't be staying here for any six hours. Get it done, Herrick." Jimmy's voice sounded like gears grinding deep inside a rusty machine. "This lawsuit of yours is as dumb as dirt, Herrick, and if you spread all that dirt out, it would cover more'n an acre."

Robert smiled pleasantly. "Let's get started. We've got a lot of wood to chop."

"If frivolous claims were electricity," Jimmy went on tirelessly, "this lawsuit would be a powerhouse."

The Booker and Bayne associates all giggled at that.

* * *

An hour later, after dozens of evasive answers, Robert finally was beginning to ask Markham Shockley about the contract that was the basis of this lawsuit. "And now, Mr. Shockley, do you recognize this document, Exhibit 12, as the contract that you signed?"

"I don't understand the question." The witness crinkled his eyes in a smile, which was probably intended to signal how everlastingly clever he was in giving this unhelpful answer.

"This Exhibit 12 has been produced from your files." Robert's voice was pleasant. "Do you recognize your signature at the bottom of the next-to-last page, right here?"

"It looks like it, but this is just a photocopy, and I can't be sure."

"O-o-o-kay, Markham Shockley." Robert smiled too. "Now, Markham Shockley, there came a time when your company did not pay Ashok Chadha's company the amount of money due under this contract. Please tell me all of the reasons you claim you didn't pay the contract. Why didn't you pay, according to you?"

"I don't understand the question."

"Why didn't Shockley Industries pay the contract price of twelve million dollars to Mr. Chadha?"

"We didn't owe anything to Mr. Chadha, not ever. That is, not to him personally. Not to Mr. Chadha. It was to his company." Clever. Again, a smile. Again, no help with the answer.

Still, Robert was patient. But persistent. And again, he smiled too. "Why didn't Shockley Industries pay the contract price of twelve million dollars to Mr. Chadha's company? To the Astin Corporation, which is Mr. Chadha's company?"

"Because the goods that Astin Corporation delivered were nonconforming."

This vague answer told nobody anything, either, because the claim that "the goods were nonconforming" was already in the suit papers in several places. In an even voice, Robert asked the follow-up question that the witness's response, or rather non-response, seemed to require.

"In what way were the goods nonconforming?"

"We were never able to get them to work right."

After dozens of other follow-up questions, Robert assembled the information that should have been forthcoming much earlier. Markham Shockley's basic story, stripped of all its evasions, was that the programmed electronics delivered by Astin Corporation required some other minor programming to perform one of the minor functions that Shockley claimed were needed.

Now, Robert asked, pleasantly: "Did you ever contact Mr. Chadha or anyone at Astin to ask for assistance in performing this 'other minor programming'?"

"No. We had lost all confidence in them by then. We just didn't trust Astin." And again, the witness smiled. Forever clever.

After five hours of this kind of questioning and these kinds of answers, Robert said: "That's all the questions I have." And he allowed himself to smile again. Mainly, because it was over. He glanced at the video camera that pointed at the witness. The jury would get an earful of how evasive Markham Shockley was, if this case went to trial. And how untruthful he was.

As he gathered his papers into his briefcase to leave, Jimmy Coleman was more deferential than he had been when he entered the conference room. There suddenly was a nicer Jimmy Coleman in the room.

Jimmy turned at the door. "Robert, we'd still like to settle this case. I'll confer with my people and call you."

"Thank you, Jimmy. I told you earlier that I was authorized to accept ten million to settle this one. Not because of the merits of the suit, but just to get it settled for my client's sake. I'll confer with my people and see whether that amount is still acceptable after hearing from this . . . this . . . *witness*." Involuntarily, Robert lowered his voice before completing the sentence, because everyone in the room knew that Markham Shockley had been a terrible witness. Not just because he had lengthened the deposition, but for himself. He had destroyed his own credibility. And he had buried any chance of defending his position.

Jimmy waddled out, followed by four other Booker and Bayne lawyers, all wearing black suits and near-identical ties.

* * *

That evening, the news anchor frowned as she looked into the television camera. "Unfortunately, my friends, we must bring you this breaking story. We all remember the terrorist explosion in Delmar Stadium. Today, a militant group called ALAP—which, we are told, stands for 'Al Likchah in the Arabian Peninsula'—has claimed responsibility for the explosion. This shadowy group called 'Al Likchah,' which means '*Brotherly Love in the Arabian Peninsula*,' is located in the troubled, anarchistic nation of Yemen, south of Saudi Arabia."

The anchor looked away for a second, with disgust. Then she read in a clear voice: "The statement by ALAP—by Al Likchah in the Arabian Peninsula—starts by saying, quote, 'Our heroic act at Delmar Stadium in America was done in retaliation for drone strikes, carried out by the United States against our leaders in Yemen. After all, the Holy Scripture tells us to *"Fight in the way of Allah."* Quran 2:190.'

"And the statement by Al Likchah goes on to say, 'This explosion is only the beginning, so guard yourselves, American infidels. Soon, you will suffocate under clouds of burning pitch. As God himself has said, "*Disbelievers are the rightful owners of the Fire.*" Quran 4:89. You will spill crimson rivers of blood, until one hundred of your lives are taken for each of our martyrs, because Allah tells us to "*Kill the unbelievers wherever you find them.*" Quran 4:89. The judgment of Allah will be carried out, and the Prophet (peace be upon him) will be avenged'. Unquote. . . ."

The camera panned outward. A co-anchor appeared on the screen together with the original speaker and shook his head. "And these terrorists who claimed responsibility are called 'ALAP?' Or 'Al Likchah in the Arabian Peninsula?' What do you suppose these 'Brotherly Love' guys are fighting in favor of?"

The anchor stopped reading and put her script down. "Nothing that we would recognize, that's for sure."

. . . Sharply, then, she went on to another story. Which was sure to be a better story.

* * *

At almost the same time, across town, the Imam at a mosque of the Islamic Society read a counter-statement to his assembled congregation, condemning terrorism.

"In the name of Allah . . . ," he began.

He paused for emphasis. Then: "We, the Islamic Society, unconditionally condemn the heinous, despicable terrorist attack at Delmar Stadium that resulted in so many murders. The Islamic faith teaches the sanctity of human life. Allah says, '*Take not life, which God has made sacred.*' Quran 6:151. If one takes a human life—much less a hundred or more lives—it is '*as if he has killed all of humanity.*' Quran 5:32.

"Those responsible for this terrorism must be brought to justice, for '*God loves those who are just.*' Quran 49:9. All individuals are responsible for their own actions, without blame being assigned to others than the guilty."

. . . At this, the Imam looked around him. He paused, perhaps believing that there might be hooligans who would assign blame to others than the guilty. To innocent followers of Islam, for example. Like the members of his congregation.

Then, he continued. "Freedom of speech and freedom of conscience are basic human rights, because the Holy Scripture says, '*There is no compulsion in religion.*' Quran 2:256. We stand in solidarity with the families of those killed in this heinous terrorist act. We wish them strength and fortitude."

Now, the Imam's voice turned angry. "Those who have pretended to carry out this despicable act in the name of Islam are liars! Instead, Islam teaches the protection of human life, which can only be taken in self-defense. '*For God loves not the transgressors.*' Quran 2:190. The Prophet (peace be upon him) said, '*The strong man is the one who controls himself when he is angry.*'

"These murderers are completely ignorant of Islamic teachings," the Imam said, passionately.

. . . But unfortunately, this statement by the Imam was not carried by any major news outlet.

4

The next morning, Robert Herrick walked quickly down the steps from the church. He wore a black suit himself on this sad occasion, but for a different reason than Jimmy Coleman's associates. He saw his old friend Elwood from law school, and he smiled for a second in spite of himself: a tight smile.

"It's Elwood R. Musgrove! As I live and breathe."

"Hello, Robert. Come on! It's not Elwood. Call me Woody."

"Hey, you know I can't call you that, after the first day of law school. You told us all, 'My real name's Elwood.' And I'll never forget what happened after your exam in the Business Torts class."

"Yeah, I got there late, real sleepy, and I parked in the Faculty Parking Lot so I'd at least get there for part of the exam. Completely illegal. Practically a death penalty crime, the professors would say, parking in the faculty lot. Got my car towed. I'd never have made it across campus to my next exam, Robert, if you hadn't given me a ride."

"And also, you were really hung over."

"More like, I was still drunk when I took that test. Both of those tests."

"It's a wonder you made it to any of your exams."

"Well, that's right, of course." Elwood smiled a tiny smile.

Then, suddenly, he was serious. "Robert, this is an occasion full of grief. I didn't know you knew the guy, Andy, who this funeral was all about. Andy, who died when the balloon hit the stadium."

"No. I didn't know him." Robert was serious now, too. "But this is one of the first funerals, and I was there in the stadium when it happened. I didn't know Andy, no; but I just felt . . . well, I felt like I ought to come to this memorial service. I feel a togetherness with all those people who died, including the ones I didn't know when they were alive."

"You were there when the explosion happened? At the stadium?"

21

"Yes. Worst thing I ever saw. Worse than the savagery in the War. . . ."

"I know." Elwood thought for a moment. Then, he said: "Robert, there's a group of relatives who want to do whatever they can about the bad guys in the Middle East who are behind this terrorism. The ones who killed Andy from a distance, with their money and their support for those on-scene terrorist guys. The financiers; the money people. These families ought to get you to represent them and file a lawsuit against those Islamic terror financiers. The Foundations or Banks or whatever they are. I'll tell these relatives about you."

No, no, no, Robert thought immediately to himself. This was an invitation to file a lawsuit worthy of Don Quixote. An opportunity to tilt at windmills. Not this time, he thought.

"No, Elwood," he said flatly. "I mean, No, Woody. No. I can't do that. I've already got more to do than anyone could list on a mainframe computer. And besides, filing a lawsuit here is a hopeless idea. I'm not into chasing unknowable international conspiracies. Especially nameless ones."

"You've done it before, Robert. With good success."

"Only if you'd lead the team, Woody. Only if you'd be the captain." Robert smiled, because they both knew it wasn't possible.

"Me! Me!? The bottom guy in the class. The anchorman. I only made it through the Civil Procedure test by smuggling in an illegal cheat sheet. Listen, Robert. You care enough to come to the funeral of a guy you didn't even know. My friend Andy. Who was a prince, by the way. You ought to represent these people! You! You're like . . . well, the great American hope. The hope for justice. For Andy. And America."

Robert just shook his head. And slowly said goodbye to his friend.

* * *

A thousand miles away, at the same time Robert was saying No to that Don-Quixote lawsuit idea, the Director of National Intelligence walked briskly into the situation room at CIA headquarters in Langley, Virginia. He sat in front of a wall that featured the eagle-star-and-shield-in-a-circle seal of the CIA.

"What do we know?" he barked.

The analyst to his right shook his head. "Not much, Mr. Director. At least, not much that we know for sure."

"Well, what do we know that's not for sure? Or what do we think we might know?"

"First thing: we don't think it was three women. The FBI spread out within a couple of hours and found witnesses who saw them. The most characteristic comment was, 'They didn't look like women, and that one guy was much too big.'"

"Who do we know who's the right kind of character for that? And who was likely to have been at this location?"

"That's the second thing. We have footage from a surveillance camera by the Holiday Inn, which is near where these guys floated the balloon. There's one really tall fellow, more'n a head taller than the other two people—the other two men, or women, or whatever they were. We've measured the height against objects nearby and against the building in the background. The big guy is about six foot seven."

"Basketball player." The Director's voice shook.

"Exactly, Mr. Director. And there's only one character we know of like that. He's . . . the guy called al Ibrahim."

"Okay," the Director agreed. "I was just thinking that. Mohammed al Ibrahim. Pakistani-American. Educated in Pennsylvania, radicalized in North Waziristan. Right there, in pissing range of the Afghan border."

"Yes, Mr. Director."

"Enough for an arrest?"

"Enough for an arrest warrant, yes. We have a wiretap set up, in fact. We ought to be getting some celebrations about 'Allah-the-Merciful' by now."

"In some people's minds, Allah is merciful enough to burn hundreds of men, women and children to death for nothing but going to a football game." The Director's voice took on a deeper sound of disgust. "All right. Let's find out who the other two fine gentlemen are who partied with al Ibrahim. And also," the Director spoke urgently at this, "let's find out who's supporting them from overseas."

"Right. The stuff they used: the balloon, the butadiene, those silly costumes; those came from somewhere. We're on it, Mr. Director."

* * *

Meanwhile, at Schilling Air Force Base in Kansas, the President climbed up the aircraft steps, wearing his jogging clothes. "The stock market is closed in New York, of course. But when it opens back up again, you know what's going to happen."

"It's going to drop like a rock." The Chief of Staff followed him, panting and sweating.

"The major news media are clueless about this. They haven't reported that the biggest impact of these terrorists is going to be the effect on our economy."

"I agree. In the long run, that will cause more deaths than the people killed in the stadium."

"Right. The gross domestic product will shrink. That doesn't just mean less money. It means less of everything. And less of everything means fewer pharmaceuticals, fewer hospitals, fewer ambulances, fewer doctors. . . ."

". . . Fewer Band-aids, even. And that way, it means more deaths."

As they entered the aircraft, they heard the noise. A kind of excitement, tempered by dread.

"Mr. President." It was a presidential adviser, a political operative, in fact; but as of now, everyone had to become an anti-terror analyst. "Mr. President, the DNI is calling. The Director of National Intelligence."

"Mr. Director?" Once again, the President displayed his uncanny way of sounding upbeat, even in terrible circumstances, which served him so well as a politician. "Mr. Director, find out who did this. Well, I already told you that."

"That's what I intend to do. And that's what I'm calling about."

"Tell me. Tell us. I'm going to put you on the speaker here, so everybody can hear."

"We have a wiretap on this Pakistani-American named Mohammed al Ibrahim. He's been talking to a whole bunch of people. There's a whole lot of praising Allah, but in between, there's conversation that al Ibrahim is having with two other fine humanitarians. Who are also known characters. A man named Hamadi, and another one named Mansouri. Those are the actors who did it on the ground, Mr. President. The ones who floated the balloon bomb. We'll get you the transcripts from the wiretaps."

"Where are these guys?"

"Best we can tell, they're headed for southwest Texas, and from there to Mexico. They talked about this border town called Del Rio, Texas, which is upriver from Laredo. Middle of not just nowhere, but absolutely nowhere. They lay low for a couple of days, holed up around Houston, which wasn't really very smart, because if they'd have taken off, they'd have gotten across the border by now. We have warrants out and no-nonsense bulletins to the Border Patrol about how much we would appreciate apprehending these three excellent scumbags. CIA is there too, at both border stations."

"Okay. Who's funding these three terrorists and supporting them? These three half-witted camel jockeys didn't do this by themselves. They getting money from The Islamic Jihad Foundation? Or maybe from the Pope, at the Vatican?"

"No." The Director laughed, a cross between a chuckle and a snort. "Al Ibrahim has been in touch with this Yemeni citizen who we think is called Sharif Malik Husan, and he is the top man in a fanatical group known as Al Likchah in the Arabian Peninsula, which means 'Brotherly Love in the Arabian Peninsula.' And this group of Brotherly Lovers, in turn, gets lots of goodies from some more fine humanitarians in the nation of Qatar. That's who we think is funding it. The money probably flows to Al Likchah from this incredibly rich and incredibly weird so-called 'charity' called The Holy Faith Foundation, but we'll have to do some work to verify that. The Holy Faith Foundation is in the little bitty nation of Qatar."

"Did the balloon design come from there?"

"We think the bomb came from Hassan al-Asiri, who is a little old bomb maker in Yemen. He usually uses solid explosives like PETN, but he'd know how to use butadiene too."

"And . . . ?" The President was impatient. "That's a lot of names that allegedly are close to other names. And so, who's providing the support?"

"Nobody's sure yet. But again, we think it looks like this foundation in Qatar. In a city called Doha, State of Qatar. The Holy Faith Foundation. Not very Holy, in fact, and not Faithful, but they've been known to do this kind of thing."

"And . . . how do they get the money to terrorists here in America? How does this Holy Faith Foundation get the money out?"

"Mr. President, we don't know yet. These bad guys in Yemen, the Brotherly Love guys, none of them talk on the phone themselves, because they know all about the Hellfire missiles we can shoot from drones. We and the Yemeni government have killed dozens of them. So, to keep themselves alive, folks like these don't use the telephone directly. They just talk to someone else who's unknown, and even that unknown someone else uses a prepaid phone that he throws away a day later."

"Let's find out. Like, right away. About The Holy Faith Foundation. And get these three mass murderers arrested. On *this side* of the border."

* * *

Meanwhile, Robert was astonished to read the headline in the newspaper. "ROBERT HERRICK SLATED TO SUE TERRORISTS."

Uncharacteristically, he spat out a four-letter word under his breath.

He sat at his big mahogany desk in his elegant office at the top of the Chase Tower. Tallest building in town. Beside him, the greenhouse-style windows stretched from the floor to the ceiling. Hundreds of feet below, the greensward around Buffalo Bayou wound its way into Memorial Park and disappeared into the horizon. It was another too-bright, blue-sky day.

Tom Kennedy looked up. "What's the matter?" Tom was Robert's favorite partner, the one he worked with most often. He sat at one of the three matching mahogany chairs, over the huge oriental carpet that shimmered with circles, diamonds, crescents, and octagons in every color imaginable.

"Let me read you a couple of choice words out of this newspaper article. It says, here, 'Robert Herrick, known as the Famous Lawyer for the Little Guy, is preparing a lawsuit against the organization behind the terrorist attack at Delmar Stadium.'"

"What? . . . Oh, no."

"It goes on. '. . . Sources close to the investigation say Mr. Herrick has concentrated upon a suit to be filed against the Holy Faith Foundation, a reclusive breakaway organization of Sunni Islamists, which operates from Doha, Qatar.' It says this organization is disclaimed by most people of the Islamic faith."

"I've never heard of them. The what? The Holy Roller Foundation?"

"Holy Faith Foundation. Whatever that is."

"Oh. Now I can pretend to understand fully. Frankly, I don't know who's a Shia and who's a Sunni. I get them mixed up. Except for knowing that they sometimes want to kill each other."

"And I bet those so-called sources close to the investigation—my non-existent investigation, that is—are just one person, and that person is my law school buddy, Elwood R. Musgrove. I told you about running into him."

"Yes. Aren't they helpful, your old law school friends?"

"Right. And it goes on to say, '. . . Mr. Herrick himself could not be reached for comment.' And I guess the Holy Faith Foundation couldn't be reached for comment either."

"Of course. That way, this newspaper story is a hundred percent legitimate. Even though it's also a hundred percent fictitious."

5

The man they called Bedouin looked satisfied. His office at the top of the Aspire Tower looked out to the east toward a forest of super-tall buildings in the heart of Doha, Qatar. From here, this man ran the organization called The Holy Faith Foundation, and he held power over it securely.

The man's full name was Sherif al Shaikh, but his public identity, the name he went by, was Bedouin. "We are all Bedouins," he was fond of saying, hearkening back to the days when nomadic tribes once scrabbled a hard living out of this desert. Bedouins were the original inhabitants, the natives of this country, and in many quarters here, they are admired. And now, the man known as Bedouin looked around the conference table at the men surrounding him and pointed at a news photograph of the damage done by the explosion at Delmar Stadium.

He smiled. "I kiss the hem of the garments of these soldiers of Islam, who took this action against the infidels. Praise Allah!"

Bedouin was unquestioned as the leader of the Holy Faith Foundation. No one knew exactly what office he held, whether he was president or CEO or whatever, because he did not believe in titles. But he did believe in projecting success, and that was the reason he had located the Foundation prominently in the Aspire Tower. This building, which is nearly a quarter mile tall, is shaped like a cylinder pinched at its curving middle, with a slanted triangle of reddish luminaries high up on its roof. These chains of lights resemble a flame, giving the building the overall appearance of a torch. Another grid of 4,000 tri-colored lamps circles the skin of the tower and is programmed to show different sliding and bursting patterns. Their dancing shapes can be seen throughout the magnificent, strange city of Doha.

"Praise Allah, who is forever merciful," Bedouin repeated. He wore a white burnoose with gold bands and a white robe with a slight overlay showing an arabesque pattern from neck to hem, like a slice of Oriental carpet. His beard and mustache were wiry and black, always under sunglasses the same shade of black; and an anomaly in the center of his forehead gave him the constant appearance of anger, of an explosive frown, even when he smiled, as he was doing now.

The seven men around him also wore white burnooses with gold bands and white robes. And they also smiled.

A newcomer to the inner circle of the Holy Faith Foundation spoke unexpectedly, across the table. Excitedly. "Bedouin, your excellency, what role did this Foundation of ours play in this wonderful act of courage?"

"Never speak these words." Bedouin's face clouded. "We deny that we had any role in this event, even though we applaud the heroes who caused it with all of our souls."

Just as quickly, Bedouin's angry smile returned. "Now. Let's get to other business. What have we done to publicize our humanitarian relief to the oppressed Sunni peoples of Syria and Iraq, who are victims of those Shia devils? It is not enough to do good works. We have to let the world know. We are a tiny pebble in the dam that holds back the Shia who pretend to Islam, and our contribution to saving our Sunni brothers and sisters is a constant mission."

* * *

Back in the United States, Jimmy Coleman entered the magnificent offices of the Law Firm of Booker and Bayne, where he was the head of litigation. He strolled through the floor-to-ceiling glass doors with their gold lettering, and he ambled slowly toward his big corner office.

All of the paneling on this floor, and on the eight others that housed Booker and Bayne, had come from a single stand of white birch, brought in from Vermont. The secretarial bays stretched as far as the eye could see, like pale boxes of marble. Inside the white birch doors to the partners' offices, Jimmy could hear Booker and Bayne lawyers, hard at work. Making money.

From the office of Bill Watson, the securities lawyer, came words that were shouted into the telephone: "Whether you know it or not, you've just confessed that your client violated SEC Rule 10b-5! Where in the hell did you go to law school?"

Jimmy smiled, because as every lawyer knows, there's not a securities broker or dealer alive who can keep from violating Rule 10b-5. The Securities and Exchange Commission has made this Rule into an all-purpose dragnet.

Next door, from the office of Janet Moxley, the oil and gas lawyer, he heard this: "If you go ahead and drill, you're going to owe everything you produce to my clients! All of that oil and gas that you think is yours, is ours. That entire lease is held by production, and it's still owned by my client."

Now, Jimmy laughed out loud. Janet Moxley was a supreme negotiator, because she was the best in the office at bluffing. Jimmy didn't know this particular transaction, but he was ready to guess that Janet didn't really believe that the "entire lease" was "held," or probably, that anything at all was "held by production."

From the office of Daniel Cordero, the bankruptcy lawyer: "You guys need to straighten up and play nice with us about this Plan of Reorganization. If you don't, you're going to get it crammed down on you by Judge Davis until your head sticks out of your hind end."

Still laughing, because he loved the backstabbing games that came out of bankruptcy cases, Jimmy reached his corner office. "Hi, Lisa," he said to his secretary in his trademark gravelly voice.

She jumped up, all six feet of her. "Hi, Jimmy." And she hugged him.

Jimmy wasn't tall; in fact he was short—just five feet seven or eight. His whitish hair had enough brown left to smear it with an ugly beige tint, and his eyes were so colorless and pale that witnesses looked away when Jimmy cross-examined them. He carried a map of his life on his face, as he grinned with brown-and-gray teeth.

Maybe it was because of his sawed-off height that Jimmy was so fond of Lisa; or, maybe, it was because she could turn out reams of dictated paper without errors, organize all of his files, and keep her cool when Jimmy started into another shady deal.

"Get me Tommy Harper over at the newspaper," he told his too-tall secretary. "Tell him I've got a response to this story about that dumbass Robert Herrick, who's intending to sue our good client, The Holy Faith Foundation."

He walked into his office and once again, for the thousandth time, appreciated the familiar, but priceless, intarsiato chest that covered one wall. Its hardware was glittering gold; its frame burst with inlays of green, tan, and red flowers. His desk had been made in modern times in the same part of Italy that had manufactured the chest centuries ago, and like the chairs around it, it was covered with colorful inlays of vines, leaves and blossoms to match the ages-old chest.

On the desk, he saw another copy of the newspaper, with its unwelcome headline promising a lawsuit against the Holy Faith Foundation.

He picked up the telephone on the first ring. "Hello, Tommy. Your newspaper carried that story about Robert Herrick intending to sue the Holy Faith Foundation. Well, the Holy Faith Foundation is one of our good clients at Booker and Bayne." Jimmy's voice grated like metal claws on concrete.

At the other end of the line, Tommy Harper knew what that meant in Jimmy Coleman's vocabulary. The Foundation was "a good client" not because it was a model corporate citizen, but because it paid bills in the millions to Booker and Bayne immediately, without question, and it exhibited no curiosity about the law firm's methods.

"Mister Herrick is making threats about a lawsuit that is *frivolous!*" Jimmy roared. Now, he sounded like hailstones in a canebrake. "The Holy Faith Foundation is a religious charitable organization. It is as remote from supporting terrorism as the Archbishop of Canterbury. If Herrick files a lawsuit, he is going to get a fine, a penalty, a sanction, that he won't be able to pay even with all the millions he's squeezed out of injured poor people."

"Oh yeah?" said the voice of Tommy Harper, at the other end of the line. It was a non-question, because Tommy wanted Jimmy to keep right on fulminating.

"The Holy Faith Foundation does good works all over the globe," Jimmy rasped. "It's saved thousands of people from starvation in Somalia. When the rebels prevented everyone else from getting to the refugees, the Holy Faith Foundation plowed through them to get there. It sends provisions to religious minorities in Syria and Iraq, in the areas covered by those butchers called ISIS. It's aided flood victims in Bangladesh and earthquake survivors in Pakistan." Jimmy's voice, now, was a high-pitched scratch.

"Oh yeah?" Tommy the reporter was scribbling furiously.

"You know what Herrick is doing? This lawsuit is going to be nothing but Islamophobia. Irrational fear of all Muslims, hatred of Muslims, just because they're Muslims. It's a holy war against the Holy Faith Foundation, conducted by this loose cannon named Robert Herrick. It's pure prejudice. Any lawsuit of this kind would be an effort at blackmail, hoping for something to be paid just because there's a lawsuit and because Muslims are unpopular. Well, we won't pay a dime! Not a dime! We'll defend this frivolous claim vigorously, and we'll make a motion for sanctions—a fine—against Robert Herrick, after we kick his ass in the lawsuit."

Tommy Harper rushed off to get it into print.

Booker and Bayne had been founded in the 1800s by Colonel Henry Anderson Booker, who always asked, "Yes, but is it fair?" in response to any proposal—but who then found a way to do whatever "it" was, for the client, whether it was fair or not. His motto was, "Find out what the client wants, and get it done!" The Colonel wore red suspenders and kept a spittoon in his office. He had long since passed on to that Great Court in the Sky from Which There Is No Appeal. But everyone agreed, if there was a living successor worthy of Colonel Booker, it was Jimmy Coleman, the present-day head of litigation.

* * *

The border crossing at Del Rio, Texas, is famous for allowing travelers to pass quickly. But today, it was blocked by barriers that let vehicles through one at a time.

The result was that a line of traffic snaked into the dust of Southwest Texas for a half mile. About a quarter-mile back, there was a stalled late model Dodge Ram, silver, that stood above the dirty ancient cars in front of the space that grew before its bumper.

"Look at that." The uniformed Border Patrol officers got ready to pull the silver truck out of line to let the rest of the line through.

"Hey. It's abandoned."

"It's stolen." The first officer was on the telephone. "It's stolen."

"I wonder. . . ."

"I wonder too. Except I more than wonder. This was the truck our three distinguished terrorists were driving, I'll bet."

Farther up the line, there were shouts, suddenly, for help. "There's a man down, here! Shot! I think he's dead."

"What happened?"

"There were three weird-looking guys on foot, running. They pulled a gun on this guy. Wanted his car. Blue Corvette. I guess he didn't move fast enough. This really tall guy . . . , he shot the man. Took the car. It was strange, seeing those three guys pile into this little bitty car, but I guess they liked the fact that it would move fast. They pulled out of this here line and turned the Corvette around, and they headed back north. Tires practically jumped off the road. I mean, they were gunning it, way over ninety miles an hour."

* * *

Five minutes later, Highway Patrol Officer D.W. Pembroke of the Department of Public Safety was in pursuit. "Throw out that tack board!" he yelled into the microphone.

And ten miles up the near-empty highway, two other DPS officers spread a jagged strip across the concrete surface. Behind it, a respectable distance away, they parked their Crown Victoria to block the highway.

A third DPS vehicle arrived, and then a fourth. Warily, the officers stood behind the cars that now straddled the highway.

They heard Officer Pembroke's siren wailing before they saw anything. And then it all happened fast. There was a sound like an explosion when the blue Corvette hit the tack strip and blew all four of its tires. The Corvette careened off a shining steel guardrail, which threw it toward the opposite side, where it also hit the guardrail. Pembroke himself edged his car up to the tack strip and stopped just short of it. He unlocked his shotgun and aimed it at the scene from behind the safety of his police car's hood.

Just past the wrecked Corvette, the other four DPS officers approached slowly, sheltering themselves behind the guardrail.

"It was almost funny," Officer Pembroke would say later. "You ever been to the circus and seen one of those clown acts, where they park a Volkswagen, and then forty or so guys in polka-dot clown suits pile out? That was what this was like. Nobody could get out until the first guy got out, because he was, like, seven feet tall. He practically had to unscrew himself from that low-slung front seat. His leg got stuck and he splattered out onto the concrete. The other two guys crawled out, but only after that. And they did what we told them on the loudspeaker, which was to lie face down. And they put their hands behind them."

Pembroke couldn't tell it without laughing. "After what I'd heard, I expected them to have burqas on. Or at least those head scarves they call burnooses, you know, that kind with the red-and-white tablecloth look. But all three of them had blue jeans on. And T-shirts. It seemed like it might be sort of disrespectful to all the other Islamic terrorists, what with these three buckaroos wearing blue jeans. And that amateur-cowboy look didn't even work, because somehow, they didn't blend with the population around Del Rio, Texas, at all."

6

The next day, inside the County Jail in Houston, three terrorists waited while authorities on several levels of local, state, and federal law enforcement tried to figure out what to do with them. Guantanamo? Supermax, in Colorado? Or where else?

They were happy, Ibrahim, Hamadi, and Mansouri. They watched their own worldwide publicity on the twenty-four-hour news cycle. Endlessly, they praised merciful Allah and contemplated the palaces they would occupy in the life to come. Still, boredom was setting in. They were in single cells. They ate what their religion demanded, but it wasn't very good. They exercised once a day in a concrete yard that they waddled to in shackles.

But suddenly, Ibrahim stood upright like a flagpole. With all of his nearly seven-foot frame. He held a newspaper in his hand and shouted at his companions in the next cubicles. He pointed, and he yelled.

"What?" asked Hamadi and Mohammed together, as they scrambled to stand up too.

"By the holiness of our beliefs." Ibrahim's face was red. "By all of heaven, and by the holy scriptures!"

"What?" Hamadi and Mansouri sounded like an echo of themselves.

"It's . . . it's . . . ." Ibrahim spluttered.

"What!"

Ibrahim showed the newspaper headline, then read it. "ROBERT HERRICK SLATED TO SUE TERRORISTS."

"What does 'slated' mean?" Hamadi asked. But nobody heard him, because Hamadi was always out of the loop.

"It's all right, Ibrahim," Mansouri interjected. "We want to get sued. We'll get this television treatment all over again."

"Not us. It's not us they want to sue." Ibrahim read on. "'The target defendant in this suit would probably be groups in Saudi Arabia, Qatar, and the United Arab Republic that supported the three on-scene actors. According to sources close to the investigation, Mr. Herrick will likely file suit against'"—and here, Ibraham could barely say it—"'the Holy Faith Foundation.'"

"The Holy Faith Foundation? The greatest soul of warriors everywhere," Mansouri wailed.

Ibrahim finally caught his breath. "Who is . . . who is this Robert Herrick, who will desecrate The Holy Faith Foundation and defile everything we call sacred?" He stared at his companions.

* * *

A few miles to the west, Robert steered his favorite antique car toward downtown. His wife Maria sat beside him. Whenever he could, he drove this car: his vintage Duesenberg. Maroon, with outside exhausts trailing alongside in gleaming chrome, and sporting a bulging hood that held way too much horsepower.

"You always look funny driving this thing," Maria laughed. "You ought to be trailing a long scarf and wearing one of those driving caps, the kind the cartoonists always picture on burglars and other choice criminals."

"I'm just an ordinary driver in an un-ordinary car. But it's the most fun to drive, of all my vehicles." He had lost count of the exact number of old cars he owned, after enlarging his garage for the third time. "These are my true loves, these beautiful cars. . . ."

Then: "Besides you, Maria," he added quickly.

Her telephone rang. "Uh-oh," she sighed. "I have to answer this."

"Hello, Mr. District Attorney," she said, with visible dread. The boss never called but for one reason.

"Maria, I need you to go to the Cop Shop. To intake the latest capital murder case. The Delmar Stadium explosion."

"I'm with Robert in the car. We're on our way to dinner and a movie. We didn't plan on papering up a death penalty case."

"Well, I'm glad it's not a Mozart Symphony that you already have tickets to, like the last time I interrupted your date night. But I need you to go to the Intake Division and prepare this indictment. I'm sorry, but . . . it's got to be done now. A matter of public confidence. And I need to have confidence in the assistant DA who prepares the indictment, because in case like this, it's tricky. Capital murder is like 'murder-plus,' or murder combined with something else that makes it worse than ordinary murder, and so it's always complicated."

"Do I get a medal for fighting terrorism, instead of having a life? Or at least a raise?"

"As high as the county will let me go." Both of them laughed at that. Maria had long since maxed out the amount the DA was able to pay.

"Al-l-l-l-l right," she said. "I suppose the indictment is going to be two counts. Or more. Capital murder is murder-plus, and the plus is, it was done in the course of committing arson by explosion. And second, the 'plus' is that there are multiple murders in the same episode. Right?"

"Right. Thank you. The voters are grateful, and since those voters voted for me, so am I." With that, the District Attorney rang off.

Maria sighed again and turned to Robert. "Drop me off at Riesner Street. The Cop Shop. The Pig Pen. The Arrest Warren. . . . Also known as The Police Station."

Robert sighed too, but he turned the car around—to do what she had told him.

* * *

"So, what do we do with these three guys?" said the President of the United States to his Chief of Staff. They both sat on elegant couches in the Oval Office, facing each other.

"I'm telling you, Mr. President. The best place is Guantanamo, however much you might not like it."

"Look. I'm trying not to put more people in that place."

"One more group of terrorists. Fly these three thugs in there on a Saturday night outside the news cycle, without any announcement. It can be done."

The President sighed. "That would be three more guys we'd have to try with military tribunals, or else try in federal court. Or, three more that we'd have to put in some not-so-friendly country, with some excuse about their being rehabilitated or something."

The Chief of Staff just waited for the President to think through to the next step. He and the President had talked about these three terrorists before.

"Can we just leave them where they are?" The President's big nose twitched, and his red hair was tousled.

"Attorney General doesn't like that idea, and for good reason. It's a county jail, the place they're in now. Very temporary quarters, and not at all tightly locked down. It's a strain on that local jail to hold them securely, and of course they really can't do it securely in that jail, and they can't comply with international law because these are enemy combatants and they get all these legalities, with treaties behind them."

"I keep coming back to it: Supermax. Or even Leavenworth. They've got lots of security, either place." The President loved to talk about Supermax, in Colorado—the tightest prison in America, where the Federal Government's worst of the worst were locked up.

"Those are places that hold convicted prisoners. That's different. But we've got to move them, because if they stay where they are, these three guys are going to be entitled to go to court."

"To court? Why?"

"Bail hearings."

"Bail hearings? But they're enemy combatants."

"Long as they're in this county jail, they're not held as enemy combatants. They're, like . . . ordinary murderers. Mass murderers, huge mass murderers, that's what they are. But they're just plain old murderers, now. And not even that, yet, because they're only being held, and they aren't charged with murder, or even spitting on the sidewalk or anything else yet."

The President just looked off in the distance. "It's not only the Holy Faith Foundation giving me trouble, it's three psychopaths we've already caught."

"I'm telling you, sir, the best solution is to spirit 'em off to Guantanamo. In the darkest, secret-est time of a weekend night."

The President stirred in his seat in a way that signaled that he had reached a decision. Or rather, a non-decision. "Well," he said slowly, "let's just leave them where they are for the time being, until I can talk some sense into the Attorney General. I just know there's someplace in CONUS that's perfect for these gentlemen"—here, he used the military abbreviation for "the CONtinental US"—"someplace that's not Guantanamo, where we can park their carcasses."

* * *

Donna DeCarlo's voice came over the intercom that sat on the big mahogany desk. "Robert, you'll want to take this one. The Governor is calling."

He picked up the receiver with a grin. The Governor was a big-time graduate of Texas A&M University. And there is nothing like an Aggie, a Texas A&M alumnus, especially one who likes to tell Aggie jokes himself: jokes about how dumb and primitive Aggies are, jokes that have mostly been invented by Aggies themselves.

"Hello, Governor."

"Robert, you know the difference between a blue-eyed Aggie and a brown-eyed Aggie?"

"Ahhh . . . no. That wasn't part of my college experience."

"The blue-eyed Aggie is a quart low."

Robert had to laugh.

"And I can see that I don't need to tell you what it is that the brown-eyed Aggie is full of."

"No."

"And that brown-eyed Aggie is proud of it, too. Now listen, Robert. I've heard about how you've been asked a bunch of times to take on this explosion-in-the-stadium case. And now, it's bringing heat down on me. I've had two senators ask me to put the arm on you to get off your ass and do it."

"I'm off my ass, Governor!" Again, Robert had to laugh. "But I've got more on my plate than J.J. Watt is going to eat for Thanksgiving dinner."

"Good. I'm glad you've got some business."

"And a wife and kids, and a life."

"Robert, are you blue-eyed? And a quart low, too? I'm asking. I'm begging. Robert! Get into this stadium case. Lots of people counting on you. Lots of my constituents counting on you. Do it for your Governor. Me."

Once again, Robert laughed. At the brazenness of the appeal. At the Governor showing, once again, how skilled he was at close-up politics.

* * *

Inside the County Jail, Ibrahim stood at his full six-foot-and-a-lot-more height. And he faced the jailer, squarely on.

"I'm supposed to dress today. For court."

"I don't have it." The jail didn't like to dress prisoners in civilian clothes. It created security risks. "I don't have it on the list."

"They foul that list up all the time. How do you say it? They screw up that list all the time. I'm supposed to dress for court."

The sergeant was passing by. "What's the problem?"

"I have to dress for court, and he"—pointing to the jailer—"won't let me."

The sergeant had recently been in court. He'd heard a harangue from a judge about causing problems for "the entire judicial system." And so, the sergeant didn't hesitate. "Dress him."

"Yes sir." And Ibrahim, who actually was scheduled only for what the courts called a "no-issue setting"— just an arraignment, to see whether he had a lawyer and so forth—retrieved his civilian clothes, even though they were unnecessary.

7

The judge stared at the tall man who stood before him in civilian clothes. Almost all of the other prisoners wore jail whites. This one had black dress slacks on, perfectly fitting his height, and an elegant soft blue shirt.

"Mr. al Ibrahim, you say you want to waive your arraignment? To give up the reading of the charge against you?"

His lawyer answered for him. The lawyer was well known to the judge: one of the most skillful at the courthouse. "Yes, your honor. He understands the charge against him."

"Mr. al Ibrahim, I need to ask you yourself, personally. Is it your wish to give up your right to an arraignment?"

"Yes, your honor." The tall man spoke quietly, in a way that was incongruous given his way-excessive height.

The judge turned to the lawyer. "I had understood that this defendant was the object of the federal authorities. They had him in custody at one time, didn't they? Why do we have him here?"

"Judge, I'm not absolutely sure, except to say that there's no federal warrant at this time."

"Mr. Ibrahim, You have a lawyer right here, correct? Do you intend to have this lawyer represent you? I mean, during your case here in this court?"

"Yes, Your honor." Politely, with a hint of a smile.

"Is there a bail hearing today?"

An assistant district attorney answered quickly. "No, your honor."

"You see, what's puzzling me, is this." The judge pushed his glasses to the end of his nose. "If Mr. al Ibrahim intended to waive arraignment, and he's perfectly well lawyered up, and he's not seeking bail today, why is Mr.

al Ibrahim dressed up in these fine civilian rags? Come to think of it, why's he even here?"

"I don't know, your honor, except to say that they screw up all the time in the jail."

"You may stand down," the judge said to Ibrahim. And shook his head. "Next is...."

The clerk consulted his docket sheet. "Billy Ray Bonebender."

"Billy Ray . . . Bonebender? That's his name?"

"Yes, your honor. Charged with aggravated assault."

The judge snickered, and several of the lawyers gathered at counsel table laughed out loud. The clerk looked puzzled.

"Okay, tell Billy Ray Bonebreaker—"

"Bonebender, your honor."

"Billy Ray Bonebender"—more laughter from counsel table—"Tell him to come up, with counsel if he has any." The judge looked off to the side, where there was nothing but the blonde wood wall of the courtroom, soaring to twenty-five feet in height: one of the old courtrooms, the kind they built way back when a courtroom was supposed to be majestic.

The judge was still thinking about the tall man in civilian clothes. That guy, Ibrahim. Finally, he beckoned to one of the deputy sheriffs who had charge of the string of prisoners. "Listen. That tall guy, al Ibrahim. Watch him. He's got on civilian clothes for no reason. I think he's a rabbit. A rabbit."

The deputy was new. "A rabbit?"

"I think he'll run, if you let him. He'll try to escape. So don't let him. I think he's a rabbit."

* * *

"Another Will-o'-the-Wisp case? Another case where we chase shadows?" Tom Kennedy was incredulous. "You want to file a suit about the Delmar Stadium bombing?"

"Well, maybe not." Robert looked sheepish, like a little boy who's been chastised for drawing on the wall with crayons. "Maybe we can just represent this one constituent of the governor. The one he called about. And let someone else carry the laboring oar, some lawyer who represents a whole bunch of people who lost relatives in this tragedy."

"Fat chance." Kennedy always wanted the firm to represent more Fortune 500 companies. The kind of clients who paid up front. "Robert, you're too quick to represent the underdog. The glamorous plaintiff. We just got finished getting a hundred thousand dollar judgment for that pet shop startup that got cheated, and that's great, except that we spent three hundred thousand getting the one hundred thousand. And you wouldn't let us even collect a fee."

"Well, but the governor's aides say they've got the goods on this Holy Faith Foundation."

"Robert . . . , the governor's aides? They're in the spin business! They're . . . politicians, for crying out loud! Their whole day is spent thinking up stuff you can sell to unsuspecting greenhorns."

"We've had a good year at this firm. Time to give something back." And it was true; the firm had more than a hundred and twenty employees now. And thirty-plus lawyers. The audio-visual department, which made exhibits and videos for use in court, had made more settlement films than anything else this year—summaries of the evidence in dozens of cases, summaries that shook loose millions from defense lawyers.

"It's been a good year, but this Will-o'-the-Wisp case will set us back a long way."

"Maybe not. The *Wall Street Journal* actually had a story that laid out the case against the Holy Faith Foundation."

Tom Kennedy just shook his head. "It's one thing to write a story in the newspapers, about the Delmar Stadium case. It's another thing to prove it all with live witnesses in a courtroom. And all the witnesses are ghosts, in this case."

* * *

Ibrahim managed to situate himself at the end of the prisoner line. He was cuffed and chained to the next guy, but he knew he'd be let loose just inside the entrance to the County Jail. The building there was modern, and it had been a source of pride when it was built, but it had some bad design features. It had inadequate elevators and stairways with narrow passages that wound around like tunnels in a prairie dog town.

The prisoners cackled on the short walk back to the jail. "This one guy I talked to, he's super-wiggy. He told me he's going to get probation for his aggravated robbery." "Yeah. He's a whale, and he's in a barrel, and he don't sense any of the bad stuff that's gonna be happenin to him." "This other guy pled to an agg rob and they sent him up for sixty rodeos." "Yeah, but that guy came from Arkansas, and besides, he did a whole lot of bizarre stuff to the female patrons." Laughter among the prisoners.

Ibrahim was quiet. When the chain of prisoners entered the inside of the jail, they stood in a vestibule in front of the elevators. One by one, the jailers let them out of the cuffs. Ibrahim was last.

He stood to the side when everyone was entering. To the side of the elevator. It wasn't easy, with his height, but he blended with the wall as best he could.

And just as the jailhouse escape advisors had told him, he made it. He didn't get into the elevator and didn't draw any attention.

He walked the few steps to the checkpoint. There were two officers. The two uniformed men sat and didn't have a lot to do, except to gossip the same way the prisoners had while they walked back to the jail; but this gossip among the guards was about their girlfriends, debts, and conditions of employment, instead of the prisoners' gossip about their pride in getting away with crimes.

"I'm A.T.W.O.," Ibrahim announced. "All The Way Out."

One of the officers stirred and faced him. "Name?"

"Manny Carranza. Or . . . excuse me. Manuel Rodrigo Carranza y Flores." It was the name of a prisoner in Ibrahim's block who was scheduled to be released but had been delayed by a foul-up in his processing.

"Yes." The man nodded, because Ibrahim was close enough in resemblance to the head shot of Manuel Carranza that the deputy consulted. The other officer pushed a button. The buzzer sounded, a loud noise that startled visitors and, for that matter, startled Ibrahim. An annoying noise, but it didn't affect the officers at all. Ibrahim pushed out.

His escape-artist teachers had told him that this simple method might work—it might—because it had worked before. Hollywood types of escapes, such as tying together bedsheets or carving pistols out of bars of soap, would just get you arrested. Simplicity was the key, they said. Let the bad design of this Jail help you.

And instantly, Ibrahim was A.T.W.O. All The Way Out.

8

Robert, the senator is here," said Donna DeCarlo's voice over the intercom. "The senator who wants to be your new client. The Governor sent her."

"Send her in."

The senator wore a dark red skirt and a matching suit jacket. "Hello. I'm Senator Ellen McKay. This is my husband, John McKay." Tall, with blonde hair, she was a charismatic woman, Robert thought to himself. She would make a good witness.

"I'm so sorry for your loss."

"Thank you. That's why we're here."

"Yes. The Governor called me. This is Tom Kennedy, my partner. Won't you sit down?"

"There isn't much to tell." The senator was poised, but obviously, she had to struggle to keep herself that way. "I filled out the information sheet you sent me. My son was watching a high school football game where his friends were playing. I still can't quite believe. . . ." The senator paused. "I still can't believe he's gone."

"Of course."

"These three terrorists were only the tip of the iceberg. We know—we *know*—that there were bigger people behind them. Respectable people in their own countries, and wealthy. But really evil people, who deserve to get sued."

Robert cleared his throat. "You should know, too, that it's a doubtful, difficult case. I mean, proving it. That is going to be next to impossible."

"We know that, too." John McKay was as elegantly dressed as his wife and just as composed. "But we want to try. And from what we hear, Mr. Herrick, you are the best. And I might add that this organization—this

Holy Faith Foundation—is the worst. If we don't do something to stop them, they'll recruit more terrorists, like cannon fodder, and do it again."

"Well, how we do that, is the question." Robert looked straight into the man's eyes. "I'm starting out from ground zero. I don't know anything about The Holy Faith Foundation or whether that's the group of bad-guy financiers who did it. For all we know, as of now, it could be The Burnoose Foundation that did it."

Robert shook his head. "I told the Governor I'd do my best. And I'll tell you two fine people I'll do my best. Together with Tom, we'll both do our best. But it is going to be hard, much harder than you'd think, to prove anything in a lawsuit like this one."

* * *

"In fact," said Tom Kennedy two days later, "it's already hard, and we haven't even finished writing the suit papers. You know, the Complaint."

"I wouldn't know about that. I'm a big picture guy," said Robert. And he grinned.

"Oh, yeah. I remember you fighting with the defendants in that last lawsuit about where the commas would go, in the jury instructions. You're a detail guy too. So, talk this through with me."

"All right. After that *Twombly* case—is the full name of it something like *Bell Telephone v. Twombly?*—after that harebrained case that the Supreme Court decided, it's bizarre. The suit papers have to be completely different than a few years ago, I know."

"After the *Twombly* case," Tom went on, "the Supreme Court says we have to put in enough facts to make it plausible—*plausible*—that you can prove a case. But at the beginning of a lawsuit, there's always a gap in your proof. You don't have the facts yet. And in this case, all we have is gaps. We've got the facts against those three on-the-scene guys, the ones who wore the fake burqas, but we don't have any facts against this other defendant, the Holy Faith Foundation. We believe they funded the explosion and laundered the money, but we don't know how they did it."

"We know enough. The *Wall Street Journal* says the Foundation quote 'financed' them."

"But that's a conclusion. The Supreme Court says we've got to have 'facts, not conclusions.'"

"All right," Robert frowned. "Here's what we do. We mention the Holy Faith Foundation up front. Then, we describe the balloon event and the explosion in the stadium at great length. I mean, page after page. Ten pages. At various points through that, while you're talking about al Ibrahim and Hamadi and Mansouri, the on-scene guys, you mention various things that required financing, and you mention the Holy Faith Foundation. Because we know that they did do that. They financed everything. And then at the end, include a paragraph about the Holy Faith Foundation, and say that they solicited, and supported, and every other synonym you can think of, this terrorist act."

"But saying they 'financed' it, and that other stuff, is not enough. It's a conclusion. We've got to say how they financed it. And yeah, we have evidence that they did, but we don't know the how."

"Attach the *Wall Street Journal* story, as an exhibit." Robert threw up his hands. "And say that they financed it with money, along with everything else."

Tom just laughed at that. So did Robert, at the majesty and, at the same time, the silliness of the law. "Okay." Tom stood up. "I know what to do now. Or rather, I guess I can sort of figure something out. Sometimes, as they say, if you can fake it, you can make it."

* * *

After his escape, Ibrahim walked briskly away from the County Jail. He headed west on Franklin Street, keeping his presence as unobtrusive as his six-foot-seven frame would allow. As soon as he could, he turned north and sprinted across the bridge over the bayou. He kept running for a mile or so before he slowed.

He opened the door to the next shop he saw. A barber shop. With a proprietor and customers who spoke mostly Spanish.

"I'm lost," he said pleasantly. "Stranded. Can I borrow a phone from someone?"

The guy in the first barber chair politely handed over his flip phone.

Ibrahim dialed his emergency number. "I am Guiding Light. I am lost in Houston."

At the other end of the line, the guy wasn't very smart. "Guiding Light, they're listening in. They've got this number surveilled."

By saying this, he guaranteed that if "they" weren't listening in yet, which they probably were, "they" would start listening now, and "they" would know that this coded conversation was important.

Ibrahim rolled his eyes. "I'm headed to the pickup spot. Send me money. Lots of money, in twenty dollar bills."

"And the National Security Agency will also have your twenty-twenty now, Guiding Light. Your location."

"I've got to get out of here." Ibrahim handed the phone back. "Thank you."

Be unobtrusive, he told himself. Relax. He pushed himself out the door and walked away. When he was far enough from the windows of the barber shop, he started running again. . . .

* * *

Later, when the sun was down and the night was full of purple shadows, Robert stepped to the podium at his alma mater, ready to deliver the graduation speech at his own law school. He set his notes aside.

"It is a privilege to speak to you on this important date," he began, "because you are about to embark on a great adventure. Congratulations on your graduation from law school! It's a wonderful time.

"I had a speech written for you," he went on, "and in fact I wrote it a long time ago. But I changed it completely, just today. Why a new speech? Well, my partner Tom asked me today, 'Why do we do what we do, Robert my friend?' And he explained that he had been mud-wrestling with this Complaint in our newest case, and he'd practically concussed his brain trying to get it done. He said, 'Why . . . I mean, why . . . do we do what we do? Why are we . . . well, why have we chosen to be lawyers, and plaintiff's lawyers at that? It sure is uncomfortable at times,' he said.

"I laughed. Because, as I said to Tom, 'I'm not sure I know.' But I've thought about it often.

"And since Tom asked, you—you new graduates—get to hear my answer. Or rather, my thoughts, because the answer remains forever beyond my reach. You get to hear along with Tom, who came here with me and is standing in the back. Here are my attempts at an answer.

". . . When I say, 'I'm a plaintiff's lawyer,' it's like saying, I resemble the railroad barons of the Gilded Age in the 19th Century, who built something by beating their way through the wilderness, who were entrepreneurs of the unknown, who created wealth out of nothing. Plaintiff's lawyers do what they do because they choose that kind of challenge. Plaintiff's lawyers dream about the chase, the adventure, the danger, and the pinnacles.

"And also, I'm a plaintiff's lawyer because my heart bleeds for people who are injured by the fault of others, and yet I can stop my bleeding heart when there is nothing to be done for this victim in front of me, who's asked me to take on an unwinnable case. Otherwise, on the one hand, I wouldn't care enough to fight as hard as I do, and otherwise, on the other hand, I'd spend so much effort on losing that I couldn't do anything for people with winning cases.

"I'm a plaintiff's lawyer because I see the law not just as a kind of oil on the gears of our economy, but as a beautiful thing that begs to be wooed, respected, and preserved. Most of the time, it shines with a brilliant, luminous purpose. And when it doesn't, I'm able to tell myself that its failures are forgivably infrequent.

"And then too, I'm a plaintiff's lawyer because I wish vehemently for justice, and yet, I know that there are injustices I can't overcome. I've taught myself, with bitter lessons, to know the difference. And to respect the limitations of my abilities.

"I'm a plaintiff's lawyer because there is something spiritual about it, as a calling. It requires a kind of self-sacrifice that returns rewards over and again. It isn't just what I do. It's who I am. I happen to be a religious guy. I go to church and I try to live it, but that's not really a part of what I'm saying. It is American, patriotic, and statesmanlike to be a lawyer, and in my case a plaintiff's lawyer. I think I would treat it as a sacred thing even if I were not religious at all."

Tom just waited. He didn't really hear the rest of the speech, because he had heard what he was here for.

But when he met Robert and they were about to leave, Tom looked at his partner and smiled.

". . . I think you're ready to try this case, Robert. To make a stem-winder of an opening statement and follow it with a final argument. But listen, Robert." Tom laughed. "I asked you this way-too-philosophical question because I've battered my mind against the wall of the Supreme Court cases while I've been trying to write the Complaint in our newest case. I guess you've shown, by this speech you've just given, that you're good with words. Why don't *you* write the Complaint? "

* * *

Across town a few days later, sitting in front of his priceless intarsiato chest, Jimmy Coleman finished reading the Complaint that the Herrick Law Firm had filed against the Holy Faith Foundation.

He laughed.

His favorite associate, Jennifer Lowenstein, sat in a chair adorned with the same flowering vines of red, brown, and green as the chest. She laughed too.

"This Complaint is ridiculous, Jennifer." Jimmy sounded like a bulldozer that needed a tune-up. "It's obviously inadequate under that *Bell Telephone versus Twombly* case."

"I know." Jennifer's memorandum had identified a dozen points of attack against the suit papers Robert Herrick had filed.

"This Complaint is no damn good, just like the Tiii-tanic was no damn good when it banged into that iceberg," Jimmy growled. "And Jennifer, we gonna sink Robert Herrick's lawsuit, just like that iceberg sank the Tiii-tanic."

9

With the shift just beginning, a classroom full of police officers milled about. They told their best stupid-perpetrator stories, and gradually, they sat down. When the big guy everyone called "Moose" started to shoehorn himself into that little seat—and he always sat right in front, in spite of his weighing 300 pounds—the lieutenant stepped up and started the briefing.

"My friends, we've got another fish fry over at Fritz's Place for Officer J. E. Moulden," he announced. "For those of you who didn't serve with him, Moulden was a prince of a guy. He slid off the road chasing a stolen car suspect. Instead of what we hope for, which is that the perp gets totalled and the officer's fine, the officer came away with brain damage in this case. We gonna pick Officer Moulden up in one a them big SUV-type black-and-whites and take him to Fritz's Place. Reason I'm telling you this is that tomorra night, we wanna see all a you there, too."

At the mention of Officer Moulden, everyone was silent. The lieutenant fiddled with his clipboard to signal that he was going on to other business.

"Now, biggest new thing we got, is about this here bean pole who is one of those three terrorists who blew up the stadium. Name is al Ibrahim. You know what kinda esteem we hold for this particular camel jockey, right? Anyhow, he escaped. Or rather, the sheriff pretty much opened the door and invited this here marplot to traipse right on out.

"Well, we need real bad to get this clown offa the streets and back into your favorite county lockup. There's been about five hundred sightings, which isn't surprising since the guy is taller'n the Empire State Building, and every Bozo out there is callin in about every guy they see who's tall. But we got nothin that means anything. We don't even know if our hero

Ibrahim is still remainin inside this metropolis, but intelligence says he prob'ly is."

The lieutenant paused. "Course I cain't even faintly imagine how intelligence would know to prog-nos-ticate where this kinda off-brand character might be visitin. But allegedly, they can."

He looked up. And paused again. "We got cartoon pitchures passin around to all of you, with a likeness 'a this fine gentleman. Mister al Ibrahim. And his identifying marks. Mostly, he's tall. If you see a dude who's six foot seven and not playin basketball, be alert."

* * *

"Okay, Tom. This funny country on the map is the middle eastern nation of Qatar. It's this pointed oval shape. And this is where the Holy Faith Foundation has its headquarters."

Robert sat at the big mahogany desk. Tom Kennedy sat across from him, looking on, as his boss turned the map toward him. Outside, it was another beautifully bright day, with puffy clouds in a sage-blue sky. The sunlight streaked onto the red, pink, and white geraniums by the window and across the huge multicolored Oriental carpet.

"Qatar looks like a football that's been squashed flat." Robert smiled at how silly that sounded. "It's actually a peninsula that sticks straight up north off of Saudi Arabia into the Persian Gulf, which is this strip of ocean"—he pointed—"that stretches between Saudi and Iran."

"And this is where those vipers at the Holy Faith Foundation are located? In Qatar?" Tom scratched his head. "And so, this is where we've got to go, to find some information for our lawsuit. Some actual evidence."

"Right. It says here that Qatar is smaller than the State of Connecticut. But it's got the richest people on earth, because it's got more than ten percent of the oil reserves in the world."

"Now, let me understand." Tom frowned. "We've already filed our lawsuit here, in America. But we have to go to Qatar to get evidence against these vicious dudes at the Holy Faith Foundation?"

"Right. We've got to get a separate hearing way over there, in the courts of Qatar, just to hope we'll be able to question witnesses."

"Do they like Americans in Qatar?"

"The answer is a clear Yes—and also, a clear No. The biggest American air base in the Mideast is in Qatar. The Al Udeid Air Base, with thousands of Americans. And also, there are tons of Americans who help Qatar pump its big-time oil. The second language in Qatar is English. And here's something you'll like. The rules of the courts are in English."

"Amazing."

"But at the same time, they really *don't* like Americans. The Qatari government supports the Muslim Brotherhood. Which is a bunch of terrorists. Qatar welcomes terrorists. The *New York Times* says that Qatar's counter-terrorism record is, quote, 'the worst in the region.' And that's saying something, since there are beehives of terrorism right next door, in places like Yemen and Iran. And the *New York Times* also says that the Qatar is, quote, 'hesitant to act against known terrorists out of concern for appearing to be aligned with the U.S.' They don't like us because they don't want other people to even *think* they like us."

"And so . . . nothing's ever easy. What we've got to do in Qatar is not going to be easy."

"No, because. . . . First, we've got to get the attention of a judge in a Qatari court, where they like terrorists and don't like Americans. We've got to get that judge, then, to order the Holy Faith Foundation to answer questions, on the ground that this Foundation is a bunch of terrorists, although the judge isn't likely to think so, offhand. Then, we've got to get answers, on the record, and under oath, in an official form . . . from people inside this vague, behind-the-scenes Holy Faith Foundation. We've got to get them to confess to being part of a terrorist organization."

"Well, maybe it's do-able." Tom sounded hopeful. "There's this thing called the Hague Evidence Convention. It's an international treaty that lets lawyers get evidence from other countries. We can use that in Qatar, right? The Hague Evidence Convention?"

"Nope."

"Ahhhh . . . We can't use the Hague Evidence Convention to get information from this blessed Foundation? . . . Pray tell, why can't we use it?"

"Because Qatar never agreed to the Hague Evidence Convention. They never signed it."

"Oh. Okay. So . . . . How we gonna do this, Chief? We gonna send out the Bat Signal and beg the Caped Crusader to go give 'em the third degree?"

"We'll have to persuade our judge here in America to write an order, and then we can ask their judge in Qatar to re-order that same order, and ask him to tell the fine folks at the Holy Faith Foundation to answer questions. We'll ask a Qatari judge, and we'll ask nicely."

"Very nicely, I'd say." Tom nodded. "Because we're going to be doing this in a country where they like terrorists, and they don't like Americans, and we'll be begging for the mercy of the local Ayatollah."

* * *

Meanwhile, al Ibrahim was well hidden away, but now, he was frustrated by what he was hearing.

"You mean, I have to just sit around? And wait?"

The man he knew only as Bedouin was patient, at the other end of the line. "We have big plans for you, my excellent friend Ibrahim," Bedouin said softly. "But now is not the time. We have to keep you safe for now."

"Big plans? But what kind of plans? I'm hanging loose in this doghouse full of American infidels that is miles from civilization, and I'd like to be doing something."

"You need to wait." Still, Bedouin was patient. He seemed to know how poorly his footsoldier Ibrahim would react to this period of sitting still. "You have a good place to live for now, near other believers of the faith. Not a doghouse, as I'm informed. You have new clothes."

"I don't like these clothes."

"It is important that you seem like other people around you. You have plenty of money, delivered to you by the command of God. You are an important and victorious servant to Him."

Al Ibrahim mumbled under his breath. And sighed. "I'm in this little place in the country. People don't speak good English, much less Arabic."

At that, Bedouin chuckled. "I know. Believe me, I know." Bedouin was a man of culture, and Ibrahim knew that, even if he didn't know who Bedouin was, or where he was, or why he was in touch with him. Both he and Bedouin used temporary, prepaid mobile telephones, and they would discard them almost daily.

"When will I be able to do something?" Ibrahim pleaded. "Or at least get out of this country that is an abomination to God?"

"Well, the answer is not No, to your requests for action, my Ibrahim. But just not now."

"What will it be? What will I be asked to do?"

Bedouin was silent for a moment, deciding how much he could tell his footsoldier friend and how he could say it. "I can't say exactly what is in your future. All I can say is that the Mother of Leaders, the Foundation of Light, in the Better Country that we know, believes that there is more to do to settle the fallout from what we have done most recently. There is more to do. You will have to wait, but not forever. There is more to do, Ibrahim. You are a servant of God. And beloved of God."

10

itting in front of his intarsiato chest, Jimmy Coleman was in a good mood. "You know, Jennifer, we're going to have a good time with this Motion to Dismiss that we've filed. I like to argue a Motion to Dismiss. Your opponent can't hurt you at this kind of hearing, and you can hurt him read bad."

Jennifer Lowenstein smiled.

"It's like the reason I liked being a safety, playing football. You get to hit other people, but you don't get hit as much yourself."

At that, Jennifer laughed.

"You did a good job writing this Motion," Jimmy went on. His voice was like a cement truck in slow traffic. "That's the way we did it back in my younger days. Get in with your best shot and keep pounding at it."

Jennifer perked up. "Your younger days?" Everyone knew where Jimmy Coleman had come from. A gang in Los Angeles. Complete with initiations that included rapes that would never be reported and with drive-by shootings from stolen cars that left no identification. Nobody knew how this violent child named Jimmy Coleman had pulled himself up to go to college and then to law school, or how he had emerged at the top of his class, or how it was possible that he'd gone to work at this big law firm. Or how he had stayed with it.

"But I still can't help hoping that they catch the right people." Jennifer shook her head. "The ones who set up this bombing in the stadium. The pictures of the people who died. . . ."

Jimmy frowned and shook his head. "Wasn't me who died," he grated. "Or you, or any of our homeboys. And all I want is to get our good client out of this lawsuit. Regardless of who did it. Getting them out would be a win, and it would be fun. Just like one of those drive-by's we did, because back then, I didn't care whether the bullets just left our calling card or whether they punctured a resident. Which happened sometimes."

His voice scratched more than usual when he added, "Jennifer, remember, I told you about how the Deacons threw me off a building, one time when I was a kid, about fifteen? The bad guys from the next territory. And you asked me, 'Why'd they do that?' And the answer was, to kill me, of course. Only it didn't. Broke both my legs, but I managed to hobble fast enough to get out of there. Well, here's what I want now. I want to throw Robert Herrick's Complaint off a building."

Now Jimmy smiled, perhaps from remembering old times. "Why? To kill it, of course."

* * *

Outside the city and thirty miles to the south, the tall man named al Ibrahim heard a commotion down in the parking lot. Curious, he dragged his six-foot-seven frame out of an easy chair and walked to the window. He parted the blinds. Below his apartment, he saw what looked like a whole fleet of police cars—deputy sheriff's cars, to be more precise—pulling together into the parking areas nearest the building. An army of deputies jumped out of their vehicles without closing their car doors. They couldn't be silent and move so quickly, but obviously, they were trying to run as quietly as they could.

Ibrahim thought fast. There was nothing he could do. There was nowhere he could hide in this apartment, even as spacious as it was. Trying to escape by boosting his height into an air intake sounded impractical, like a losing proposition; and even if the possibility existed that he could do it, there wasn't time. His eyes dilated from momentary shock.

Then, he relaxed. He made himself comfortable and waited quietly, because there was nothing else to do.

The officers disappeared behind the first floor landing. From Ibrahim's window, he couldn't see the first steps, where they would start up the stairs toward him.

Suddenly there was a lot of shouting, but the sound was muffled by his window. It was followed by a breaking noise that could have had many possible causes, including a boot kicking a door. Then, the shouting continued inside, down below.

Finally, two officers emerged in the parking lot, pushing a scruffy subject wearing socks and dirty blue jeans, with his hands cuffed behind him. Ibrahim heard some of the next words clearly enough. ". . . Warrant for your arrest. . . . Jason, we got a warrant. Outstanding warrant . . . been outstanding more'n than a year. Robbery, six cases. And plus, you gonna have some extra trouble, Jason, because it looks like you been keepin a private drugstore full of amphetamines and quays in this apartment too. Possession with intent to distribute, is what you'll be hearin about yourself."

He breathed his realization with relief. It wasn't . . . about me. At all. These cops weren't here for me! . . .

He stood looking down for a long time. The deputies cleared the scene. Al Ibrahim stood still and watched closely.

Then he sat down.

Half an hour later, he reached for his prepaid, throwaway phone that was new today and would be gone soon. He dialed the number. "Bedouin . . . . Bedouin," he whispered.

"Bedouin is unavailable. Message?"

"Message? Message. . . . You've got to get me out of here. I'm going nuts. At least . . . you've got to move me away from here or give me something to do."

* * *

Robert Herrick left his office late and finally went home. He went to bed at 10:30. "I'm as ready to oppose this Motion to Dismiss as I'll ever be," he told Maria.

He was asleep by eleven o'clock. But an hour later, he drifted to his past. The dream came back, the dream he dreaded . . . .

As Lieutenant Robert Herrick, he began to feel and see what he had come to call "the disaster dream": a dream that was both a fallout from the stadium bombing and a nightmare from the worst period of his life. From the War. It was a strange dream. He was experiencing his role years earlier in the hills near the "DMZ"—the Demilitarized Zone—and at one and the same time, he was narrating the event to Maria, his wife. The words he dreamed were inadequate to convey the horror that he was seeing.

. . . "We were plodding through jungle." He imagined himself seeing it and describing it at the same time. "Cutting our way through, sometimes. It was a world full of green, an unearthly green that seemed like the color of the green in hell, the kind of green that wraps around you, strangles you, so that every step is a leafy bundle of claws and teeth that slashes you. All of a sudden, I burst out into the clearing behind my other guys. On this grassy plain, the clearing stretched maybe a couple hundred yards, the length of two or three football fields. We all knew that this clearing was a whole mass of danger, a catastrophe. Danger you could feel and smell.

"I was the eighth man. I had shed my insignia, my lieutenant's bars, of course. If they can identify the leader walking in a string of men, the bad guys will shoot that leader. If they can't, they sometimes shoot the man with the radio. We rotated the assignment of carrying the radio and tried to cover it, to hide it. This was decades before they invented cell phones, and the radio was a big heavy bulk that you carried on your back.

"The guy we called 'Wise Man' was at the point. In front. His real name was Danny Wise, from Steel Bluff, South Dakota, but it got shortened to Wise Man, of course. Wise Man was always on point. It was crazy dangerous, but he just did it, every time, until it got to be an automatic thing. Wise Man was little, about five feet seven or eight, and he was quick. Wiry and skinny, you know? He could move faster than anyone else if the jungle turned into an ambush. He was a splib dude. A 'splib' is a black guy, but the word isn't negative; it's neutral, the same way that a 'chuck dude' is a white guy.

"Our objective was to search and destroy. A 'Search and Destroy Mission,' meaning that we knew they were out there and we had to find them. It was known that the enemy had been on Hill 861, ahead of us, and we were on the saddle, the ridge, that dipped between 861 and Hill 558, where we had come from. These were just nameless bumps in the earth, near the Demilitarized Zone. I should say the *so-called* Demilitarized Zone. Search and destroy was a common mission but a scary one. In officer school they called it a 'meeting encounter,' meaning that chance and the enemy controlled the meeting—and more importantly, the timing. Our job was to push forward through that bushy, growing, crawling hell until we saw them or they saw us.

"The clearing was more than dangerous. We had to cross it, but it was deadly to have to do it. We would stagger a few stooping, bent-down steps and fall—and then squirm ahead. That was the plan. A clearing isn't what you want, because the enemy can lie concealed in the jungle while they see you clearly, and they can cover you with bullets and RPG's, which are grenades, all at once, while you're a stand-up target.

"All of a sudden, Wise Man dove down into high grass. In a single motion. I don't know what he heard or saw. It may have been some sort of clinking sound like metal on the metal of a SKS, which was the enemy's standard semiautomatic, or it might have been movement in the brush that wasn't wind. He was quick. Almost immediately, the noise was thunderous, of automatic fire and RPG's and God knows what else. The second guy, this time, was Garey Pogue. A big guy. He didn't make it to the ground before he spun around. His mouth was wide open, and his face was intact, but it was a curious shape and covered with a sickening spread of red, red blood. Redder than you've ever seen. The other guys were down by now, faster than Garey.

"Wise Man was well on the way to emptying his M-1 and probably was fingering a new magazine. Thank goodness for him.

"I was busy calculating. Not calculating exactly, but figuring. Could we call in "CAS," which means close air support? A helicopter, like a Huey gunship? It was a clear-enough-but-cloudy enough day. It's a paradox: if there's too much in the sky, visibility won't support a helicopter, but if there's not enough cover, it's harder for those guys, and no one will let them fly if it's too dangerous. A fighter-bomber like an F-5 would be welcome, and the bad guys probably wouldn't be too close to us for that kind of firepower. Still, I worried about the likelihood of the fighter-bomber dropping ordnance on the friendlies, of course. Namely, us. Bombing us, our own friendly selves.

"'This is Alpha One Actual,' I shouted into the radio. 'Requesting air support.' You see, that word, 'Actual,' means that I'm the specific individual commanding the unit. If someone just said Alpha One, or Charlie Two, it could be anyone in that unit. 'Actual' means that I'm the serendipitous gentleman in charge during this developing disaster. I gave them the coordinates of the enemy. 'Nowhere near the clearing,' I added. 'Away from the clearing! Tell them that. That's where we are, your friendlies, so drop the stuff far away from the clearing.'

"We maintained fire for what seemed like forever. Maybe it was twenty minutes, maybe it was forty. The aircraft came out of nowhere. Really welcome. An F-5, carrying high-drag 500 pound bombs and a lot of other toys. I just prayed that they didn't make a mistake, like getting the coordinates off just a little, or thinking that they were supposed to bomb the clearing instead of stay away from the clearing. We didn't see the bombs drop, of course, or the napalm, but they did drop. And suddenly, the jungle in front of us was orange fire, orange with black outlines, orange the color of implements in a Satanic ritual, rising to the sky like steam from a full smokestack. We never knew what happened to the enemy because we didn't find anyone dead, when we moved on after it was quiet, and they may have dee-deed out of there safe and unmolested.

"We were able to use our clearing as an LZ, a landing zone for a helicopter. We got Garey Pogue out within an hour. He lived, and that was miraculous.

"But in my mind, the whole time, the fireball grew. And grew. And then, the whole scene changed. The fireball from the F-5 was replaced, in my mind, during my dream, by . . . the image of Delmar Stadium during the football game, with the explosion in the end zone. It transformed. And once again, I saw a vision of helpless people becoming victims, trying to run, trying to squat down, burning, dying, there in the stadium. My dream about the War had been transformed, taken over by a different war, the war against random innocent people in the stadium. . . ."

* * *

. . . And that was when Robert woke up, panting and bucking. Maria was shaking him.

After he settled down, he said to her: "This is what that explosion in the stadium is doing to me."

She corrected him: "To us." And she added, "This lawsuit is going to remind you every day about this dream. It's going to remind both of us. Get out of this case! Give it to someone who wasn't at the stadium and didn't see it. This lawsuit's going to bring back the dream over and over."

Maria shook her head. "But now you've got to get up and go argue your case. The Motion to Dismiss is on, today. I wish it weren't."

11

There were three loud knocks from outside of the back door to the courtroom. It opened suddenly, and a law clerk stepped out.

"Order in the Court. Everyone rise, please. This United States District Court is now open, according to law, with the Honorable Elsa Domínguez presiding. God bless the United States and this honorable Court."

The law clerk pronounced these standard words the way law clerks always did: loudly, distinctly, and with conviction.

"Be seated, please," said the judge pleasantly.

She looked down. "How are you, Mr. Coleman?"

He smiled his dirty smile. "Very well, Judge Domínguez, thank you."

"Mr. Herrick?" The judge was formal but friendly.

"Just fine, your honor. And you?"

"Bouncy and fun, like always." She laughed, and so did the lawyers. "Now, Mr. Coleman, you're the one who filed this Motion to Dismiss. I'll hear from you first. But let me tell you something before you start. I've read the briefs filed by both sides, so tell me something new."

"Your honor, I'll do that. Our brief doesn't count all the inadequacies we found, but I can tell you, we've identified more unsupported conclusions in this Complaint than there were in the Complaint that the Supreme Court threw out in the *Twombly* case. *Bell Telephone versus Twombly*. The central piece of vague groundlessness is Mr. Herrick's disconnected allegation that the Foundation, here—the Holy Faith Foundation—somehow, in an unspecified way, *'financed'* that terrible bombing that took place in our football stadium. Without any facts, just a mile-wide conclusion that my client 'financed' it."

Jimmy's voice scraped with disgust. "The Holy Faith Foundation is one of the biggest charities in the Mideast. It does good works all over the

58

world, with scores of millions of dollars. Mr. Herrick's Complaint also uses a lot of synonyms for 'financing' something. He says that this charity 'funded' that deplorable act. He says that the Foundation, quote, 'gave money through other entities' to the terrorists. He never backs up these conclusions, or the other conclusions in this Complaint, with any facts. And I have to add: The Holy Faith Foundation condemns that terroristic act, just as I do."

"Mr. Herrick?" The judge's voice had an edge of accusation to it. "Isn't that true, about the unsupported conclusions in your Complaint?"

"So far as it goes, your honor. Let me point out, first, that we're at the beginning of the case. The Supreme Court didn't say we had to stuff all of our evidence into the Complaint. That's impossible. All the Court said was, we have to provide facts that make our claim, quote, 'plausible.' If you were to say, 'Defendant X committed a crime, and Defendant Y financed his committing it,' wouldn't that make it plausible that Defendant Y was involved too?"

Robert wore a pinstriped suit with a dotted tie. The lawyer's uniform. He stretched to his full height. "Your honor: Look at the kind of system Mr. Coleman is advocating. It would make it impossible to even begin a claim against any defendant that did some basic money-laundering. It isn't until later stages of investigation, that a plaintiff can trace all the shell corporations and individuals shifting their cash and credit, that even a simple money laundering case involves. You can't do that until the lawsuit's been on file, and you've obtained the documents that prove it from the defendant."

"Well, Mr. Coleman, that's true too. Isn't it?"

"Not according to the Supreme Court, your honor. The Court pointed out how expensive that kind of document-production is. It would cost hundreds of thousands just to find and produce and read all of the documents that Mr. Herrick would want us to give to him, and that's why the Supreme Court said that Mr. Herrick's got to have something tangible, something concrete, something more than the gossamer tissue of imagined vagueness in this Complaint that he's filed."

Jimmy's grating voice dipped down and rose high as he denounced the "leaps of logic and foolish speculations in this disgrace of a Complaint." And then his voice dripped staccato sweetness. "The Supreme Court intended the Motion to Dismiss for exactly this kind of case, which would waste the gifts of a worldwide charity on a wild goose chase."

Robert stood. "Again, your honor, what the Supreme Court said was that the Complaint has to contain a 'short and plain statement.' Yes, it has to have facts. But the kinds of facts it has to have are just those that are sufficient to make the claim, quote, 'plausible.' Plausible, that's all. The Supreme Court specifically said that it doesn't even have to seem probable, just 'plausible.' We've said, in the Complaint, based on a *Wall Street Journal* report that is attached as an exhibit, that the Foundation, quote, 'financed the actions of the three co-conspirators by parceling money into cooperative corporations, partnerships, individuals, and other entities in a manner designed to conceal the origin of the financing.' That's enough to make the claim 'plausible.' And if that isn't enough, nobody will ever be able to file a Complaint in a case involving money laundering."

The judge was quick to speak at this point. "All right. I think I have your arguments. You're both starting to repeat, and I think I've heard enough. This case will send me back to the law books, not just to reread that *Twombly* case, but also other cases. And to read and reread the Complaint.

"I can only add, Mr. Herrick, that whether you're right about the Supreme Court making claims impossible or not, one thing is sure. Conclusions are not enough. That's what the Court said. The Court was aware that it would be making the claim in the *Twombly* case unprovable even if that claim was as good as gold. And later, it did the same thing in a civil rights case, recognizing that it was killing what might be a valid claim. And so, Mr. Herrick, as for your argument that it's hard to plead a money-laundering case, well, the Supreme Court has said, in effect, 'We know that, but that's tough.'"

Jimmy Coleman was experienced enough to stay quiet now, while he was winning. He just nodded. Robert looked miserably in Jimmy's direction, and then he looked away . . . when he saw that same, dirty, lopsided smile.

* * *

Eight time zones to the east, the man named Sharif al Shaikh, who called himself Bedouin, sat again at his conference room at the top of the Aspire Tower. The building that looked like a torch; the building designed to signify that the light of the world is right here, in the sumptuous city of Doha, Qatar, the capital of the country that God has blessed.

"We have this . . . this court case, in America." Bedouin's forehead was misshapen so that he frowned even when he smiled, and his jaw came to a point beneath those constant black sunglasses that hung on a bigger nose than fit his face. "We have this . . . ," he spit out the word, "this lawsuit. We have a very good lawyer, of course. A lawyer who will fight the other side and give no space to anyone. And our lawyer has filed a Motion to Dismiss the lawsuit."

"Are we really concerned about a lawsuit?" The Vice President wore a white burnoose and a white robe with arabesque trim, just as Bedouin did. "The courts don't do much, do they? As far as I know, the main active courts here are the sharia courts, and they are occupied with family relationships and crimes. Traditional crimes. Sharia crimes. In America, I know they don't have sharia courts, and it's a shame that they don't, but are the courts in America so different?"

"Yes, absolutely!" Bedouin practically shouted it. His ample belly quivered. "The courts are crazy in America! That's the hellish land of infidels, the place where the unholy take their most protective refuge. They think, in America, that blasphemy and insults to the Prophet are perfectly all right . . . ," here Bedouin stamped his sandals, "and that all kinds of sinful horror are just something they call 'freedom of speech.' And the courts go along with that, and with other deranged behavior."

"But can the courts do anything to us here? Our courts cannot say anything that commands the Amir, or that contradicts the Amir. Surely they cannot do that to us here, from America."

"No. Even in America, they cannot do that and make it happen here, in our country. But if a court in America issues a fatwa against our Foundation, a judgment, it can mean that we will be harassed all over the world. I have seen it. Our holdings will be threatened with seizure in Germany, and our funds will be vulnerable to confiscation even in Switzerland."

"But my Bedouin, you said that our lawyer has filed a motion to dismiss this lawsuit," said the Comptroller. "Won't that get rid of it?"

"Our lawyer says, maybe. And maybe not. That's the way things are in America. You can't tell anything about the law, in America. He doesn't know whether the judge will dismiss this disgusting lawsuit or not."

"So, what do we do?"

"That is why I have called this meeting. I think the Motion to Dismiss has to be granted; I cannot imagine otherwise. But our lawyer has suggested that we pay a piddling amount. A few million dollars. And call it a gift, a charitable contribution, to the survivors of people killed in the explosion at the football stadium."

"Why?"

"In America, they say that in this way, we will be paying the 'nuisance value' of the lawsuit. The nuisance value means the amount we would pay just to defend the lawsuit. The amount we would pay just to get rid of the nuisance. I like that. It shows that even American demons can produce some interesting twists. Even Beelzebub turns out felicitous phrases. More importantly, our lawyer says that a well-timed offer of nuisance value will often work, especially if the lawyer on the other side is greedy and wants to collect a quick fee."

The burnoose-topped gathering around the conference table all laughed at that. Everyone here knew that Americans were greedy. They knew it, because they knew that Americans shared every other negative quality.

"And after all, American lawyers must be even more greedy than the average American." Bedouin smiled his angry-looking smile. "Even here in Doha, in God's kingdom, the lawyers are soaked in avarice. Lawyers everywhere are loquacious, mendacious, and avaricious."

When some of the faces around the table looked blank—as if to say, What do those words mean?—Bedouin added: "That means they are talkative, untruthful . . . and most of all, greedy."

12

Tom Kennedy stepped into Robert's office looking like a man who just swallowed a tree full of lemons. "The judge says . . . our Complaint is insufficient and subject to being dismissed."

"I know. I read the order."

"Is this the end of this magnificent adventure? Is this the last chapter in our long-shot lawsuit against the Holy Faith Foundation?"

"It may be."

"How could it not be? Judge Domínguez's order is pretty clear."

"We can file an Amended Complaint. The Judge has pointed out a couple of things we need to be more particular about."

"But how can we? We put everything we know into this Complaint."

"I think Judge Domínguez knows that. She's pretty smart. She's even suggested a way for us to salvage the Complaint, by using the Federal Rules of Civil Procedure."

"I must have missed that."

"Look here. The order refers us to a section of Rule Eleven of the Federal Rules of Civil Procedure. And that Rule says, if we think we will discover evidence but we don't have it yet, we can say that in the Complaint."

"Well . . . , I've never done . . . that kind of Complaint before. I guess that's why your name is on the door to this law firm, Robert, instead of mine."

Robert laughed. "There still is a lot of stuff that I should know too, but I don't. And it's pretty unusual to use this Rule, so don't feel bad about not knowing it."

"Okay, O Wise Leader. So, how do we amend the Complaint?"

"Well, here's the Rule." Robert pointed to a page in a thick paperback book with the title, Federal Rules of Civil Procedure. "Here's Rule Eleven.

This Rule says we should just go ahead and make the allegation. We say what we think is correct, and what we think we will be able to prove. Even if we don't have the evidence yet. And we should 'designate' it as coming under this Rule. Then the Rule says, we should add a sentence saying that we believe that we'll be able to discover evidence to support what we have said. We think we'll discover it from the defendant and from other sources."

"All right. I get it. So, we say that The Holy Faith Foundation's financing was delivered through another company or individual, whose name is unknown as of now. And we add, 'Plaintiffs designate this statement as one for which evidence is now unknown. But Plaintiffs expect to obtain evidence through discovery.'"

"That's right. This Rule fits our situation exactly. Sometimes, the details of exactly how a defendant did something wrong are known only to that defendant. Here, we don't know how the Holy Faith Foundation funneled money to the terrorists, or the exact money trail that the Holy Faith Foundation used, because we can't be expected to know. But we can find out, using the other Rules in this Rule Book. The drafters of the Rules didn't want to make it impossible to bring a case like this. That would end up rewarding money launderers."

"Will this Rule, this Rule Eleven, do the trick, then?"

"Well . . . ummmm . . . I don't know. That's why I've always said, this is an awkward lawsuit."

* * *

Jimmy Coleman was in his office when the Amended Complaint came in. He was sitting at his flower-printed intarsiato desk, talking to one of his Booker & Bayne partners. They had been talking about a lawsuit, but their conversation had dissolved into a discussion about fly fishing for brook trout. Lawyers' conversations tend to do that. They intended to bill the client for the entire discussion, of course, including the part about fly fishing.

"Okay, so what you're saying is that you jerk down twice when the fish hits." Jimmy smiled.

"Well, yes. But the first time, not so hard. You gotta pull real light."

And that was when six-foot-Lisa-the-secretary knocked. "I thought you'd want this right away. Here's an Amended Complaint from Robert Herrick."

"Yes." Jimmy scanned the Amended Suit Papers to find the parts that the judge's order had said were inadequate. He read some of the words out loud. "Plaintiffs designate this allegation . . . do not now have evidence

... expect to obtain evidence through discovery ... attached Exhibit is a *Wall Street Journal* article that supports Plaintiffs' statements ... Plaintiffs intend to find ... evidence .... will support these statements ..."

Jimmy stopped reading and said, "Lisa, find me Jennifer Lowenstein. Right away."

"These are ridiculous allegations," said Jimmy's partner. "You'll just file the same kind of Motion to Dismiss, won't you?"

"Oh, we'll file a Second Motion to Dismiss, all right. It won't be quite the same, and that's what I'm going to ask Jennifer Lowenstein to do. She's the associate I have the most confidence in. But I can see what Robert Herrick is doing, unfortunately."

"Robert Herrick is just an ambulance chaser who's gotten as rich as King Nebuchadnezzar from the chasing."

"We'll certainly treat him that way in our Second Motion to Dismiss." Jimmy glanced at the Amended Complaint. "But I see what Herrick is doing. He's using the Rules—a part of Rule Eleven that doesn't come up much, but I'm familiar with it. And even though we'll deny it, I think that worthless son of a bitch, that Herrick, might be doing it in a way that will succeed, unfortunately. We may lose the Second Motion to Dismiss. We may be stuck. Hooked." Jimmy laughed.

"And if the judge overrules this Motion to Dismiss," Jimmy grated, "We'll just have to beat Herrick the traditional way, in front of a jury." He grinned. "Because as far as the Motion to Dismiss goes, we may be caught. Hooked, just like that brook trout that you and I were having so much fun talking about."

"And then, you can bill those rich Arab clients a whole lot more," his partner said, by way of consolation. Jimmy laughed harder.

* * *

The day after Booker and Bayne's Second Motion to Dismiss hit the courthouse, Judge Domínguez issued her ruling.

IN THE UNITED STATES DISTRICT COURT
FOR THE SOUTHERN DISTRICT OF TEXAS

SENATOR ELLEN McKAY, et al.,	)	
PLAINTIFFS,	)	
V.	)	CIVIL NO. 22835
THE HOLY FAITH FOUNDATION,	)	
DEFENDANT	)	

<u>ORDER OVERRULING FOUNDATION'S SECOND MOTION TO DISMISS</u>

The Holy Faith Foundation's Second Motion to Dismiss came on to be heard this day, and the court having considered the pleadings and arguments of counsel, it is ORDERED that the Amended Complaint is sufficient, and the Second Motion to Dismiss is overruled.

Elsa Domínguez,
United States District Judge

Robert saw Tom getting ready to celebrate, and so he immediately interrupted. "Don't feel good, yet, Tom. There's an opinion of the court that goes along with this order. And unfortunately, the opinion takes away a lot of what the order seems to give us."

He picked up the opinion. And said, "The court's opinion goes through each passage that the First Motion to Dismiss challenged, and it explains why our Amended Complaint answers the problems. But in nearly every instance, the opinion uses words like, 'just barely,' or 'meets the lowest, minimum standards.' The court is saying that our Amended Complaint is enough to keep us in court, but the judge knows it's going to be hard to prove. And then, the opinion adds these words, which are not very helpful to us.

"'The Court warns Plaintiffs that they face obstacles in presenting the evidence that they must produce. This Court will not hesitate to dismiss the Amended Complaint if the conditions for dismissal appear later. Further, the Court directs the parties to be sparing with expensive discovery or depositions as they search for the elusive evidence that Plaintiffs so boldly predict that they will find.'"

He put the opinion down on his desk. "Tom, I've heard of courts telling plaintiffs to go light on the discovery. To avoid expense. But I've never faced it in any case of mine. And to us, this opinion is really bad news."

"It sure is. We need real depositions and discovery, good discovery, to find what we need."

"Well, let's get started on it. I've asked a team of associates to find out how we can question people in Qatar. Specifically, I asked them to research a procedure called 'Letters Rogatory,' which is the fancy name for a method of asking foreign courts to let us ask those questions. That's something most lawyers never hear about, these blessed 'Letters Rogatory.' And I've asked the associates to write us up a Motion to be filed with Judge Domínguez, which is called a 'Motion to Issue Letters Rogatory.' That's so that we can go to Qatar and present these Letters Rogatory, this request for questioning, to a court there, and hopefully, get permission to take a deposition or two, directing our questions to people at the Holy Faith Foundation."

"Oh. Great." Tom shook his head. "I had forgotten about that. Judge Domínguez tells us to be simple about the discovery, and our first act is going to be to ask her to order a complicated process for taking a deposition overseas. And to talk about 'Letters Rogatory,' which is a fancy name that most lawyers have never heard of."

They both looked out at the horizon, through the tall windows and across the expanse of green that faced them, but they didn't find any inspiration there.

13

At eighteen thousand feet above the Persian Gulf, the G-II aircraft belonging to Robert Herrick and Associates broke through a bank of altocumulus clouds.

Robert pointed down. "Look at the color of the water. We're making this trip for business, to get information from the Holy Faith Foundation, but the country and the ocean are going to be beautiful."

"Amazing." Maria was still moving around, but now she sat and put on her seat belt. "It's a pure, sparkling baby blue color, in this light. Really nice. Can we go swimming?"

"You can. As for Tom and me, we came to work." Hurriedly, he added, "And the legal assistants, too. Don't you go luring these legal assistants away from the job, Maria."

Maria laughed at that. "You're not coming with me to swim? Then I guess I'll go shopping instead." She had a stack of catalogues. "From what I understand, this place has the best of the best, because the Qatari people can pretty well afford it."

"Well, Robert, you'd better re-evaluate the whole mission." Tom shook his head. "That is, if you still want to be able to afford things like this airplane, after Maria gets through with Qatar."

"I guess this airplane, this Gulfstream II, is your prize possession. Your baby." Maria laughed at him again.

"No. That would be you, Maria."

"Besides," he added, "this G-II is not a toy. It's a tool, and it helps me to do the job of a lawyer."

At that, both Tom and Maria laughed, and so did Robert. "But serious-ly, I think we come out ahead, the law firm does, with this airplane. As compared to commercial flights. It's not the newest model, and I've had it a long time. I'd never get rid of something just because there's a newer one."

"Yes, your tight-fistedness is well known. And also, it is known far and wide that you're miserly. And parsimonius."

"Okay, Maria, so I'm careful about spending." He saw that she was looking at him skeptically. "And anyway, you know what my prize possession is, in terms of things instead of you, my forever love. The Duesenberg. The 1931 Stutz. The '38 Packard, '30 Bentley, '30 Cadillac, and my forty-two other fine cars. It's my one indulgence."

"Your one indulgence? What about the vineyard, the winery, the ranch, the horses, the chamber orchestra. . . ."

They both laughed.

"It's a long flight," Tom said. "I had no idea we'd go over Canada. And Greenland. Or that when we refueled, it would be in Paris. A loooong flight, and you two are getting punchy."

Suddenly, a sliver of land was visible in the fuzzy distance. Robert spoke over the intercom to the pilot. "Randy, tell us what we're seeing."

"Sure. This sandy brown patch in front of us and to the right is the northeast tip of Qatar. This strange kingdom is a peninsula that sticks out into the Persian Gulf, shaped like an oval that's pinched at the ends."

The aircraft continued to descend. "Now, what's coming up underneath your side is a town called Ar Ruwys. We're heading right between that little place and another little burg called Al Klawayr."

"Why can't they have names I'd recognize for the towns?" Maria laughed, "Like Boston or Havana?"

"Baby, these are Arabic people."

"Okay, so couldn't these little burgs be called Omar Khayam or something?" She was still having a good time being silly.

The pilot broke through her attempts at humor. "See the things that stick up, there in Ar Ruwys? Those are minarets. That's the main mosque at Ar Ruwys."

"Looks like an oil field town, from the pipe racks," Maria said.

"And now we get a lot of sand," Randy-the-pilot went on. And it was true. The land was almost colorless, just a mild-almost-white light tan, with lines that might be roads and an occasional slight bump of a hill. Here and there, they could see a housing compound, with green inside the walls. Other than that, the sand went on forever. "Almost nobody lives inland, in Qatar," Randy added.

Tom looked at Robert for a moment. "Are we going to meet with our local counsel tomorrow, before going to the Qatari court? Is that right?"

"Yes. Mustafa Abboud, our Qatari lawyer. He's filed our request for questioning the officers of the Holy Faith Foundation. He thinks we have a decent chance to get something—some kind of order to the Foundation and its officers, to provide some sort of discovery to us. But the question is, what will it be, if we do get it?"

"Right. Questioning some low-level flunky won't help very much. And if all we're allowed to do is to use written questions, that won't help at all."

Randy, the pilot, broke in at this point. "The City of Doha is in front of us, on the far edge of Qatar. The western coast. It's the capital and one of the most deluxe, opulent cities in the world. Up to the north is West Bay Lagoon. Pricey real estate. The circular bay has a swanky drive along its coast called Al Corniche Street. That's where Maria will go, because it's like Rodeo Drive or Fifth Avenue. Or the Galleria. You can drop a big bundle of wampum in a short time. There's an artificial island called 'The Pearl,' and you can't go there unless you're certifiably a zillionaire. And off to the left, you see that spectacular sight? That amazing building is the Aspire Tower, almost a quarter mile tall and shaped like a torch. That's where your defendant is: the Holy Faith Foundation."

Now, the aircraft banked hard to port—a hard left turn. "We're going over the Ras Abu Expressway. And next . . . here we go over the ocean again, but this time on the west coast. . . . Turning still, to port. . . . And now, we're heading north, just the short distance to Hamad International Airport."

A minute later, the G-II glided onto the runway. "Wow," Maria said, sitting still for a change.

* * *

"I'm Mustafa," the Qatari lawyer said with a smile. "Mustafa Abboud."

Robert shook his hand. He said to Tom, "Mustafa went to school at the University of Illinois. And got a law degree at Pennsylvania, in America."

"Good. Maybe we can understand each other." Tom laughed.

Mustafa smiled. "Well, but I also went to Qatar University Law School. To get some on-the-ground training, you know."

"And I guess your training includes knowing how to tie on a burnoose." Tom laughed as he looked at the pictures on the wall, showing plenty of burnoose-topped lawyers. But for now, Mustafa wore an elegant pinstriped suit instead, with a dotted blue tie. His teeth gleamed, and his hair was close-cropped.

"Well, today I'm dressed down, to help the foreigners feel comfortable." Mustafa laughed too.

Robert had a single thought. "What do you think of our chances with the court, Mustafa?"

"Impossible to know. We don't get a lot of these requests for discovery from other countries. Oh, we get enough so that the judges know about them. Fortunately, we have Judge Massad, and he probably won't like what happened with this explosion in the stadium. He's American-educated too. Went to Emory Law School in Atlanta. Biggest problem is that everybody knows the Holy Faith Foundation, and here in this country, it has a reputation for attitudes that the people share."

Mustafa's office was upscale, with mahogany brown trim and light green walls matched with an oriental carpet that echoed these colors. His desk was ornate, but the group sat in an area with a table and plenty of gold-colored chairs with curlicues carved into them. Through the floor-to-ceiling window, the Qatari skyscrapers were visible: a riot of colors and strange shapes, looking like something out of a Dr. Seuss cartoon. Here was a building shaped like an elongated thimble, with an hourglass structure next to it, and next to that, an enormous asymmetrical edifice with spiral stripes around it.

"Tell us about the courts, please," Robert asked. "I've heard on the one hand that the judges are pretty up-to-date and fair. And I've also heard the opposite, that they are medieval, too, and that stoning is still a sentence for certain crimes."

Mustafa smiled. "Both true. On the one hand, we have the sharia courts. But they won't be involved. They apply the traditional law of the Prophet to family law, inheritance, and crimes. They pronounce the 'verdict of God.' Stoning is still on the books, but it's pretty well obsolete and doesn't get ordered much nowadays. Instead, what will be involved in your case is the 'Adlia' court. AD-lee-ah court. It's the court of commerce."

"And I guess—with so much dependence on contractors and trade, Qatar had to develop commercial courts that are fair, or at least sort of fair."

"That's right. Judge Massad is one of the judges of the Civil Court, Second Department. Heavily westernized. We have a split in Qatar, with Fundamentalists claiming that the power of law comes only from God, and frankly, the Fundamentalists are on the rise. But the elite judges of the Civil Court are well established and are in fact elite. There are seven very large law firms here that practice in these courts, including of course my own."

Mustafa outlined the events that would likely occur in the court. "Stand whenever you address the court," he concluded. "And speak only when you are spoken to."

14

May it please the court, My Lord," said Mustafa, the Qatari lawyer, to the judge. Both of them wore traditional dress, with burnooses, although there were lawyers in business suits present as well. Evidently, it was proper to wear either. But Mustafa had told Robert, "I'd probably better dress the part of the humble local, in this particular case."

"M'Lord, May I present Mr. Robert Herrick," Mustafa went on. "He is a very honorable lawyer from the United States, and in fact he's from Texas. Stand up, please, Mr. Herrick."

"Good morning, Mr. Herrick." The judge was genial and urbane. "From Texas? Do you have a monstrous spread and abundant cattle? Like everybody else?"

"Well, ah . . . , yes, My Lord. Maybe not exactly monstrous."

"He happens to have a ranch," Mustafa added unnecessarily.

"Oh, I was just kidding." The judge's smile grew, and he laughed. "As you were, Mr. Herrick. Don't let me embarrass you."

"My Lord, I just didn't want you to think I was 'all hat and no cattle,'" Robert said. And laughed too. If the judge laughs at something he himself has said, it's a good idea for the lawyer to echo the humor in the judge's remark, whether it's funny or not.

The judge apparently had never heard this saying about hats and cattle, and now he threw his head back and laughed out loud. "That's a good one. Probably comes from the folks in the wide open spaces, I guess."

Then he turned to the other side of the courtroom and went through the same kinds of pleasantries. Well, Robert thought to himself, judges are alike all over the world. They're almost all good politicians.

This courtroom, he thought, was surprisingly simple. Clean and solid, and sparkling with upkeep, but with plain blond wood paneling up to the height of the chairs and white walls above that, unadorned except for a large photograph of the Amir of Qatar behind the judge.

"I've read your memorials," the judge pronounced. He turned to Robert and explained: "Memorials are what you would call 'summaries of evidence' in America." He looked down at the papers and paused. "It will not be difficult in this case. Qatar is a powerful country, but we're small, and commerce is essential here. We must respect courts in other countries if others are going to respect our courts. I have read the order of the court in America, which requests the taking of four American-style depositions. I am inclined to grant the request, but possibly not for all four depositions. Counsel for the Holy Faith Foundation, what say you?"

"It's an outrageous charge against our Foundation," said the defense lawyer, "and every burden placed on the Foundation means less that it can perform of its charitable activities. The request should be denied outright. At most, there should be a limited number of written questions."

"Well, you can't get much with written questions in this situation," said the judge. Thank goodness, Robert thought, this judge went to law school in the United States. The preference for oral questioning before trial is an American obsession.

"We all know what a scourge to the world this kind of terrorism is," the judge went on. "And we all know that sometimes it originates in Arab countries. Peace be to the Prophet! I don't start with any opinion that the Holy Faith Foundation would have done something like this—it's a pretty foreign idea to me—but it behooves us to be sure that we're open about it. And you can't investigate a case by assuming, at the beginning, that one party or the other is right."

There was a pause. Then: "Two depositions," offered the judge, and smiled.

Judges are the same everywhere, Robert thought again. If there is a satisfactory way to compromise, a judge will prefer that rather than making one party win.

"As long as they are of financial managers at the top level," said Mustafa, "we can get by with that, although we'd be more sure with four."

"All right." The judge was ready to rule. Judges everywhere looked the same, when they were ready to rule, Robert thought to himself. "Two depositions." The judge looked down at the defense lawyer. "At least one is to be the top financial officer: the CFO or equivalent. And one is to be an upper level operations officer, knowledgeable about how the Foundation's funds are spent."

At that, Robert almost high-fived Tom. The rest of the hearing was details and pleasantries, ten minutes long.

* * *

Maria met them at the hotel. They sat in the lobby, looking up at the arabesque designs. The elevators were glass cylinders with starry inserts at top and bottom that looked like marble inlays, and the china on the table was gilded.

"Okay, Maria, looks like you made a pretty good haul." She had shopping satchels from Gucci, Versace, Chopard, and other places with elegant European names that Robert didn't recognize.

"Best find was this purse." She opened the Gucci bag and showed it. "This purse is discontinued, and I've always wanted it."

"I guess it cost less because it was discontinued." Robert sounded hopeful.

"No, it cost more because it was discontinued. The good news is, it only set us back eleven hundred dollars. Look, Robert, at home I work my tail off, like you. This is one of the only chances I get to be a silly, wasteful chick. A Valley Girl hanging in the mall."

With only the slighted wince, Robert turned to Mustafa. "Ahhh. . . . Well. . . . Umm. Mustafa, I'm happy with what we got today in court. We don't know for sure how helpful it will be in the end, because you never know. Still, I think we can get some of what we need with this order from the judge. But, Mustafa, you seem less sure. Tell us what we really got. And more important, what we didn't get."

"We got basically nothing. Except the right to start all over again. Robert, remember, please. This was just the 'Court of First Instance.'"

"I know. And there's a 'Court of Appeals,' too."

"Right. And a 'Court of Cassation.' That's the highest one in the chain, unless we happen to see the Presidium Adlia Court intervene, which is unlikely."

"Okay. Nothing's ever easy. But . . . won't those courts follow the decision today, unless they know for sure that it's wrong?"

"No. Maybe that's the way in America, yes. But this is a real Court of Appeals. Remember, we don't have juries, and almost everything about the evidence is in writing."

"So, what we've won today . . . is like nothing. It . . . really . . . is. . . ."

"All we've won is a suggestion to the Court of Appeals from the Court of First Instance. Really, I suppose today's order is only a limitation on what you can hope to get. You won't get more than two depositions. And you might get a whole lot less. Maybe nothing."

"Oh. . . . Great."

"Well, but there's one good thing."

"What's that? I'm not sure I want to ask, at this point."

"Our system in Qatar doesn't take as long as appeals do in America. Since everything was already written in advance, the memorials and briefs are probably on their way to the Court of Appeals now. You'll know soon."

"Oh. . . . Oh. Great."

15

By now, Ibrahim was so stir-crazy that he had started talking to himself. "I've got to get out of here. I've got to do something! I'd rather be in jail than in this royal doghouse of an apartment."

After all, it certainly was a nice apartment. Beautiful gold and white patterned cloth on the wall. Dark brown furniture in a middle eastern style, of fine material. Neutral carpet, only a little darker than the sand in Qatar. Ibrahim was well taken care of. But he had grown so, so weary of these surroundings.

He walked from the couch to the window. He half expected to see a posse of sheriff's deputies swarming the scene again. This time, he imagined, they'd be here to arrest him. He almost hoped for it, just to experience some kind of change.

Seeing nothing, he plodded back to the couch. Here was his Quran. Dog-eared, marked, and bedraggled. He usually could occupy himself with reading a few of his favorite pages, with the possibility that he would see something new in them. Now, he turned to some of them, slowly:

> *"Disbelievers are the rightful owners of the Fire."* That came from Chapter 7, verse 36.

> *"Those that the Muslims have killed were not really killed by them. It was Allah who did the killing."* . . . That page was almost too worn to read.

Ibrahim loved that last one. It came from a passage in the Holy Book that he had marked prominently. He stared at the words idly and thought about how well that passage fit his own great moment, recently, at Delmar Stadium during the football game. "It was Allah who had launched that balloon. It was Allah who did the killing."

Suddenly, there was a loud, unfamiliar sound. . . .

Ibrahim's throwaway telephone rang. An unreal sound. It was a traditional, old-fashioned telephone ring that was well known fifty years ago, but that Ibrahim was not accustomed to. He looked at the telephone for a moment without moving. Just . . . daydreaming.

Finally he picked it up. And just listened without saying anything.

"Is this al Ibrahim?" asked a familiar voice, in Arabic.

"Yes. Yes, . . . Bedouin?"

"Are you all right, my son? You sound . . . well, distant."

"Yes, Bedouin, my honored leader. I am . . . fine. But my heart is boiling. I need to act, to do something."

"And it is time for us to plan the next move. Please listen carefully."

Ibrahim listened carefully. He listened eagerly.

*   *   *

Bedouin had barely put the phone down from calling al Ibrahim when he asked his secretary to place another call.

He reached a woman who answered softly in Arabic and who passed him on to a man who passed him on, after a long pause, to the powerful person who was the real object of the call.

The big man, the magisterial man, answered in Arabic. "Hello, Bedouin, my brother."

"Hello, my beloved leader, and honored servant of the Amir, as his Minister of Justice. I need your help in a matter that is of national importance. Only you or the Amir would have the authority to do what is needed. Only you can intervene with your judges, in your Courts of Appeals, to do what is just."

"Tell me, my Bedouin. Your services are valued, and so are your requests."

*   *   *

On the far side of the globe, in Robert Herrick's office, the usual hundred geraniums bloomed in all of their colors above the huge Oriental carpet. Robert looked out the window, and so did Tom, sitting opposite him. The day outside was gloomy, dark even in midday, and rain came and went. The mood inside was gloomy too.

"I'm sorry, Robert." Mustafa Abboud was calling, and his voice came over the speaker from Qatar.

"Mustafa, what time is it where you are, in the Persian Gulf?"

"It's about eleven o'clock in the evening. Don't worry. I work late, and I called you now because I know the time difference. Anyway . . . again,

I'm sorry," Mustafa went on. "We did our best. The Court of Appeals decided our case on the accelerated docket—in other words, very quickly—and they decided it on the written memorials alone, without any oral argument."

"Yes, they do that here sometimes, too. They decide appeals just by the written briefs. Always makes you feel incomplete, even if you win, when there's no possibility for speaking live with the appeals court."

"Well, that's what they did here."

"The bigger issue, though, is the result." Robert read it aloud. "Here's the key part of the Court of Appeals opinion. 'The honorable Court of First Instance gave correct deference to our sister nation of the United States of America. Speedily, we affirm that Court's decision to allow the questioning of two officers of the Defendant Foundation. It is in one minor respect that we disagree with the honorable Court of First Instance. The questions to be answered should be presented to the Court of First Instance in writing, to be asked by that Court of the two officers, with responses in writing by the officers of the Holy Faith Foundation. This is the method provided by our law absent exceptional circumstances. This case does not present exceptional circumstances.'"

Robert and Tom both groaned at that, just as they had upon first reading it.

"Again, Robert, I'm sorry." Mustafa's voice was quiet.

"Oh, don't apologize, Mustafa. We saw you in action. You've done a fine job in this case. It just didn't come out the way we had hoped."

There was a pause. Then, Tom asked the inevitable question. "Is there such a thing as a Motion for Rehearing in the Court of Appeals in Qatar? And if there is . . . , would it do us any good to try that?"

"If you want to keep appealing, I think it might be better to go on to the next higher court. The Court of Cassation."

"All right. You're the expert."

"But I wouldn't do that either. That doesn't usually change the result. And actually, here's what I would suggest that you do, instead."

Mustafa paused, then went on. "If I were you, Robert, I'd start composing the written questions that you'd like to ask. And I'd assume that that's all you'll get, because I think it is all you'll get. Now, the good news, is that at least the Court of Appeals has ordered the Court of First Instance to pass on the questions and receive the answers. The judge in the Court of First Instance is more favorably inclined toward your case. Maybe Judge Massad, the judge in First Instance, will insist on complete answers. And if you ask the questions now, he will remember you, and you'll have the momentum. He may be diligent about getting real answers instead of getting stonewalled."

Robert paused too before answering. "That's probably . . . good advice. We won't be able to try the next higher court if we do that, but asking questions now sounds like the best option."

16

You can serve God in the greatest way, Ibrahim, by doing what I tell you," said the distant voice of the man called Bedouin. "I have already told you that we have more to do. What might be called tying up loose ends, except that our remaining issues are much bigger than loose ends to tie."

Ibrahim spoke eagerly into the disposable telephone. "Tell me, my beloved Bedouin. I wish more than anything to help."

"Good. You are a faithful follower of the true religion. Of the Prophet."

"Peace be upon him."

"Peace be upon him. And praise be to Allah, the Most Merciful."

They both were silent for an instant.

"Now," Bedouin went on, "I suppose you already know about a court action undertaken in the United States, not far from where you are located. It is a usurpation of the power of any court, as the courts in our country would well know. The idea that a court would have power to disturb a public organization such as our Holy Faith Foundation is outlandish. We are under the protection of the Amir, through the power of God."

"Of course. Praise Allah."

"The court in the United States is built and operated by the basest kinds of infidels. That court has allowed lawyers in the United States to maintain a suit against our Foundation."

"It defies belief, but yes, I had heard that."

"And there is more. The American lawyers have come here, to our beautiful and sovereign nation, and have invaded the courts here. In the emirate of Qatar!"

"Is that true, my Bedouin?"

"Yes. And their actions here made it necessary for me to contact the Minister of Justice to straighten it out. So far, there is no harm done. We will contain it, at least in Qatar. But it is embarrassing to the Holy Faith Foundation for us to have to answer these kinds of charges, at all."

"I understand."

"And now, there is some sort of 'investigator' that the American lawyers have sent here. Twice already he has visited our humble operations in the Aspire Tower, right here, in the middle of Doha, Qatar. Or rather, he has attempted to visit."

"Do you want me to take action here in America, where I am now, against the unholy figures who are maintaining this interference? It would be my honor to serve in that way."

"Well, yes and no, my Ibrahim. We do indeed need your services against these unholy figures, as you so accurately put it. But it is time for you to come home. To come to Qatar. We have developed a strategy for dealing with this bumbling investigator and for opposing the entire operation against us."

* * *

Sitting at the big desk, Tom and Robert put their heads down and, once again for the third time, studied the answers from the Holy Faith Foundation's officers. "This is all we've gotten from our written questions, the questions the Court of Appeals in Qatar let us ask," Robert said finally. "It's a masterpiece of not answering, while using words that appear to answer."

"Man, that's the truth. These responses give us a mouthful of empty nothing."

The sky outside was dismal, cloudy and gray. The greensward stretching west, far beneath the high windows, glistened with moisture. The gray, white and brown towers to the south were a little darker than usual, and even the huge Oriental carpet on which they sat was duller than it had been yesterday.

"Here's a question, for example. 'Please provide Balance Sheets and Income Statements for the Holy Faith Foundation for the past three years, or if the financial statements of the Foundation are not precisely called "Balance Sheets" or "Income Statements," please provide the similar or analogous financial statements of the Foundation for the past three years.'"

"I see it. And the answer the Chief Financial Officer has provided to us is, 'We do not maintain any financial statements called "Balance Sheets" or "Income Statements," and we do not maintain any financial statements called "similar or analogous financial statements," but it should be sufficient to say that the Foundation has significant assets and makes charitable contributions in the many millions of dollars or their equivalent each year.'"

"Which provides us no information whatsoever."

"But it is accompanied by a very long translation of our question into Arabic calligraphy and a long Arabic answer, just to make it clear that the CFO made a big effort."

"Which actually had nothing to do with answering the question, because the answer, in English, uses the same terminology as the question, identically, to evade the question."

"Here is another choice sample. The question asked for transfers of funds by contribution, expense, or otherwise to other entities within the last three years. The answer contains a list of multiple-million-dollar expenditures and multiple-hundred-thousand expenditures, mostly to Qatari and London banks and well-known Qatari organizations like the Red Crescent, which is their equivalent of the Red Cross. And it lumps together, then, '*All other contributions or expenditures of less than one hundred thousand dollars.*'"

"There is one expenditure to a subsidiary of a bank in Yemen. Is that promising?"

"No."

After a pause, Tom asked, "Will the judge of the Court of First Instance in Qatar order them to file more complete responses?"

"Mustafa, our lawyer, will make a request for that kind of order. But he's already been told that the judge is very unlikely to order anything more. Remember: the Qatari courts operate mostly in writing and aren't used to this kind of questioning."

Another pause. Then, Tom asked, "Robert, we have the usual economic clause in our contract with our clients in this case, don't we? The provision of the contract that allows us to withdraw from the case, if it becomes so unlikely of success that it is uneconomical in our judgment?"

"Well, yes. And I've thought about that. I've even discussed it with our lead Plaintiff, Senator McKay. We've kept her up to date about what's been happening. And maybe now's the time to consider that economic clause carefully. I can't . . . see what more we can do in this lawsuit."

"We need to get out of this quagmire. And dismiss this suit."

* * *

The flight attendants on the Qatar Airlines flight were all very attractive women. Evidently, this little country wanted to impress in that way. They wore crisp suits with skirts in a snappy, dark red color and matching red hats that covered uniformly dark hair above dark eyes.

The tall man in seat 2A sat back as the aircraft taxied on the runway. He enjoyed hearing the announcement of arrival at Doha in Arabic, followed by the same message in English: "Ladies and Gentlemen, welcome to Doha. . . ."

Al Ibrahim was traveling on a false Qatari passport, as he usually did. He felt an extra spring to his step as he unfolded his huge frame and stooped to pass the galley. "Thank you, Mr. Hassan," the first-class attendant said to Ibrahim, and smiled. "And welcome to Qatar."

Al Ibrahim, known temporarily as Mr. Hassan, smiled broadly. "Thank you, and thank Allah, for bringing me home."

17

There are probably a hundred thousand black Mercedes vehicles in Qatar, most of them in Doha. That is a large number for a country of just over two million people. Qataris appreciate these German cars, and they can afford them.

The man known as Chipmunk drove a rented Mercedes, for now. An M-Class SUV: a big chunk of shiny black luxury. He had been in the country for about two weeks as Robert Herrick's investigator, assigned to find out what he could about the shadowy finances of the Holy Faith Foundation. The M-Class was mildly impressive in Doha, if only mildly, and it was helpful to his efforts to befriend ridiculously rich natives.

Chipmunk had his name because of his enormous cheeks. "That guy looks like . . . a chipmunk," was a not-uncommon description of Chipmunk from a distance. His real name was largely forgotten by now within the law firm where he worked, and he had long since lost all memory of where the nickname had originated. "Hi. I'm Chipmunk," was his usual greeting to a new acquaintance, "and if you look real close, you can prob'ly guess why."

The big M-Class glided gracefully out of the Sheraton Doha parking facility. Which was itself ornate and palatial, but not nearly so much so as the hotel interior, with its atrium lined with greenery and arabesque patterns. Sheraton in America is a mid-level hotel. In Qatar, Sheraton is opulent.

Chipmunk had been flatly unsuccessful at asking questions of personnel at the Holy Faith Foundation itself, on two different visits. He had gaped at the Aspire Tower—the building that looks like a torch—just as any tourist would have, and he had admired the gold-leaf patterns on the direct elevator that served the Foundation. But security guards in resplendent black uniforms had kept him from coming within earshot of anyone inside the Holy Faith Foundation.

Now, as Chipmunk exited the Sheraton parking lot, another black Mercedes followed. It was driven by Al Ibrahim, who zoomed around in an E350 sedan. Not quite as chunky as Chipmunk's M-Class, but still big and impressive. His goal was to shadow the American investigator for now. If more was needed—if the man called Chipmunk stumbled across information that he shouldn't have—Ibrahim might have a bigger job to do. For now, he just followed.

Chipmunk was full of hope about this particular day. He had made contact with the local office of the International Red Crescent, which is the organization in Arab countries that does what the International Red Cross does. The written answers that the Foundation's Financial Officer had given to Robert and Tom's questions were not very useful, but they did show some of the larger contributions that the Foundation had made. In the last three years, the Foundation had given millions to the International Red Crescent—as well as millions to the Local Red Crescent, which served Qatar, just as the American Red Cross serves the United States, separately from the International organization. Chipmunk had simply dialed the number in telephone records for the International Red Crescent and had found a friendly ear in a woman named Maryam who seemed to know the International organization's finances.

Now, after giving his Mercedes to the valet in front of a tall building with spiral stripes—one of many unique and strange structures in downtown Doha—Chipmunk dialed the number once more. Maryam would be waiting upstairs. Chipmunk took the elevator up to the seventeenth floor.

"Hi." The woman named Maryam laughed. "You're Chipmunk. And you're not hard to recognize."

Chipmunk laughed too. "I guess not."

At the same moment, Ibrahim crossed the first floor lobby after leaving his black Mercedes. He saw the floor that Chipmunk had selected. Impatiently, he waited for the next up elevator.

There was no one there when Ibrahim exited the elevator. But he had served his mission, so far. He immediately dialed the number for his leader, the man called Bedouin, and reported where he was.

* * *

As soon as he heard from Ibrahim, Bedouin told his secretary to "Get our guy on the phone at the Red Crescent. I forget what his name is." He relied on his very efficient secretary for contacts.

An instant later, the line came to life. "Yes, sir! This is Abdul. I'm the General Manager of this office." The man's voice was enthusiastic. Evidently, Abdul knew the importance of hearing from the Holy Faith Foundation. "He'd better know," Bedouin thought to himself.

"This is a delicate matter," Bedouin explained. "There is a man who is dangerous to both the Red Crescent and to my Foundation. I am afraid that he wants to find out operational details to attack both organizations in ways that I do not foresee. I am told that his name is Chipmunk, and that he is American; and here is what he looks like. . . ."

"I will summon security and identify him," said Abdul, again enthusiastically. "And get rid of him by turning him over to the police, with instructions."

"That is what I suggest. I had thought at first about contacting all of the recipients of our contributions in town by email, but we decided that this would not work. An impersonal message of that kind would not convey the urgency of the situation, and it would broadcast information about a problem that we would rather not distribute throughout the country. Or the world."

"I understand. And thank you, once again, for your generous assistance."

"You are more than welcome, for the good works that you do. And I appreciate your help in this important matter."

* * *

"Here is the book that we maintain to answer donors' questions," Maryam told Chipmunk.

"I'm interested in one recipient of your donations, in particular. A group in Yemen. It is called 'Al Likchah in the Arabian Peninsula,' or ALAP. Meaning, Brotherly Love in the Arabian Peninsula."

"I can find that. What a nice name!"

"Would the contribution that it came from have been earmarked, or would it just have been general funds?"

"Here it is. And see there: remarks. 'Contributed on Suggestion of Donor Foundation.' Now, that would mean a particular Foundation suggested it to us, specifically. The Holy Faith Foundation. So, what that says, to me, is that the Holy Faith Foundation conferred with our International Red Crescent and told us to make a gift to the group called 'Al Likchah in the Arabian Peninsula' out of the money the Foundation had given to us. I've never heard of any Al Likchah, or ALAP, as you called it, myself."

"And here is something written in pencil. In Arabic, I guess."

"Yes. It's Arabic. Translated, it says, 'Personal, from Bedouin.'"

"And Bedouin is. . . ."

"That's right. He is the top gentleman in the Holy Faith Foundation. So this means that the instruction to send the money to Al Likchah in the Arabian Peninsula came to us as a personal instruction from the head of the Foundation."

Chipmunk grabbed his camera and snapped pictures. "I am impressed with the International Red Crescent. I will be sure that my company makes a contribution. It will be modest compared to what that Foundation has given under Bedouin, but an amount that will help. And Maryam, you have been so kind that we will give it in your name and make sure that the boss here knows."

"Thank you." She blushed.

Ibrahim sat in the lobby and watched Chipmunk leave. He wondered, somewhat idly, why this investigator had been here so long, since he knew that Bedouin had called the Director here. But that wasn't his department, so he stood up and began to shadow Chipmunk again.

18

Chipmunk was excited, all right, about what he'd found in Qatar."
Tom laughed. "But he didn't realize what a hero he was."
"He didn't? I'm surprised."
"No. He knew he'd found something valuable, because it connected the Holy Faith Foundation to an oddball organization called 'Al Likchah in the Arabian Peninsula.' But he didn't remember who Al Likchah was. We picked him up at the airport, and we explained it to him."

"Well, he is a hero. It's the best lead we've got."

"Yes, but here's the next problem." Tom frowned. "How do we connect Al Likchah, or ALAP, to the terrorist bombing? We've got to complete the chain, the conspiracy, by connecting the Foundation all the way to the bombing, and that's going to mean we've got to prove that Al Likchah is guilty of the terrorism in the stadium."

"Well, yes, that's a problem under the rules in court. Al Likchah is already convicted in the newspapers, because they've claimed responsibility. But we can't recover anything from a shadow organization like that, in a disorganized, violent country like Yemen. And in our lawsuit against the Holy Faith Foundation, the claim of responsibility by Al Likchah or ALAP probably won't be admissible in evidence . . . unless we have some other independent evidence linking Al Likchah and the bombing."

"Right." Tom lifted a pencil. "Al Likchah's claim of responsibility in the newspapers is a classic example of hearsay. It's what someone else said, not what the Foundation said, which is the actual Defendant."

"So we have to complete the last link in the chain," Robert answered, "by producing independent proof that Al Likchah financed the stadium bombing. Then we have a conspiracy, and it's no longer hearsay."

"What a silly problem! Al Likchah has said to the press that it's guilty, but we can't use that statement in court, because we're suing the Foundation, which is a separate defendant. And we can't use that statement because it's a statement by someone other than our defendant, someone who's not testifying, and so it's hearsay, even though it doesn't seem like it, and even though every juror would probably think that it's just plain crazy that we can't use it."

"Well, this is where we need an expert witness. An expert witness about terrorism, who can link Al Likchah to the Delmar Stadium bombing."

"And then. . . ."

"And then, the law gets really strange. Then, we can show that there's a conspiracy between the Holy Faith Foundation and Al Likchah." Robert stared at the ceiling. "First, the expert testifies that Al Likchah is the band of terrorists who did the actual bombing. The expert uses his expertise about the methods and history of Al Likchah. And then, second, we use the evidence that Chipmunk found, the records, to prove the connection of Al Likchach back to the Holy Faith Foundation. And then, suddenly, we have independent proof of a conspiracy, and then . . . Presto! Third, like magic, now we can offer more evidence of the conspiracy, such as the claim of responsibility by Al Likchah, which is no longer hearsay, because it's part of a conspiracy. Pretty convoluted."

"The law makes us run around in a circle."

"And, of course, our expert will have relied on what he's read about ALAP, or Al Likchah in the Arabian Peninsula, to figure out that Al Likchah is the guilty party. In other words, our expert will have relied on hearsay, even though we ourselves can't offer hearsay as evidence. It's so inconsistent that it's wacky. Just bonkers."

"So, we can't tie together the conspiracy with just the claim of responsibility by Al Likchah, because that's hearsay. But we can hire an expert to say that Al Likchah did it, and the expert can base that testimony on hearsay. And then, we can tell the jury about the claim of responsibility by Al Likchah, because then it's part of a conspiracy and therefore, no longer hearsay."

"That's right." Robert smiled. "It's a long and winding road. Not exactly common sense."

"Charles Dickens said that 'The law is an ass,' and maybe he was right."

"Yes, and in fact, Tom, watch out! The law is an ass, and it's contagious, and you might have already caught it!"

* * *

On the other side of the world, in Qatar, the man known as Bedouin stood beside his secretary, talking by telephone to al Ibrahim. "By now, that infidel is long gone. That investigator. And we don't know what he has learned."

"Yes, the man they called Chipmunk took a plane back to America the same day." Al Ibrahim was puzzled. "I don't understand what happened, my beloved Bedouin. You called and told the Director to kick the guy out. But I checked later, and this woman named Maryam had shown him her accounts. Only Allah knows what he might have found out."

"But I talked to this Abdul, the Director. He told me no one from America had come by at all."

Ibrahim was still puzzled. "Abdul? Abdul ... ? The Director's name was Mohammed, I think."

"Here it is, the telephone number." The secretary pointed. "Red Crescent of Qatar."

The light began to dawn on both Bedouin and Ibrahim at the same time.

"But I was at the offices of the *International* Red Crescent. . . ." Ibrahim's voice was strained. "Not the Local Red Crescent. . . ."

"The International is separate from the *Qatar* Red Crescent . . . ." Bedouin's voice was angry. "You gave me the wrong Director," he said to his secretary. "The wrong telephone number. . . ."

There was an awful silence. Finally, Bedouin spoke again, in a tightly controlled voice. "You are relieved of duty," he said to his secretary. "Go to Human Resources and wait for my directions."

"It probably wasn't her fault . . . ," Ibrahim began.

"Quiet! Be silent," Bedouin practically shouted, now. "I would have told you to take this man out, this man called Chipmunk, if I had known something like this was going to happen."

The terrified secretary left quickly, with her hand covering her eyes.

19

've talked to a possible expert witness for our case. An expert about terrorism," Robert said. "He sounds like a good one. Of course, we never know how good any expert is until we see the guy's testimony."

"Absolutely right," Tom Kennedy agreed. "And Jimmy Coleman will help us with that. He'll make sure we see the negative aspects of this witness, or any witness."

They sat on opposite sides of Robert's big mahogany desk, with the shimmering, multicolored carpet below them and a hundred geraniums in red, pink and white beside them. Outside the greenhouse-style windows, hundreds of feet below, the evening rush hour was beginning, with tiny cars clumping and entering freeways. It was a cloudy, misty day, but Robert was upbeat.

"Well, I actually expect that this expert will, in fact, turn out to be a pretty good one. We've disclosed him to Jimmy Coleman, and he and I have both agreed to present the witness by deposition for what we call a *Daubert-Kumho* hearing. To present him to the judge, to decide whether he's got enough expertise."

"I kind of remember the *Daubert-Kumho* factors, but it's been a while . . . ."

"The Supreme Court said in the *Daubert* case that if it's a scientific expert witness, you have to show that the witness fits the scientific method, with opinions that are testable by experiments. And there are other factors—such as the amount of publication that's been done on the issue. And how generally and widely the scientific method has been accepted by other experts. Those are the most important *Daubert* factors."

"Okay. I remember, now. But if it's not a scientific witness, if it's a terrorism expert, like here . . . ."

"A witness about terrorism isn't a scientific witness and won't be using the scientific method." Robert shook his head. "Right."

"Then, in that case, it's the later decision of the Supreme Court that controls, the *Kumho* case. . . ."

"Right. And unfortunately for us, *Kumho* just happens to be a terrible decision by the Supreme Court. Those Justices got lazy. They said we have to use the same factors, the same scientific factors, but with 'leeway.' Not a very legalistic decision, to say that 'leeway' in applying the factors is the so-called legal standard."

"The terrorism expert can't be expected to conduct scientific experiments to test opinions or conclusions about terrorism. Obviously. Crazy thing is, the judge is supposed to consider scientific experiments anyway—but then, the judge has to give 'leeway' to the witness. And how can a witness figure on quantifying the science, when explaining theories about terrorism, where it's not scientific at all? And how can the judge do that, even with 'leeway,' anyway?"

"That's what we're up against, thanks to the Supreme Court. Those Justices are just plain sloppy sometimes. And nonsensical. And that's the way they were in the *Kumho* case."

"So, who's this terrorism expert?"

"His name is Professor Andrew Edmonds, and he teaches at the University of Virginia. He's a former professor at the United States Military Academy at West Point, where he taught courses on Terrorism, Weapons of Mass Destruction, and Terrorism Financing and Recruitment. He has a Ph.D. from Stanford, and he also directs the Center for Terrorism and Security Studies. Has testified multiple times before Congress and in twelve court cases involving terrorism issues, either in trials or by deposition."

Tom seemed impressed. "Sounds . . . pretty good." Robert's upbeat attitude was infectious, and Tom was starting to share it.

"Here's what's even better. Professor Edmonds looks great for the part. A former military man. With short, well-combed hair, gray at the temples. A military bearing and sharp attention to dress. In excellent physical shape."

"Looking the part is always a big part of playing the part, for a witness. Right?"

"Right. And I'm giving Professor Edmonds over to you, Tom. We've got to question him in a deposition, and he has to be cross-examined by Jimmy Coleman. We've got to be able to show that his opinions are based on sound methods—not scientific methods, obviously, but when he testifies about ALAP or Al Likchah and about The Holy Faith Foundation, we've got to have him explain his methods, in detail. And he's got to be ready to discuss the scholarly publications in the area. And to tell us whether other experts would agree with him."

Robert looked out the window for a moment. "In front of the jury, what we're going to ask Professor Edmonds is whether the claim of responsibility by Al Likchah is realistic, is accurate; and also, to trace the funding back to The Holy Faith Foundation. But for now, for this deposition. . . ."

"I get it. For now, for this deposition, the key thing isn't his opinions, but how he arrived at them. His methods, and how solid they are. And also, scholars' publications about the methods and the amount of agreement by other experts about the methods. These are the *Daubert-Kumho* factors."

"Right." Robert smiled. At last, it looked as though this case was on a solid foundation.

"The law is obsessed with indirect things," he added. "Not the actual testimony of the witness, because that would be too straightforward. Instead, the law forces us to dance backward a couple of steps, away from the testimony, concentrating not on the terrorism, the horror, the deaths, the despicable actions of the defendants—but instead, on issues that are unemotional. Bloodless. Antiseptic. And incredibly dull. Such as, academic methods. But sometimes, that's just . . . what the law is like."

* * *

On the other side of the world, Ibrahim found himself once again pleading with Bedouin for action.

"You understand, Bedouin, that I have dedicated my life to Islam. And I would like to be doing something."

"Stay patient, my son, my Ibrahim." Bedouin's voice was soothing. "You are safe here in Qatar."

"I have the opportunity to lead a mission into Spain. Into Barcelona. As you know, Barcelona was once a stronghold of Islam, dedicated to the Prophet (peace be upon him). The missionaries known as Al Likchah in the Arabian Peninsula have asked me to lead a team of three other warriors. We would use a completely different technique from the explosion at the stadium in America. It would be low-tech. And inexpensive."

"That's fine, but. . . ."

"Bedouin, we would destroy a so-called newspaper, in Barcelona, that actually is a nothing but a blasphemous collection of lies, operated by scummy Christians and Jews, who constantly misrepresent the face and nature of Islam. Our plan would involve only the simplest of weapons, just assault rifles and grenades. And we have a clear escape route. The escape would be the easiest part of it. We have all the details worked out with Commandant Sharif Husan, who acts on behalf of Al Likchah."

"A good escape plan is one thing, my son. But think, what a good escape plan is not. It is not a guarantee of a good escape. Listen to the Holy Scripture. 'The strong man is the one who controls himself when he is angry.'" Bedouin's voice was still even, still soothing. "You are easily identifiable, my Ibrahim. Your God-given height is a signal, as vigorous as a neon arrow, and it announces your presence. It is an advantage for many things, your height is; but it is not an advantage for a man who needs to remain unknown. Stay here, and you can remain free and undisturbed in Qatar."

Ibrahim was silent for a moment. His respect for Bedouin, like that of other followers, was immense. He struggled to accept what he was told.

* * *

Back in America a few days later, the deposition of Professor Andrew Edmonds had begun. It was going well, Robert thought. He had opened with the Professor's background, which he knew would sound impressive. He had asked the Professor about his ultimate opinions, as briefly as possible: the sponsorship of the stadium bombing by Al Likchah in the Arabian Peninsula, and the sponsorship, in turn, of Al Likchah by The Holy Faith Foundation.

Now, it was time to turn to the real battleground. The methods that the Professor had used to reach these opinions.

"I considered the facts known in this case, of course," Professor Edmonds testified. "And I also considered publicly known facts about both Al Likchah in the Arabian Peninsula and The Holy Faith Foundation."

"Now," Robert began, "how did you go about considering these facts, so that you could figure out that the Delmar Stadium explosion was financed by Al Likchah in the Arabian Peninsula, and so that you could trace the funding back to The Holy Faith Foundation? We need to know your methods, because the Supreme Court said so in the *Daubert-Kumho* factors."

"I considered many kinds of information, all of which pointed to these two groups. First, and most obviously, claims of responsibility. Some terrorist groups claim responsibility for their violent acts. Some do not. As for Al Likchah in the Arabian Peninsula, that group is known to claim responsibility. It makes sense: they are hard to locate, so there's no danger, and publicity helps them. Al Likchah regularly claims responsibility, with pride. Just as it did here. The message from Al Likchah was written

with lots of flourishes, and it quoted the Quran, and it was issued promptly after the event. That's all characteristic of Al Likchah, like a signature.
The Holy Faith Foundation is entirely different. It cloaks itself in the
appearance of a charity, and it maintains that appearance by making
many charitable gifts each year. It never claims responsibility for terrorism."

"Besides claims of responsibility, are there any other factors?"

"Of course. You can't rely solely on claims of responsibility. Sometimes groups claim responsibility falsely. Another factor is communica-
tions. Chatter. It is well known that the chatter from Al Likchah is intense
before a terrorism incident that it sponsors. Oftentimes, it's in code.
Before this event in the football stadium, there was a lot of chatter from Al
Likchah, and some of it was coded. And there was chatter from The Holy
Faith Foundation, consisting of calls to Yemen."

"What else?"

"Access to funding. Al Likchah has good funding, from The Holy Faith
Foundation. And another way to trace terrorism funding is participation
in other terrorism activities, such as recruiting, training, and furnishing of
weapons. Al Likchah is well known as doing all of that. The case facts,
here, show that The Holy Faith Foundation shifted more than a million
dollars to Al Likchah shortly before this. Al Likchah, that group, has very
sophisticated bomb-making capacities that would have been able to
generate the relatively complex weapon that was used in the Delmar
Stadium explosion. And Al Likchah constantly recruits. And trains its
rookies."

"Any other factors?"

"Yes. Travel to and from Yemen, where Al Likchah group is located.
The main subject in this case, Ibrahim, made several trips to Yemen. He
was there long enough to be steeped in the methods of Al Likchah, and he
traveled there just before this event. Religious agreement is another
factor. Both Al Likchah and Ibrahim are Sunni Muslims. They share
beliefs, closely."

"Now, Professor, I need to ask you about some other issues under the
law. Under the *Daubert-Kumo* standard. The methods that you've used
here, could other scholars disprove them, if they were untrue? That's one
of the indicators of real expertise, says the Supreme Court."

"Yes. Another scholar could take any one of my reasons and use evidence to disprove it, with evidence that is known about terrorism. But I
doubt that will happen."

"And these reasons you've used, are they the subject of extensive publication? Widespread publication by other scholars about the methods is one of the factors that the Supreme Court mentioned in the *Daubert* case."

"There's a huge amount of publication about tracing sources of terrorism. Nobody could read it all, it's so extensive."

"And finally, here's another one of the *Daubert* case issues. Would other experts on terrorism agree with you about the indications of responsibility that you've identified?"

"There is never perfect agreement in this field. But yes, I would expect most scholars studying terrorism to agree on the methods."

Now, Robert turned to Tom and whispered, "Have I covered everything we planned?" He looked once more at his notes. Then: "I pass the witness."

20

Robert Herrick had taken just over two hours of deposition time to question Professor Edmonds.

Jimmy Coleman took about thirty minutes to cross-examine the professor. But it was a very effective thirty minutes.

Jimmy's starting point was unorthodox. "In order to have sound methods in a field of expertise, Professor, you first have to have . . . a field of expertise. Isn't that right?"

"What?"

Jimmy asked the court reporter to read back the question, just to emphasize that the professor had missed the question entirely.

"Ahhh . . . I suppose so," was Professor Edmonds's answer. "You have to have a field of expertise to have . . . expertise in a field."

"Would you say that Professor Pamela Styrsky, at Columbia, was an expert on terrorism?"

"Yes, certainly."

"And this expert, Professor Styrsky, says that, quote, 'Terrorism is not a coherent field of intellectual endeavor, because it has no uniform means of certification, no generally shared rules of reason, and no universal methods.' According to that, terrorism isn't a coherent field. Right?"

"Well . . . , but . . . you're ripping that one sentence out of context. Professor Styrsky also says that it should be regarded as proper academic inquiry, even though it obviously involves scholars of different subjects."

"And if we accept Professor Styrsky's statement, and combine it with your admission that you have to have a field to have sound methods in a field, then there are no sound methods in terrorism. Right?"

"Well, . . . but I wouldn't put it that way." The professor's head bobbed with disagreement.

"It sure shows that there isn't universal agreement in the field, in spite of your testimony earlier that there would be. Right?"

"No, there's not . . . universal agreement on everything. Still, there is a lot of agreement."

"And you heard from Mr. Herrick that general agreement among experts is one of the factors that the Supreme Court required, in the *Daubert* case. So, with general agreement lacking, that's one of the requirements that your testimony is missing, right?"

"I'm not a lawyer and I can't say that."

"There are terrorist groups that don't claim responsibility for their actions, right? And so you can't tell one way or the other from claims of responsibility. Isn't that correct?"

"From that by itself, no."

"There are terrorist groups that don't get money from charities, and don't do training, and don't do recruiting, right? So you can't tell anything from any one of those factors, right?"

"From any of those things by itself, no. You can't tell a duck only by noticing that it happens to have feathers, but feathers are one factor you'd look for."

Jimmy ignored that statement as if the professor hadn't said it. "It's possible for a terrorist to get money from someone who doesn't share the terrorist's intentions, and doesn't even know what the terrorist plans to do, right?"

"Certainly. A terrorist can get money from people who don't intend to support terrorism, and they do it all the time."

"The Holy Faith Foundation is a major charity that gives out many scores of millions of dollars, isn't it?"

"That's right. But I can tell you this. Charities in the Mideast, some of them, are heavily involved in terrorism funding. There are so-called charities that do good works on the side because it helps to shelter their terrorist activities. The fact that the financier is a charity some of the time doesn't mean that it doesn't sponsor terrorism. And that's certainly true of the Holy Faith Foundation."

Jimmy ignored those statements, too. "And the dollars the Foundation gives to legitimate charitable purposes—well, those dollars overwhelmingly outnumber the relatively tiny amount that the Red Crescent gave to this group called"—Jimmy ground out the words with contempt—"Al Likchah in the Arabian Peninsula, right?"

"Oh, yes."

"Isn't it possible that The Holy Faith Foundation didn't know exactly what this group, Al Likchah in the Arabian Peninsula, was going to do?"

"Is it possible? Anything's possible. But I don't think it's likely. In fact, it's overwhelmingly not likely."

Jimmy went on in this vein. A few minutes later, he had asked about each of the methods of tracing terrorism that Professor Edmonds had identified, and he had obtained an admission that it, alone, meant nothing. And for most of the methods, Professor Edmonds was forced to say that some of the other experts disagreed with him.

"I got no more questions for this . . . witness," said Jimmy, finally.

At that point, everyone took a twenty-minute break to allow the court reporter and the videographer to reload their instruments.

* * *

Robert spent another half hour doing a redirect examination. But his confidence was way, way reduced.

"Professor," he asked, "even if one of the methods you used would not have been enough by itself to trace the terrorism activities in Delmar Stadium to their roots, what if you took all of them together?"

"It's when you put them all together that they matter." The professor nodded, firmly. "And if you take all of them together here, the conclusion is inescapable that the group called Al Likchah in the Arabian Peninsula supported this terrorism, and The Holy Faith Foundation deliberately financed it all."

"Can you imagine a doctor trying to diagnose a particular kind of cancer by just one external symptom?"

"Of course not. And that wasn't what I was doing."

"Now, the fact that someone may disagree with some of your methods, does that mean that nobody agrees? Is there still general agreement to the methods you've told us about?"

"The indications of terrorist activity that I've testified to are generally agreed to by experts on terrorism. There is some disagreement about some of them. Of course! Isn't there disagreement in most fields?"

"Now, has the Council on Foreign Relations written about the frequency with which charitable organizations have supported terrorism?"

"Yes. It's generally recognized that many terrorist groups are financed by organizations that do charitable activities too. And the linkage between charitable organizations like The Holy Faith Foundation and terrorism is so well known that the Council on Foreign Relations has recognized it, in a publication called 'Tracing Terrorist Funding.'"

Finally, the deposition ended. Jimmy didn't do any more cross-examination. He knew he had done enough for his underlings to write pages and pages of briefing, to argue to the judge why this professor was a terrible expert. And why he shouldn't be allowed to testify, at all.

And as he left the conference room, Jimmy had the last word. "It looks like you got another sorry-ass case here, Herrick."

His army of black-suited associates laughed as they followed him.

21

His forged passport identified him as a man named Hassan, and his ticket said he was the Vice President for Personnel of Agrwal Petroleum Corporation. He sat back comfortably in his seat as the 787 Dreamliner began its takeoff run. He was six feet seven inches tall, but the individually enclosed seats in first class gave him plenty of room.

Actually, Mohammed al Ibrahim had nothing to do with any oil company or personnel department. Qatar Airlines was returning him to the United States with a new mission from the man named Bedouin.

Ibrahim fingered his individual remote control for his electronic surroundings, which hardly seemed necessary since he had his own monitor right in front of him. The flight attendant, resplendent in a dark red suit that was unusually feminine for an airline, appeared immediately because Ibrahim had accidentally touched the call button. She smiled and asked what she could do, with her dark red hat bobbing respectfully. The Qatar Airlines symbol, fashioned into a pin on the top of her headgear, gleamed.

"Nothing . . . really," said Ibrahim, a little sheepishly. But then: "Actually, I was wondering about the time for breakfast service. I'm getting hungry."

"Of course!" The smiling attendant was boundlessly enthusiastic. "No particular time. It's Qatar Airlines, so breakfast is when you want it. Dining on Demand, we call it. What would you like?"

Within five minutes, he was wolfing down a feast that included an enormous waffle with strawberry preserves and whipped cream, eggs, turkey sausages, apples, pears, bananas, and various unknown fruits. And champagne, of course. The real stuff, from the Champagne Region of France, poured slowly into an oversized glass by the ubiquitous attendant.

He thought about his meeting with Bedouin in the ornate conference room. "It's a beautiful airline and a wonderful service, and you deserve it, al Ibrahim, my son." They had had tea together and talked the small talk that Bedouin had chosen, while his leader confirmed and reconfirmed the appreciation he felt for Ibrahim's service.

"And now, it is important for us to take care of issues in the United States," Bedouin had said finally. "Ibrahim, it is not ideal that we send you back, because you are so recognizable. But the need is great, and your loyalty is proven beyond any inquiry. Perhaps enough time has passed, and we will keep you under cover until the time comes. Now, listen. As service for the Prophet (peace be upon him), here is what you are called to do. . . ."

And now, here he was, as the Dreamliner mounted toward the sky and left the Capital of Qatar behind.

* * *

"When the judge calls a 'status conference,' and actually names it that—a status conference—you never know what to think." Robert exited the elevator in the Federal Building and stepped toward Judge Elsa Domínguez's courtroom.

"Exactly." Tom frowned. "Sometimes, it's really just that, a status conference, where the judge says, 'What's the status of this case, lawyers? You gonna be ready for trial, maybe, on the date this case is set?' But sometimes it means the judge is going to give the plaintiffs, namely us, a lot of unnecessary homework. She might say, 'Please rewrite the pretrial order to provide issues and sub-issues and sub-sub-issues for each of the contested matters of law, and rewrite the exhibit list to tell what each exhibit shows, why it's relevant, and which Rules of Evidence might be involved in it.' And we've got dozens of issues and tons of exhibits, so those choice tasks would take hundreds of hours."

"Well, I hope it's not that. Remember that time we had to describe all of the exhibits in detail? And the judge decided we hadn't been detailed enough and excluded some of the exhibits?"

As they entered the courtroom, they saw Jimmy Coleman with his usual coterie of four black-suited associates. Jimmy, of course, had a choice greeting. "Hello, Herrick. You gonna tell Judge Domínguez the status of yo' doggy-ass case, here?"

"Hello, Jimmy." Robert laughed. "As usual, I don't know about your case, but you've got the talking part down just right."

Almost immediately, there were three knocks on the back courtroom door, and Judge Domínguez's law clerk appeared. "Order in the Court. Everyone rise, please . . . ."

Judge Elsa Domínguez ascended to the bench. Federal courtrooms are built to emphasize the power that the United States of America reposes in its judges, and this one had a huge granite backdrop that dramatized the point. "Be seated, please," said the judge pleasantly.

She got immediately to business. "Is discovery complete?"

"We think so," said Jimmy immediately.

"Not exactly," said Robert. "There are twelve of our document requests still unanswered, for reasons that we think are inadequate. We have two more depositions to take that have been set and reset at the request of Mr. Coleman."

"And what is the remaining status of those document requests?"

"We have worked with Mr. Coleman, and we have not been able to resolve all of them."

"We are prepared to supply documents for five of them, but the others are just unreasonable, judge." Jimmy made his plight sound forlorn and bitter. "It would cost us thousands of dollars to collect those documents in the other seven, and they don't have anything to do with anything. They're irrelevant."

"All right." Judge Domínguez scowled. "Mr. Coleman, you will answer those five that you've collected by day after tomorrow. And by day after tomorrow, Mr. Herrick, you may designate two more of your document requests, with which Mr. Coleman, you must comply, within one week of the designation."

"Good grief," said Tom under his breath. "The judge makes that kind of ruling without asking what the documents are?"

The judge looked sharply at him. It didn't appear as though she had heard the remark, but she could tell it was unfavorable.

But Robert was full of pleasantness. "Yes, your honor. It is less than we think is due, but we certainly will live with that order of the court."

"Thank you. And there is one more piece of business I need to conduct with you." The judge put on a stern face. "This case will be tried two months from now, come Hell or high water. There are certain cases that need to be tried and resolved promptly, no matter which way they come out, because they are important to the United States. There will be no continuances. If you think you want to reschedule the case at the last minute, think again. Nothing short of every single lawyer being so ill that every one of you is on your deathbed, certified by a battery of Board Certified doctors, will be considered. Are both counsel blessed with a clear understanding of what I've just said?"

"Yes, your honor."

"Yes your honor."

"Order in the Court," announced the law clerk again. "Everyone rise, please." And Judge Domínguez disappeared into chambers, while the lawyers filled their files with the treasured mounds of papers they carried with them.

22

When he walked into his home through his kitchen, the first thing Robert saw was the gun. He jumped. A Glock 41, a weapon that enthusiasts would call a superb gun, and the favorite of many police officers, in spite of an annoying kick. Made in Austria and equipped, in this case, with a laser tracer that shined a spot of light over Robert's heart.

With his hand behind his back, Robert nudged Maria so that he covered her. They had come into their home through the back door, which was their usual point of entry. Robert's favorite car, the burgundy Duesenberg, sat in the driveway behind them. Boxer the dachshund trotted up to Robert's feet, happily unaware of the threat facing his humans. Robert thought for an instant about a means of escape but saw that nothing could work.

The man behind the gun was huge. Six feet seven, with mideastern features, dark eyes, and a white burnoose. He was expressionless and held the gun steady.

"Good evening, Attorney Herrick."

Robert just waited.

"I am Mohammed al Ibrahim. You no doubt remember my name. You probably recognize me. Just to be sure that you recall, I recently engineered the deaths of more than a hundred people in the football stadium. Which is beside the point here, except to emphasize that I can kill you. And I will, happily, if it is needed.

"My people have sent me to talk to you," Ibrahim went on. "Just a conversation, this time. Not to kill you, although if that were my assignment, you would already be dead. It turns out that my people need you to remain alive, at least for a while. And to resolve a disagreement between you and them. To be specific, it concerns a certain piece of litigation that

105

you have brought against a charitable foundation that is anchored in Qatar. Do you understand what I am talking about?"

"Yes, of course." Robert's voice was tight.

"Splendid. If you didn't I would have to assume that I had found the wrong home." Ibrahim laughed without a smile at his own witticism, such as it was. "Now, this unnamed Foundation is not concerned about the outcome of this court action, because its people are confident that they have done nothing wrong, and you cannot prove that they have done anything wrong. But the very existence of a lawsuit brings its own troubles. Auditors are interested in lawsuits. Auditors love lawsuits, because lawsuits justify their existence. They spend hours figuring out an amount a foundation must set aside unspent, because of each lawsuit. A 'reserve,' the accountants call it."

Ibrahim stared at Robert. "And the reserve is an unfortunate restriction on the activities of the company or charity. In this case, the result is that the Foundation that you have targeted is unable to perform its good works to the fullest. It has had to set aside too much. Not because it is guilty, but because of the mere fact that you have written false accusations against it. Various other worthy associations are receiving less money than they have received in the past, and less than they need, because of you. Do you see where this conversation is going, Mister Attorney?"

"Yes. I do."

"Good! I had heard that you were an intelligent individual. In a moment we will see how intelligent."

"You are going to subtly invite me to dismiss this lawsuit."

"Certainly not! Then, all it would take would be for you or others like you to file a duplicate lawsuit the next day. No, not at all. My people don't want your clients to go away empty handed." At this, Ibrahim smirked. "They want to settle the lawsuit. They see themselves funding a charitable contribution to your clients."

"What?" Robert was startled.

"The lawyers have told us that the American way is that if you settle it, it goes away, and no other duplicate lawsuit is possible."

"Well . . . that's . . . that's true."

"Pay careful attention, Lawyer Herrick. You will receive an offer soon to settle this lawsuit for a cumulative total of fifty million dollars. Fifty million. Generous, don't you think? I should add that the lawyer who will convey this settlement offer does not know of my visit to you right now. He has no idea, except that his client has instructed him to make this offer. And here is the real point. Your future depends upon the acceptance of this offer. Your continued *existence* depends upon the acceptance of this offer."

Ibrahim paused, to let that sink in. "The settlement of this lawsuit is to be a normal settlement. My visit is confidential, not to be disclosed to anyone: police, or the other lawyer in this case, or anyone. Your course of action is to listen to this offer of settlement from the mouthpiece on the opposing side and accept it in the normal manner. Otherwise, your future will be short. Do I make myself understood?"

"Perfectly."

"All right. You've responded in an amiable way to all my questions. I like that. Come with me. We will put you in a place in the front yard where you cannot see. And I shall take my leave."

Ibrahim stood aside in the kitchen, with the gun still lasering Robert. As Robert passed into the hall, Ibrahim suddenly bludgeoned him across the side of his face with the gun barrel. A sucker punch. Robert recoiled and instinctively positioned himself to fight back. But then he stopped. His nose was dripping blood. Maria, who now was in front of him, made a sound like a stifled scream and had her hand over her mouth.

"You are a wise man, to keep walking forward quietly." Ibrahim laughed again. "So, be wise about the subjects we've discussed tonight. If you do not, my instructions are to visit you one more time. And to make that unpleasant visit the last."

Just as they reached the front door, Ibrahim discharged the pistol once. The tiny dachsund yelped once, then fell into a heap, bleeding from his back and stomach.

Robert gritted his teeth. Maria cried out, "Boxer!"

"Go to that other side of the house." Ibrahim ordered. "Count to two hundred slowly, and then you can come out. If you come out faster than that, or if you try to run for it, I will be watching, and you will not survive the event."

Robert did as he was told, with Maria beside him.

When he and Maria came back to the front of the house, Ibrahim was gone. So was a gray car, a Toyota, Robert thought, that had been across the street.

* * *

Maria ran inside to do what could be done for Boxer. But the little dog was lifeless, and Maria fell into a mass of sobs and tears. Robert called 911 and asked for a patrol car, then said, "Please! Every available patrol car." Then he called the police station and asked for Detectives Derrigan Slaughter and Donnie Cashdollar.

"We be comin fast as can be," said Detective Slaughter quickly.

The first patrol officer was there within five minutes. Fairly prompt, but Robert knew the bad news: even prompt response time usually isn't fast enough. Five minutes gives time for a perpetrator to travel miles away, in an unknown direction. Still, there was a chance, and the officer drove away, guessing at the direction. A second car arrived, and the officer shouted that he had received the first officer's call. There would be others.

It took eighteen minutes for Detectives Slaughter and Cashdollar to get there from downtown. Derrigan Slaughter was an always-elegant African-American officer, dressed now in a perfectly cut, pearl gray double-breasted suit and a maroon solid tie. He could have been photographed for *Gentlemen's Quarterly*. Donnie Cashdollar was a study in contrasts, with his usual mixture of mismatches: green pants, a pink-and-black plaid shirt, a blue tie, and a brown tweed jacket. This was the sartorial look that these two partners were famous for. The other officers were so familiar with this odd couple that they had long since stopped kidding them about it.

"We gonna be the case officers to take this here repo't," Detective Slaughter announced. "It'll be within the sphere a' influence of the Homicide Division, so we got jurisdiction."

"Man, am I glad to see you two gentlemen." Robert almost smiled, in spite of the situation. "We've been through the wars together, you two guys and I." And it was true. The two partners had handled the criminal sides of three or four of Robert's cases, and they had developed a relationship of affection with him.

When their business was through, Donnie Cashdollar shook his head. "We gotta catch this guy. I know it's occurred to you, Robert, that he has no reason to leave you alive even if you do settle this lawsuit."

23

Jimmy Coleman's call came at nine o'clock the next morning. Because of the events of last night, Robert was still at home.

"Robert, I apologize for calling you there," Jimmy rasped. "But I think you'll appreciate the reason."

Jimmy cleared his throat, dramatically. A long, hacking process. Then:

"My client has instructed me to convey an offer of settlement for this entire case of fifty million dollars. Fifty million! In all candor, my client astonished me by making this offer, because the Holy Faith Foundation vigorously maintains that your allegations are untrue, and the Foundation believes there is no evidence that you have that even comes close to the kind of proof that would be sufficient in a courtroom."

Jimmy's voice still had its guttural quality, but now, this morning, it was soothing. Even friendly. "So you see, my client does not fear this lawsuit. But that is not the whole story. The people behind the Foundation are kind people, with feelings, and they care about other people like your clients. Because after all, the Holy Faith Foundation is not in the business of fighting lawsuits. It gives money to worthy causes, rather than taking money. It is in the business of creating a better world. It makes charitable contributions to deserving people everywhere. It finds itself outside its charter, now, and distant from its purpose, while it is defending against fellow citizens of our world in a lawsuit, rather than helping them."

Jimmy spoke slowly and respectfully, now, as he went on. "And your clients have undergone a tremendous loss; there's no question about that. The Foundation has set aside fifty million dollars, which is in a reserve overseen by its accountants, even as we speak. Fifty million dollars, as a charitable contribution to assist these people who have lost so much."

"I don't quite know what to say," Robert responded. For once, he truly didn't know what to say, even as a response to a huge settlement offer.

"It's a generous offer. You should take it. Your clients will benefit from it. Of course, I've bushwhacked you with this offer, and I understand your consternation. And you're still at home. My client instructed me to convey this offer immediately, so I did. Call me from the office later."

"Wait a minute, Jimmy. Do you know the story behind your settlement offer? Do you know about the visit I received last night?"

Jimmy didn't. "What visit, that you received last night?"

Robert filled him in. "I ought to be scared, but mostly I'm mad."

"Herrick, that's the most bizarre story I've ever heard. I know of no such person as this 'Ibrahim' you describe, and I don't believe my client has anything to do with this sort of activity. The Holy Faith Foundation is exactly what it sounds like. It's a charitable foundation."

There was a pause. Then: "Call me later, Herrick. And realize, this is a great opportunity for your clients. And for you. Fifty million."

* * *

"Settle it," Maria said. "Settle it. I know you're mad about last night, but *settle* it."

"Should I settle this case at the point of a gun?"

"That's beside the point. Your clients would receive large amounts of money for what is at best an uncertain claim, with sketchy evidence. It's a good deal."

"But the whole thing is just . . . wrong. What would happen then? Would the story of the Holy Faith Foundation's involvement in terrorism be told? Would the world know who financed the bombing and deaths in the stadium? No."

"It's not your job to change the world. It's your job to represent your clients. And that means, settle this lawsuit!"

Robert finally drove to the office. He wrestled with his conscience the whole way. "If it's right to settle the lawsuit, it's right to settle the lawsuit. And that's true in spite of the crime that was committed against me and Maria last night," he told himself repeatedly.

He told himself, but he still was unconvinced.

* * *

Tom Kennedy was all business, with none of the hesitation that Robert had been feeling. "First thing we have to do is to notify all of our clients immediately about the settlement offer. That's the duty of any lawyer, whenever you receive any offer of compromise."

"Well, that's right, of course."

"So, we have to notify everybody about the fifty million. Immediately. And that can't be all. Every client is going to want to know whether we recommend accepting it. Every client is entitled to our advice about that, regardless of the circumstances."

"That's right too, of course."

"So far, all I'm doing is repeating what's in the disciplinary rules for lawyers. Our ethical duties."

"Again, yes."

"And I think we should recommend the settlement," Tom went on. "Every single one of these people should know that there is a big chance they'll get nothing—nothing at all—from a trial. We've fought the good fight. But we haven't gotten many breaks. And our case, frankly, isn't very strong."

"Well. . . ."

"Robert, be a counselor about this, the way you ought to be, instead of a gunslinger. Advise them to accept it. Because there are other issues about the duty of a lawyer that we have to discuss."

"For example . . . ?"

"For example, there's the problem that under our law, in this state, every single client has the right to decide, individually, whether to accept the settlement or not. Some will accept it. Some won't. And the ones that decide they won't—those clients are entitled to our continued advice and representation, until and unless we withdraw from representation with the permission of the court. And I can assure you, the court won't allow us to withdraw on the eve of trial, and so you can count on trying this case in front of a jury. We'll still have plenty of clients who won't settle, who'll want to take this thing to trial."

"And that's . . . that's right too."

"There's one more thing. . . . Robert, do you have a conflict of interest?"

"What? No."

"It's not the usual kind of 'conflict of interest.' It's not the slap-you-in-the-face kind where you have two different clients with conflicting strategies. But remember what the disciplinary rules say. You cannot represent a client if the representation, quote, *reasonably appears to become adversely limited by the lawyer's own interests,* unquote. That's section 1.06 of the Rules."

Tom's voice rose. "And that's the problem here. The visit you got last night and the threat from this Ibrahim, that threat gives you an interest in getting rid of the case—maybe. Your interest in staying alive . . . is a conflict, however unfamiliar this kind of conflict is, as a conflict of interest. And that fits the disciplinary rule. Maybe."

"I don't have a conflict of interest. I'm not motivated in the least to throw this case because Ibrahim visited my home."

"Well, here's the problem. If you try the case and lose it and later a court decides that it '*reasonably appears*' that you shaped the way you represented your clients just a little, or nudged the result so that you lost, then you're liable to your clients for the loss. And that means, *you*—or rather, *you* and your *whole law firm*—end up owing the clients everything they should have won."

Robert thought for a minute. "It's amazing," he said finally. "Most issues of legal ethics have a simple answer. 'You must do this.' or 'You must not do that.' But then, every so often, legal ethics dilemmas arise for which there's no answer. No answer at all. No answer, no matter how you look at it."

"Well, that's this case. There's no answer. You might have a duty to withdraw, if you have a conflict of interest. But also, you might have a duty *not* to withdraw, because we're on the eve of trial and it would hurt your clients. And even if you tried to withdraw, Judge Domínguez is certainly, for sure, not going to allow you to withdraw on the eve of trial."

"So, what do we do?"

"Also, Rule 1.03 requires us to communicate this kind of development to our clients, to keep them 'reasonably informed.' I mean, we've got to notify them about the fact that Mr. Ibrahim visited you and threatened you. We have to tell every client that you had a gun pointed at you. That's what the Rule means."

"And that's right too. Wow, Tom. It just gets better and better, doesn't it?"

24

This is what some people call a 'ghost meeting,'" the President said. "It means that the agenda doesn't appear on any records, and we're all here without assistants or deputies."

Then he added: "Except me, of course. I can't navigate my way out of the Oval Office without an aide."

Their tight smiles flickered.

"We all know that this terrorist named Mohammed al Ibrahim has resurfaced. He's had only one known sighting, where he threatened a lawyer after breaking into his home. The lawyer, whose name is Robert Herrick, is performing a national service, actually a major service, by trying to hold the financial conspirators liable in that terrible stadium bombing."

The President looked around the Cabinet Room before continuing. The portraits of former presidents seemed to look down suspiciously, as if asking, "Are you doing your best for this great country that we have bequeathed to you?"

"The reason for this meeting is to figure out what else might be the intentions of this terrorist." The President sounded upbeat, the way he always did, but his forehead was wrinkled in a frown. Observers could not help noticing that his red hair was heavy with gray now, after three years in office. "Our discussions are off the record so as to avoid tipping anyone, including foreign governments, in ways that might inform Ibrahim and his pals. So, let's figure it out. Mr. Director, what do you know?"

"Mr. President, we find no evidence of any new planning of episodes within the country," said the DNI, the Director of National Security. "There are ongoing investigations of groups ranging from the clownish to the dangerous, but nothing about Ibrahim. We even brought in a red team—you know, a team of security professionals from outside the agencies—to second guess us. They found nothing significant that had been overlooked."

"It's an inexact science, of course. But all right. CIA?"

"I'd just have to echo what the DNI has said," the CIA Director agreed. "It always feels strange to have made such a big effort and to conclude that there's nothing we can find, but it happens."

"General?"

The representative of the Defense Intelligence Service shook his head. "We don't have any contacts with Ibrahim from outside the country."

"What do you think he's doing?"

"It's a guess," the DNI said, "but this man is experienced at avoiding electronic trails. He probably spends money only in cash or with turnover credit cards. He uses prepaid phones, and he only uses them miles away from the place where he usually stays. He does most messages through unknown partners. He speaks English on the phone. We've got electronic ears in the territory listening for common Arabic words on telephone calls—you know, they'd recognize the sounds for 'the' or 'is' or 'Allah' in Arabic—but all we've captured with that has been ordinary people's conversations, immediately erased."

"All right. Maybe this Ibrahim just came here to threaten the lawyer. Could be, if the lawyer has actually tracked down the right terrorist financier. But I don't like it. Mr. DNI, let's do the full court press. Let's find this Ibrahim."

* * *

A thousand miles away, a knot of lawyers had assembled in Judge Elsa Domínguez's courtroom.

"No, Mr. Herrick," said the judge firmly. "No. I'm glad you have said you are not moving to withdraw, but only notifying the court, because the court will not allow you to withdraw. The trial of this case is a week and a half away."

"I understand, your honor. Now, there is one further issue. The court has a gag order in place in this case, and your honor has explained your reasons for that. We have concluded that we, as lawyers, have a duty to disclose this threat against their lawyer to all of our clients."

The judge looked startled. Then thoughtful. And then, she nodded. "Yes."

Then, the judge said, "Mr. court reporter, put this on the record. Mr. Herrick has notified the court of a threat he has received and of his duty to notify his clients."

"And your honor sees the problem immediately. We have this duty, but with a group of clients numbering over a hundred, there is no chance of perfect compliance with the court's gag order. Someone among the clients is too likely to tell the media about a matter as explosive as this. Someone is going to tell the media. It could even be innocent, someone not understanding that they're not supposed to do."

"I will order what you may and must say," said Judge Domínguez emphatically. "It's totally an unfamiliar situation, but I can see how you need it. Mr. Coleman, any objection?"

"Your honor, I have had no role in any threat. My client vigorously denies it and believes it did not happen. We wish that to be part of any communication."

"Don't leave here, either of your gentlemen, until you have agreed on language for me to order Mr. Herrick to issue to his clients. Something like, 'To all of our clients in this case: This is to notify you that your lawyer, Robert Herrick, has received a death threat in connection with his maintenance of the lawsuit on your behalf. The defense lawyers and defendant deny any participation in this threat. Death threats against lawyers are rare but they certainly happen. Your lawyer, Robert Herrick, has assured the court that his representation of you as clients will not be compromised by this threat.'"

The judge looked at the lawyers. "Something like that."

* * *

"Well, we didn't get much in that pretrial hearing," said Tom Kennedy. "The judge ordered responses from Coleman about two of our outstanding document requests, and that's all."

"Maybe they're the most important ones. Our terrorism expert, the Professor, thinks so. Look at the bright side."

"We've got a lot of work to do to get ready for this trial. On one big issue. How do you present a case involving more than a hundred wrongful deaths with so little evidence about who did it?"

"Well, we'll have focus group results to tell us. Thank goodness for that."

"And we've got to get the right jury," Tom said. "But even then, the fact remains. We don't have a lot of evidence."

25

At the elegant offices of Booker and Bayne, the Foundation's trial team gathered in the big conference room. "This is Doctor Randolph Murphy," Jimmy told them.

There was an enthusiastic response.

"This is the age of consultants. Jury psychologists. And Dr. Murphy is a good one. We usually consult him before a big trial. He can tell you, like a sorcerer, whether left-handed Lutherans will be biased against your airline when it's been accused of negligence in a plane crash. Or whether Republican lesbians would give big damages for a slanted oil well. Dr. Murphy is the best there is at that."

Dr. Murphy had coke-bottle glasses and a head as bald as a frankfurter. He looked like a jolly genie standing there beside a TV screen with a collapsible metal pointer in his hand. He was wearing a bright yellow jacket over his chubby frame, with blue and yellow plaid slacks and Hush-Puppy-style shoes. "Dr. Murphy could consult a psychologist himself, to tone down his wardrobe a little," Jennifer Lowenstein thought to herself. But she knew from experience that there was no denying this man's professional expertise. He was extraordinarily effective at what he did.

"Don't lay it on quite so thick, Jimmy," the good doctor said. But he was obviously pleased.

"Now, here's what we did," he went on. "We surveyed two hundred fifty people in this county, where the jury will be selected. We used a telephone survey, and we presented a kind of neutral scenario involving the evidence in this case. And what we found is surprising. You don't want the usual kind of defendant's jury in this case."

"Why is that, Dr. Murphy?" Jimmy was listening intently.

"Usually, the defense wants people who make hard decisions. Upper-class people. Educated. A banker, who knows how to say 'No' to a loan application. A geologist, who tells the oil company to 'Drill here,' on the basis of incomplete information from seismographs. Or a doctor, who does exploratory surgery on a patient who might be injured by that surgery. The plaintiff, instead, usually wants people who decide things on a humanistic basis. People pleasers. A beautician. a shoe salesman. The defense wants hard decision-makers, and the plaintiff wants sympathetic caregivers. Usually."

"And you're saying that this case isn't like that?"

"Exactly. We think it's because the plaintiff's proof is circumstantial. Indirect. For the plaintiff to win, the plaintiff's got to get the jury to put all the pieces together and say something that's hard to say. That the defendant, which is a charity, committed a massive crime. The easy way out is to make a non-decision by saying, 'There just isn't enough evidence.' And that's why this case is different.

"And here's what our surveys showed," the colorful bald man went on. "Professional people were good for the plaintiff in this case, relatively so. Educated people tended to side with the plaintiff, too. The folks in the people-serving professions, the hairstylists and waiters and the like, these people were better for the defendant, for the Foundation. They tended to look at the case as an incomplete puzzle, rather than wrestling with the meaning of the evidence."

"Were there differences on account of age? Or social class?"

"Yes. Exactly. Young people, who tend to decide quickly and holistically, were more favorable to the defense, this time. To the Foundation, because they saw the picture as incomplete. And so were older people. That's a big reversal. Usually, old people who have made their peace with the world are sympathetic, humanistic decision-avoiders, and usually, that helps the plaintiff, but not here. And then, upper class people—those with wealth or education or prestige—tended to identify with the plaintiff, here. Usually, those would be defense jurors, but not here. We think it's because they were more likely to put together the evidence, recognizing that nothing like this is ever free from ambiguity, and they could make a hard decision."

"Listen up, everybody." Jimmy grinned with his usual eve-of-trial enthusiasm. "We've got the recipe for a big win. Because thanks to Dr. Murphy, we've got a description of our ideal jury."

* * *

But the defense was not the only side using jury consultants. Robert Herrick had just received a report from a firm called Calkins Jurimetrics. Professor Alistair Calkins was the chair of the sociology department at

Rice University, but he earned most of his income from researching and preparing reports like this one. It was called, "Jury Presentation Considerations for the Trial of the Delmar Stadium Attack: Survey, Focus Group Results, and Analysis." It was accompanied by a videotape that was titled, simply, "Focus Group."

Robert and Tom sat across Robert's desk, along with two associates who would help with the trial. They didn't notice the beautiful day outside, and they didn't look at the lush green of the grass along Buffalo Bayou or the trees of Memorial Park that faded into the horizon. They sat beside rows of flowers and above a huge, colorful Oriental carpet, but no one paid attention to these things.

The jury selection survey had produced several hours of wonder and planning. The best jurors for the plaintiff, against the lawyers' instincts, were educated, upper class professionals and managers. Professor Calkins's survey also showed that service workers were bad for the plaintiff, even though in most other cases they would be good for the plaintiff.

"All right," Robert had said finally. "We know what kind of jury we want. The problem is, Jimmy Coleman's probably also had this kind of workup done, and he'll be trying his best to get the kind of jury that's the worst for us."

"Well, that about says it all," Tom agreed. "So, how do we present the case to this ideal-or-not-so-ideal jury? That's what this Focus Group tape is about."

"Yes. We've all read the Focus Group Report. It's strange. There are two ways to approach this case. One, that it's a case of Islamic terrorism. Or, second, that it's not a case involving Islam or religion so much as people accused of crime, so we have to prove their guilt securely. And the Report says we have to take both approaches. We have to use the words, 'Islamic terrorism.' Otherwise, there will be jurors who will wonder why we didn't say that—are we wimps, or blind, or what? The other is that in trying the case, we have to stress what happened and who did it, without trying to use religion as a club. Otherwise, there will be jurors who will decide that we're relying on religious labeling instead of providing proof."

"Let's look at the videotape," Tom said.

Helpfully, the videotape began with a table of contents. Selection of a given section allowed the lawyers to consider the discussion of the focus group about the events in the stadium, the answers provided by the Holy Faith Foundation, the documents, and other issues. Including a section titled, "Discussion of Religion and Islamic Terrorism."

"This focus group was put together in the usual way," Robert told the two associates. "Professor Calkins uses five or six individuals. More than that makes some members of the group shy and prevents them from talking, but with fewer, you don't get a range of opinions. The professor is good at getting people from different professions. In this case, he had"—Robert looked at the Report—"a schoolteacher, a nurse, a retired financial analyst, a construction worker, and a worker who called himself an accountant but who was really just a bookkeeper."

"They put them behind a one-way mirror and videotape them discussing a summary of the evidence," Tom added. "At first, it's a free-form discussion. Then, when they wind down, Dr. Calkins gives them a set of specific questions."

"All right." Robert pushed buttons on the remote. "Here's the discussion about the 'Islamic terrorism' issue."

On the screen, a man was speaking. "That's probably the financial analyst," Robert said.

". . . They've got the money flowing into this group called Al Likchah in the Arabian Peninsula. And it looks like money-laundering, the way they did it. It went through another group, the International Red Crescent, which wouldn't seem to have much to do with a group like Al Likchah. And from the Red Crescent, it was directed, how? By a phone call from this guy Bedouin, who's with The Holy Faith Foundation. Bingo. It's clumsy money-laundering, but it's money-laundering. And the last group is the one that actually funded it. Al Likchah."

"Well, and plus, they're all Islamic or Muslim groups," said the man who seemed to be the construction worker. "It's a case of Islamic terrorism."

"Everybody's Islamic or Muslim in that part of the world," answered the financial analyst. "That doesn't mean much."

"But we know that it's Islamic terrorism. Why can't we call it that?"

Robert paused the tape momentarily. "There you have it. To some jurors, it's wrong to rely on the fact that it's Islamic terrorism. To others, it's wrong not to call it Islamic terrorism, and you may look silly enough to lose credibility."

"A frequent kind of trial dilemma," Tom agreed. "We have to provide some expression that it's Islamic terrorism. But we can't lay that on too heavily, because we don't want to turn off the more thoughtful jurors, who might think we were trying to short-circuit the proof."

"We have to provide just a touch of Islamic terrorism," said Robert, and in spite of the seriousness of the subject, everyone laughed at the irony in that phrase. "We have to give 'em . . . just a touch."

26

All right, Mr. Bailiff!" Judge Elsa Domínguez announced. "Bring them in."

And a surge of excitement rushed through the courtroom. Most of the benches were crammed full of news reporters, lawyers, and curious onlookers, and this was the moment they had been waiting for.

The door to the courtroom opened. The first member of the jury panel walked in: a balding man wearing work clothes. The others streamed in behind him. At the front of the audience section of the courtroom, the bailiff pointed, and the first potential juror, the balding man, obeyed and sat at the end of the center bench. The others, in a row, followed suit. And then the bailiff started a second row, with all of the line of citizens sitting in the proper order. Courtroom regulars will tell you that, for bailiffs, keeping the potential jurors in the proper order is the overriding objective, and ironically, at this point it doesn't matter whether these people are intelligent, or impartial, or educated, or anything else that would make them good jurors—as long as they line up like sheep.

It took about fifteen minutes just to seat all of the potential jurors. Judge Domínguez had summoned more than a hundred potential jurors for this panel because publicity about the case meant that many citizens would be unable to serve. The bustling of the potential jurors taking their seats was the only sound in the courtroom. The spectators just stared.

"Not a good jury panel," whispered Tom Kennedy. "Not good at all."

"Shhhh," Robert responded. But it was true. The first potential jurors fit the types that the Calikins Jurimetrics Study had told them were bad for the plaintiffs. Number one, the balding workman, was an operator at a chemical plant along the ship channel. Not educated; not professional; not the type who made hard decisions based on available evidence. Bad for the plaintiffs. The second was a saleslady for a restaurant supply company. In a people-pleasing job, and again, not the type who made hard decisions based on limited information. As Robert read the juror information forms that these citizens had filled out, he realized that most of the first row was populated by people who the surveys had said would be bad jurors for the plaintiffs. A quick scan of the jury information forms hinted that the other rows would be filled with similar people.

The judge had already begun her introduction to the jury panel. "Good morning, ladies and gentlemen. . . . It's a trial about the explosion in Delmar Stadium. . . . The plaintiffs have the burden of proof, but only by what's called the 'preponderance,' or greater weight, of the evidence. . . . You are the exclusive judges of the evidence. . . . But you must follow the law given to you by the court. . . . Jurors perform a service that only free people can perform. . . ."

It was all standard stuff, and Robert concentrated on reading the jury forms.

Finally, the judge told the jurors, "The attorneys have the right to ask questions. . . . Do not withhold information. . . . The attorneys will now begin their examination."

And that was Robert's cue to stand up. "Good morning, ladies and gentlemen of the jury panel!" he said, with an enthusiasm that masked the nervousness he felt at the beginning of every trial. "Every time," he told friends bluntly, "I feel like going to the bathroom and losing my lunch." He had learned, contrary to public expectations, that this kind of fear was characteristic of most good trial lawyers.

He wore a pinstriped charcoal suit and a blue tie with tiny dots. The lawyer's uniform. He pulled himself to his fullest height, and his blue eyes steadied. Now, as he faced the jury, he felt his adrenalin flowing, and his automatic response settled his stomach.

"Good morning," a chorus of voices answered him. Solidly. That was a good sign.

"I am Robert Herrick, and as the judge told you, I represent the plaintiffs in this case. Stand up, please," he gestured, and two of his clients stood at counsel table, by the bench. Then: "Will you please stand up too?" he said to a part of the courtroom, and another group of plaintiffs stood. "These are some of the relatives of those who were killed, and some of those injured, in this case. There are many more. They are watching us in a large room with closed circuit television because"—and here, Robert emphasized the next words—"*there are too many people injured or killed in this case for all of them to be present in one courtroom.*"

He was glad to hear a murmur from the potential jurors. They could not avoid understanding how big this case was.

"Now," Robert said, "can you promise me, all of you, that you can be fair to these injured and surviving people, if you become jurors? And more importantly, can you promise all of *them* that you can be fair to them? Is there anyone who cannot?"

It was an old-fashioned jury selection question. No one on the jury panel ever said no, but that was not the point. After silently committing to be fair to the plaintiffs, the hope was, the ultimate jurors would indeed be fair to them.

Robert held up three fingers. "We will show you three kinds of facts in this case," he told them. "First, that the terrorism in Delmar Stadium was financed by the defendant, The Holy Faith Foundation." He pointed firmly at the counsel table next to Jimmy Coleman, where a vice president of the Foundation also sat. The vice president, who had been conscripted against his will for this role, cringed at being identified in this way.

"Second"—and Robert pointed again, emphatically—"that this defendant, the Foundation, *knew* that its financing would result in the deaths of many innocent people." He paused, while the vice president looked as though he wanted to sink under the table. "And third, we will show you that on average, the compensation that the law requires for each plaintiff is ten million dollars, although it will vary for each plaintiff."

He walked slowly toward the other end of the bench to let these themes sink in. The jury research, he knew, said that jurors define the case early. They don't necessarily "decide" the case in terms of who should win, but they decide on a "framing" of the case. They decide what the issues are, or what the case is about. And the lawyer who defines the issues often has an advantage.

"Is there any member of this panel who believes that there is some reason why he or she should not be a juror in this kind of case?"

Hesitantly, a few members of the panel raised their hands. And there was a forty-five minute period during which the judge questioned these panel members outside the hearing of other potential jurors. By the end of that time, the judge had removed eight members of the panel whose answers showed that they could not judge the case impartially. Robert was glad to see that the potential jurors who were let go were all of the type that Calkins Jurimetrics had said would be bad jurors for the plaintiff.

Most of the rest of Robert's jury examination went by in a blur, as he asked question after question designed to root out jurors who could not or would not accept his evidence. And he eliminated a dozen more unfavorable panel members.

Toward the end, there were fireworks.

Robert spoke deliberately as he began the wrap-up of his examination. "I think you will find this awful event, at the end, to be a chain of connections between like-minded organizations and people, all of who shared attitudes of dislike or hatred for America and our way of life." He was trying to follow the suggestion that he mention Islamic terrorism but not rely on it. "I think you will find that the chain, from the Holy Faith Foundation through the International Red Crescent to Al Likchah in the Arabian Peninsula, all the way to the man named Ibrahim and his two co-felons, to be a case of Islamic terrorism."

Jimmy Coleman erupted. He was on his feet immediately. "Your honor, I object strenuously to Mr. Herrick's improper attempt to attack the defendants because of their religion! He has no evidence. He has no proof of wrongdoing by this Foundation. It's a charity. I ask that these remarks be stricken from the record and the jury instructed to disregard them, because they are deliberate attempts by Mr. Herrick to create religious prejudice and hatred."

Robert was not surprised by the objection, but he was surprised by Jimmy's vehemence. Apparently, so was the judge, who arched her eyebrows but remained calm. "The jury will judge the evidence," she said. "This is only a preview of what Mr. Herrick says he will prove. You cannot judge the case by any sort of prejudice, but it will be up to you, as the sole judges of the evidence, to determine whether the plaintiffs have proved their case. The objection is overruled."

Robert sat down. The judge had handled the issue in a way that didn't hurt him. Maybe. But he knew that Jimmy had gotten the jury's attention, and ironically, during Robert's own time to speak, Jimmy had already gotten across his point.

* * *

Jimmy's jury examination had Robert constantly gritting his teeth. Again and again, Jimmy skated right up to the line that divided proper remarks from improper ones. But Jimmy was as skillful as his reputation, and he never said anything that Robert was confident would get the judge to rule against him.

"In response to Mr. Herrick's three points, we have one point," Jimmy thundered. "And that is that Mr. Herrick has no credible evidence against this major charitable organization, The Holy Faith Foundation. None whatsoever."

Jimmy sounded like a cement mixer. "Can you, as jurors, say that there is no evidence, if in fact there is no evidence? Is there anyone who cannot?"

Jimmy paused. "I didn't think so. If the case isn't proved, you must say so. Our system depends on it. And I think at the end, you will see that this case boils down to a heap of imagination combined with a lot of religious prejudice against Muslim people. Prejudice, like the kind that you just saw from Mr. Herrick a few minutes ago!"

Jimmy went through all of the questions that his strategy would have said should have been asked. And every time he made a point, he returned to his main point. Which was that Mr. Herrick didn't have any evidence, and he was relying exclusively on religious prejudice.

By the time the jury examinations had ended, and the judge had dismissed the jury for the day with warnings not to talk to anyone or view any news media, Robert felt that the tables had been turned. This was a trial, all right, but *he*—Robert Herrick—was the real defendant.

Robert, himself, was really the defendant on trial.

* * *

Jury selection is not really a process of "selection," but rather a process of elimination. The clerk gave Robert and Jimmy each a list of people who remained in the jury panel: the panel members who hadn't been removed by the judge for one reason or another. Each of the lawyers went to a separate room to "make their strikes" by drawing lines through the names of three people on the list—the three they wanted most to get rid of.

The process was short, because the judge hadn't given them much time. "Twenty minutes," she said. "Fifteen if you can." The two groups of lawyers practically ran to their places, followed by the two client representatives in Robert's case.

"We need to cross out that first guy," Tom said. "The bald guy. The one who's a plant operator. A bad juror for us, according to the study. And when you talked to him during jury examination, Robert, he didn't seem to like our case, either."

"Agreed," said Robert. And he drew a line through the man's name, eliminating the first potential juror.

"Okay," Tom said. "The second one isn't very good either. The saleslady. Bad for us, according to the jury study. But I wouldn't strike her, because she seems harmless."

"Right. I think she is a follower instead of a leader. She will go along with other jurors, and we have only three we can take off, so we'd better just leave her on the jury."

... And in this way, they went through the so-called "live list"—the people left from the original jury panel, who could still serve as jurors. And Robert drew lines across three names.

"Well, do you think we've got a good jury?" one of the clients asked as they walked toward the clerk to turn in their strike list.

"That would be nice." Tom laughed, unhappily. "But Jimmy Coleman's doing the same thing we are, right now. The ones we want the most are the ones he wants to get rid of most. He'll have struck the jury so that we get something in-between: not the worst possible, but not what we want, either."

And a few minutes later, Judge Elsa Domínguez swore in a jury that fit that description. Not horrible, Robert thought, but also not very good.

27

'm going to play baseball tonight, Tom." Robert was definite. "It's what keeps me sane. It's Friday night, and we have the weekend to work. My team needs me, and I need them."

And so, in spite of Tom's protestations that there was "a ton" of work to do, Robert was here, at Clemens Field, to pitch for the Cardinals. Against the menacingly named Colt .45's. An unusual hobby, maybe, playing baseball in later life, but it worked for him.

"You ready?" Bill Garza, his catcher, laughed. "Because I've seen you when you were ready, Robert, and I've seen you when you weren't ready. And when you aren't ready, it doesn't work out very good."

Robert laughed too. "I'm ready. Man, I'm ready."

And he thought he was. But the first inning, as Garza might have said, "didn't work out very good." Robert started the first Colt .45 hitter, a left-hander, with a low inside fast ball. Usually a decent way to begin. But the guy went down and got the ball and lined it into the right field corner for a triple. He waltzed home when the next batter hit a single.

"Now Robert, you told me you were ready. Okay, maybe so. At least you're not walking these guys. But maybe you're not ready."

"I'm ready." Both of them knew, though, that pitchers habitually claim they've got their best game even if they don't, and if you just give them the next batter, they'll get him out.

"Here's an idea. Throw the curve. Outside. Mix up whether it hits the plate or if it doesn't. Let's change from this strategy of too-many-fastballs. Throw the fastball for a ball. Don't throw it for a strike."

Robert stared at him.

"When what you're doing's not working, you try something else. That's the idea."

Robert thought about it. "O-o-o-kay," he said finally. It made sense. "When what you're doing isn't working, you try something else."

The Colt .45's jumped on the Cardinals for two more runs that inning. Then Robert settled down, alternating curve balls thrown for strikes with curve balls thrown outside. Finally, the bleeding stopped.

"Good job, Robert," Garza said three innings later, when the Cardinals were ahead six to three. "You finally found your balls, so to speak."

A teammate came in as a relief pitcher after the fifth inning. The Cardinals won by a score of eight to five. Robert sat the last innings, with his arm wrapped in ice. He kept thinking to himself, "When what you're doing isn't working, you try something else." It was worth remembering.

* * *

"I labored hard in your absence, Mister Nolan Ryan," Tom said the next day. "I sure hope you had a good time."

"Indeed I did," Robert answered. "The baseball gods were guiding every pitch."

"More likely, it was your catcher."

"That too."

"Well, I'll tell you what." Tom grinned. "I have an idea. A departure from what we had planned, but a good one. Why don't we call the medical examiner first? Doctor Brczykowski." He pronounced the name carefully: "BAR-chee-KOW-ski."

"That . . . is an unorthodox beginning."

"Here's why. Dr. BAR-chee-KOW-ski actually made the scene, himself, personally. He went to the stadium and saw everything before any of the bodies was moved. That's really where this story begins. We can tell the whole story, then, by witnesses who will tell how the police discovered who did it, and finally, by how we discovered the role of The Holy Faith Foundation."

"Well . . . maybe. I see what you're getting at. It's definitely unorthodox."

"We wouldn't try to tell the whole story through Dr. Brczykowski. He's the set-up guy. We'd have to call various assistant medical examiners later, who did the individual autopsies."

"Well . . . maybe. . . ."

"And I'll tell you what, Robert. One advantage of this approach is that it doesn't emphasize the Islamic angle. It's a different approach. We can come back to that then, later, after the Islamic angle is well established by other evidence."

Robert immediately imagined himself listening, once again, to Bill Garza. His catcher. "When what you're doing's not working, you try something else."

"Okay," he said finally. "Let's do it."

* * *

The judge gave each side two hours to make opening statements. They were uneventful. Robert told his story, and Jimmy told his, which consisted mostly of attacks on Robert's story as being unsupported by evidence, together with assertions that it was based entirely on prejudice.

"Call your first witness," said Judge Domínguez finally.

"Plaintiffs call Dr. Bill Brczykowski," Robert announced.

Jimmy looked stunned for a minute. He stood up. "Your honor. . . ."

"Yes, Mr. Coleman?"

"Dr. Bill is the medical examiner."

"Yes. I know who he is. In fact, I know him."

"There's been no predicate laid. No indication of any wrongdoing. It's unorthodox and improper. . . ."

"Is that a substitute for a formal objection?"

Jimmy looked like he was thinking hard about how to put an objection into formal language. But then: "No, your honor. I would only point out that calling the medical examiner first is no substitute for evidence showing who allegedly did it."

Dr. Bill Brczykowski was already approaching the witness stand. Robert noted, with approval, that Dr. Bill was wearing his usual cheerful, wildly colorful clothes. He sported a blue and white seersucker jacket, with dazzling awning stripes. A matching pair of powder blue pants. A yellow shirt, festooned with a big red polka-dot tie. White socks and white patent shoes completed the outfit.

"Welcome, Dr. Brczykowski," the judge greeted him with a smile. "You've been sworn. Please take your place on the witness stand. And Mr. Herrick, you may begin your examination."

28

Dr. BAR-chee-KOW-ski," Robert began with the medical examiner, "would you please tell us your qualifications?"

"Certainly!" The pathologist with the unpronounceable last name smiled with all thirty-two teeth. "I have a medical degree from the University of Wisconsin and am a diplomate of the University of Tennessee post-graduate program in pathology. My internship was at Harvard in Massachusetts and my residency at Baylor Hospital in Houston."

He paused and looked pleasantly at the jury. "Pathology, by the way, is the study of disease and injury. And how they affect the body. Forensic pathology uses medical science to consider these things in the context of the law. For example, we determine cause of death in suspected cases."

The witness smiled again at the jury. "The medical examiner for the county is like what's called the coroner in other states. It's a public office occupied by a forensic pathologist who directs other assistant medical examiners."

When the jury stared at Dr. Brczykowski, Robert wasn't sure whether they were impressed by his credentials or blinded by his clothes. The man's awning-striped blue-and-white jacket shone like the sun in the light of the courtroom, especially when combined with his matching blue trousers, his bright white shoes, and his floppy red bow tie.

"Is it okay if I just call you Doctor Bill?" Robert grinned.

"Certainly!" enthused Dr. Bill, who was used to difficulty with his last name. The jurors appeared to enjoy this moment.

"All right, Dr. Bill. Did you have occasion, on the night of the Delmar Stadium disaster, to visit the scene at the stadium, as part of your duties?"

"Yes, sir." The pathologist smiled as if recalling a lighthearted moment, because he loved his work. "It's unusual for me personally to go to a crime scene, because ordinarily one of my investigators goes. But in this case, we had four investigators there, and it took some coordination. So I went too."

"Please describe what you saw."

"It was like a battlefield. Worse, maybe, because of the burns." The doctor looked at the jury and smiled broadly. "Bodies were strewn where they lay. Burned to the point of carbonization of the entire clothing and epidermis, many of them. The edges of the burn pattern showed evidence of individuals who had tried to escape but who had been overcome by spreading flames."

"Now, ultimately, autopsies were performed. But . . . did you personally perform the autopsies, Doctor?"

"Not most of them. There were too many. We have other doctors too, my assistant medical examiners, who are highly qualified pathologists."

"We will call the other pathologists later, most by deposition, to testify about those autopsies. For now, we want to get information about your investigation of the scene. By the way, was this scene something that you were accustomed to, in your work?"

"Frankly, I'd have to say no." Again, the doctor wore a happy smile. "I'm used to death and to a whole range of causes, but I've never seen anything like this."

"Were you able to determine what sort of agent brought about the event?"

"Undoubtedly, it was an incendiary device. We located the remnants of a set of canisters and connectors in the middle of the scene."

"Doctor, I won't ask you the cause of death for each individual at this point, because that depends on the autopsies. But in severe burn cases such as this, what is the usual cause of death?"

Jimmy Coleman halfway stood, apparently to object. But then he thought better of it and sat down.

"Often, the actual cause of death is asphyxiation, sometimes combined with shock or cardiac arrest." The genial pathologist favored the jury with another cheerful look. "The arterial blood within the lungs may even literally begin to boil, meaning an inability to take in oxygen. The heart doesn't receive the arterial blood it needs. Then, the cause of death is asphyxiation. Oftentimes."

"Doctor, are these the kinds of injuries that would be painful, for the time during which the individual would be conscious?"

"Yes! Certainly!" The pathologist wore a big smile in spite of the horror of the subject. Death, for him, was a professional subject that came in various ways, and all of them were just facts for clinical inquiry. "This event would be extremely painful to the individual, for however long the process of death lasted."

* * *

Jimmy paused for a moment before cross-examining Dr. Brczykowski. Momentarily, Robert hoped that his rival was shaken by the testimony. Maybe Jimmy was having trouble thinking of an approach.

But unfortunately, that was not the case.

"Dr. Brczykowski, let's be clear." Jimmy's voice sounded like a grindstone turning against a chisel. "You're not saying that this defendant, The Holy Faith Foundation, is in any way responsible for this awful incident, are you?"

"What? No. Of course not. I'm not a witness to that kind of thing; I'm a witness to what the scene was. It's a part of my job, to investigate the scene."

"Right. That's my point. You can't add anything to answer the question, 'Who did it?,' can you?"

"No. Of course not." A big smile.

"The kinds of incendiary materials that could be used to build what you call an 'incendiary device' of this kind are available easily to millions of people, aren't they?"

"I suppose so. Yes, of course they would be."

"In fact, you probably can buy the materials for this kind of device on the internet. Right?"

"I suppose so."

"There have been American citizens who have built incendiary devices, haven't there? And they've just used commonly available materials?"

"Yes. Of course!" The doctor still sounded relentlessly cheerful.

"And there have been American citizens who have used easily available materials to build devices that have attacked government buildings, right?"

"Yes."

Jimmy did his best to wave his hand in a throwaway gesture. "I've got no further questions of the doctor."

The jury looked confused. If, as Jimmy had suggested, this doctor had nothing to add that connected the defendant to the case, . . . then, why had the doctor been called as the first witness?

Robert looked on, in confusion himself. Starting with the medical examiner had seemed like such a good beginning point.

But Jimmy had shown everyone that . . . it wasn't.

* * *

"We're not going to get much sleep tonight," Tom said. "Or this week, or next."

"That's just the way it is, being in trial," Robert answered. "During the day, you beat your brains out trying the case in front of the jury. Then you hotfoot it back to your office and stay up all night getting ready for the next day."

"Too bad the jury doesn't know. Or appreciate it."

"Well, maybe they'll appreciate it if we can figure out what to do next, after what happened with Dr. Brczykowski."

"They'd probably like to have someone who could put the case together a little more clearly, or advance the story."

"And so: change of plans. We call Chipmunk as our next witness. He doesn't know the whole story, but he can tie together several pieces. And during that, we can have Chipmunk tell the jury that our expert witness, Professor Edmonds, will tie the rest together."

"So, we'd better get Chipmunk in here." Tom called him on the intercom. "Good. He's still in the office."

Several hours later, they had outlined the questions they would ask Chipmunk, and they had gone over his answers. And a couple of hours after that, they had anticipated questions that Jimmy Coleman might ask on cross-examination.

"Let me ask one final question," Robert said. "Ahhh . . . Chipmunk . . . we know that even your wife calls you Chipmunk. But when we call your name to come to the witness stand, we have to be a little more formal. So, let me ask you this. Chipmunk . . . *just what is your real name?*"

It wasn't very funny, but they all were feeling featherbrained, and it was nearly ten minutes later before they all stopped laughing and making silly follow-up jokes. The pressure of trial brings out an unnatural sense of humor.

29

Well, it's hurry up and wait." Tom closed the door to Robert's office behind him.

"What's that mean?"

"They just called from Judge Domínguez's court. No trial today. We get a day off. Something happened with the court reporter and she's not available."

"Well, I'll be darned. And it couldn't have come at a better time. I got a message from the Cop Shop. Donnie Cashdollar and Derrigan Slaughter— you know, the two homicide detectives—they called. Something about us needing to go to the jail." He looked at his partner's face and laughed. "No, not for us to be locked up in the jail ourselves, Tom."

Robert pushed the intercom. "Donna, please call the detectives. Our favorite homicide detectives."

"Who knows what's going on?" Robert laughed. "These guys are wonderful. They always surprise me."

"Cashdollar! Homicide!" The detective's voice came across the telephone, clear and confident.

"Donnie, it's me. Robert Herrick. With Tom Kennedy on the speaker."

"And I be on the line too," said Derrigan Slaughter's voice. "Robert, you gonna like this."

"What's going on? You guys want to let me know I won the lottery? And I didn't even enter."

"Even better. There's this guy Hamadi, and he plans to plead guilty to them stadium murders. He was one of the three perps who done it, Hamadi is, but he's probably the least one of 'em, and he's likely looking to get life in prison for pleading and testifying. And right now, he's blabbing his head off."

"Wow. Not something I expected."

133

"Right. But since it's done happened, you might as well mosey over to the jail and hear what old Hamadi got to say. Maybe around ten o'clock. We know you got this civil lawsuit, and we know you gonna give us whatever you find. So, we gonna meet you there at the jail. Hamadi gonna perk up your testimony."

"It's a deal. We'll be there. Thanks, gentlemen."

* * *

Derrigan Slaughter was wearing a navy suit with a navy-and-silver striped tie. As elegant as the prince of Monaco. Donnie Cashdollar had maroon pants, a gray jacket, a blue shirt, and an orange tie. As sloppy as Bozo the Clown.

Robert laughed silently. These two guys! Always a study in contrast.

"I've never been inside a jail I liked." Robert frowned in spite of himself.

"We're going to protect you," said Detective Cashdollar, with mock seriousness. "We're here in case you get jumped and humped."

"Great."

The elevator seemed to take forever. It was huge, and it rocked past floor after floor. "Here's the place," Detective Slaughter announced, finally. "Nice and high up. Just so it ain't easy to skate out on rollerblades, I guess."

They walked beside single cells in a row. "Careful. I know you know this, but some 'a these guys, they be th'owin' stuff at you. Like excess baggage. I mean, fee-cees."

"Hamadi!" Slaughter shouted. "You got a visit from yo' fan club. This here is Robert Herrick. He got a few questions for you."

"You gonna get me outta here? I wanna go somewhere that isn't here."

Robert looked at the two detectives, who shrugged.

"Not right away." Robert shook his head. "It's a long process. Hamadi, you were there at the stadium bombing?"

"I was there." And over the next twenty minutes, Hamadi narrated the story.

"Okay, Hamadi. Now, what we want to know is, how did this all come about? Who sent you?"

"The Holy Faith Foundation." Hamadi's answer was immediate.

"How do you know that?"

"Al Ibrahim was the boss. He told me."

"Did you ever talk to anyone at The Holy Faith Foundation?"

"Once. It was a call that came for Ibrahim on the phone, actually. I answered. It was a guy named Bedouin. That's what he said. 'Tell Ibrahim, this is Bedouin.'"

Robert and Tom looked at each other.

"Did you talk to him any more than that, Hamadi? To Bedouin?"

"Yes, 'cause it took Ibrahim a minute or two to get there. Bedouin congratulated me. He congratulated us, all of us, about the stadium. He knew all about the details in the plan for the stadium. And he talked to me about the Holy Faith Foundation and how proud they were of us, and how we ought to keep drawing the money we needed from Al Likchah in the Arabian Peninsula and he, Bedouin, would make sure Al Likchah sent us the money. Ibrahim was always talking about Bedouin. Ibrahim talked about how that gentleman named Bedouin ran The Holy Faith Foundation with an iron fist."

Fifteen minutes later, the lawyers and the detectives left.

"How about getting me outta here?" Hamadi wanted to know. "Some place a little nicer, even if it's still on the inside."

"We be workin on it," Detective Slaughter promised. "We gonna work harder for you now. We don't got the stroke to get it done by ourselves, but we gonna work on it."

*　*　*

"Okay. So what did we get out of that meeting with Hamadi?" Robert asked, when they were back at the office. "If anything? What I mean is, we can't use any of that connection with the Foundation unless we tie down the fact that it was, in fact, Bedouin. We've got to authenticate the fact that it was Bedouin he talked to. We've got to offer some *evidence* that the voice on the other end of the line was Bedouin."

"Right. And . . . I'm not sure we can do it," Tom admitted.

"Otherwise, this guy Hamadi, the fact that he says it was The Holy Faith Foundation, that's just his guess, or it's hearsay. And inadmissible."

"Well. . . . Maybe we can use the co-conspirator exemption from the hearsay rule. Like, Ibrahim was a co-conspirator with Hamadi—not much trouble proving that—and our expert testimony and the money trail show that The Holy Faith Foundation was part of the conspiracy. And so was Bedouin."

"Maybe . . . or maybe it's enough if we use this one conversation that Hamadi had with Bedouin on Ibrahim's telephone. It's not enough, maybe, that Hamadi identifies him, because he'd never heard or talked to Bedouin before. But the voice on the other end of the line knew enough about both the stadium plans and the Holy Faith Foundation, so that it's impossible that it was anyone but Bedouin."

"Well. . . ." Tom looked skeptical.

"Or at least, it's not very probable that it wasn't Bedouin. Or it probably was *someone* with the Foundation. Maybe we prove it that way."

"Or maybe, it doesn't work."

"Or maybe, it doesn't work," Robert frowned. "Right. Maybe we can't use this conversation at all, under those kooky Rules of Evidence. And we'll sure try, but maybe we just don't have enough evidence to make this case. And well, we . . . knew that. . . . From the beginning."

30

A courtroom full of spectators and lawyers stood while Judge Elsa Domínguez ascended to the bench. "Be seated, please. Good morning, gentlemen. I hope that you got some of the usual work done yesterday without having to stay up all night."

"Yes, your honor. Thank you," was the reaction from both sides.

"Well, good. But we need to get on with it and get this case tried. Mr. Herrick, you ready to call your next?"

"Yes, your honor."

And then, everybody in the courtroom stood again, as the bailiff brought the jury in.

"Your honor, ladies and gentlemen of the jury, plaintiffs call Steven Kallstrom."

This name, unfamiliar as it was to Robert and Tom, was Chipmunk's real name. And with this cue, the man everyone knew as Chipmunk—and even his wife knew him as Chipmunk—approached the witness stand.

"Please state your name for the members of the jury."

"Steven Kallstrom."

"Now, I've always known you by your nickname. And just in case I slip and call you that name, let us tell the jury that you are known to everyone as"—Robert paused for effect, here—"'Chipmunk.'"

"That is true." Chipmunk smiled.

"And just why do you have that name, Chipmunk?"

Chipmunk puffed up his cheeks and looked toward the jury. Several of them laughed. That was fine. Jurors like it, when a lawyer or a witness gives them a few lighter moments in the heavy mass of boredom that makes up a trial.

But the court reporter wasn't amused, and she wasn't putting up with this. "You've got to answer in words that are audible, please!" Her tone dripped with annoyance.

"Excuse me," Chipmunk said quickly. "The answer is, my cheeks. They make me look like . . . well . . . a chipmunk."

By now, the jurors found this exchange uproariously funny. The courtroom is a grim place, and even weak humor can burrow through to its audience.

"Very well, Mr. Kallstrom . . . or Mr. Chipmunk. And how are you employed, Mr. . . . Chipmunk?" More laughter from the jurors.

"I am an investigator for the law firm of Robert Herrick and Associates. Your law firm, Mr. Herrick."

Robert got Chipmunk to tell the jury his background. A degree in Criminal Justice. A number of years working for the Drug Enforcement Agency: The DEA. A whole raft of in-service training programs, ranging from accounting to ballistics.

"With respect to this particular matter at trial, Chipmunk—and for goodness sake, I'm just going to call you Chipmunk, if that's all right—did you have occasion to travel to Qatar to investigate the connection of The Holy Faith Foundation to this case?"

"Yes. I did."

"Please tell us what happened when you went to Qatar and attempted to visit The Holy Faith Foundation."

"On two occasions, I was turned away at the door and told that no one would talk to me."

"Did you find publicly available information about grants made by the Foundation, and if so, what?"

"The grants are publicly available on a web site. I found that the Foundation, this defendant, had made gifts in the multiple millions to the International Red Crescent, which is the counterpart to the Red Cross here."

"Nothing wrong with making those grants. Is that right?"

"Nothing is wrong with giving to the Red Cross, no. Or the Red Crescent. But what I found out in visiting the Red Crescent really surprised me."

"Did you have occasion to view the books and records of gifts made by the Red Crescent? And did you obtain any of those records, or copies?"

"Yes. I was given assistance by a lady who maintained the records, a Ms. Maryam Latifah. The records were obviously business records, made by someone who knew of the transactions shown there, and the dates showed that they were made regularly, soon after each grant."

"I'll show you what has been marked as Plaintiff's Exhibit 16 and ask you whether you can identify it."

"I can. This is a copy of a business record showing a particular set of gifts made by The Holy Faith Foundation to the International Red Crescent and, a few days after that, a gift by the Red Crescent of a slightly lesser amount that went to someone called Al Likchah in the Arabian Peninsula."

"Your honor," said Robert, "I offer Exhibit 16 into evidence."

Jimmy was on his feet. "Your honor, the proper predicate has not been laid to show that Exhibit 16 could even possibly be a proper business record. The people who made the record haven't testified. The people who kept the record haven't testified."

"Well, but the Rules of Evidence say that a business record can be admitted on the testimony of any 'other qualified witness.' I've never seen a predicate for a business record set up in exactly this way, but he's a qualified witness. We routinely admit records on the testimony of people with no more qualifications than being file clerks."

"Your honor!" Jimmy's voiced sounded like a chain being pulled on concrete, except it was a little higher in pitch than usual. "I have to protest."

The judge looked at him for an instant. "Plaintiff's exhibit 16 is admitted."

"Now, Mr. Chipmunk," said Robert, still unsure what to call this witness, "I'm going to show the pages of this document, Plaintiff's Exhibit 16, one at a time on the screen so that the jury can see each page clearly. First item, a page from the Red Crescent showing that it received a grant. Did you copy this?"

"Yes, with a camera."

"What does it show?"

"That The Holy Faith Foundation put a million and a half dollars into the Red Crescent for what was called a 'program grant.'"

"Now, look at this next page. What does it show?"

"It shows that three business days later, the Red Crescent made a grant to an organization called 'Al Likchah in the Arabian Peninsula' of almost exactly the same amount, just barely under a million and a half dollars."

"Now, we will connect this up later, but have you come to learn what this organization, 'Al Likchah,' is?"

"It is an organization that sent funds to the three individuals who bombed Delmar Stadium."

Jimmy was red-faced. "Objection, your honor! This is not on personal knowledge or from an expert witness."

"That's sustained. The jury will disregard the last question and answer."

"As I was saying," Robert went on, "we will connect this up later, through another witness, namely, Professor Andrew Edmonds. Now, Mr. Chipmunk. Do you see some handwriting on the page?"

"Yes. It's Arabic. It is written right next to the record of the grant to Al Likchah in the Arabian Peninsula. Translated, it says, 'Personal, from Bedouin.' In other words, an individual named Bedouin personally requested or authorized this transfer of funds from the Red Crescent to Al Likchah."

"And do you know, of your own knowledge, who 'Bedouin' is?"

"Yes. He is the head of The Holy Faith Foundation. He is called Bedouin by everyone. Just as I'm known as Chipmunk to such an extent that everyone knows me by this name and no one knows my real name, so, he's known to everyone as Bedouin, and if he has a real name, most people don't know what it is."

There was a rippling commotion as dozens of news reporters ran out of the courtroom to get this information, from this famous trial, into the newspapers and onto news broadcasts. And the rest of Robert's examination of Chipmunk was uneventful.

* * *

Jimmy Coleman started his cross examination of Chipmunk by saying, "Look again at this handwriting in Arabic that you have claimed to translate for us. As I read it, it says, 'Merry Christmas.' Now, look, Mr. Kallstrom. Doesn't it say 'Merry Christmas' to you?"

Uselessly, Chipmunk stared at the dots and squiggles that were penciled into the document. Finally, he said, "I can't read Arabic. I don't know."

"I can't read Arabic either," Jimmy admitted. "But I think what it really means is, 'Mister Herrick and the witness named Chipmunk tried to put one over on this jury by pretending they could translate something that they couldn't.' No matter how you read it, isn't that what this hand-scrawl really means, now?"

Chipmunk was uncomfortable, and he blurted out several "Ahhhs" before speaking. "I answered honestly. I've been told, and I believe, that the Arabic translates to say, 'Personal, from Bedouin.'"

But some of the jurors were frowning, as if Chipmunk and Robert had pulled off a prank.

"Now, let's get out some other facts you don't know." Jimmy sounded like a roadster with a busted muffler. "You don't know anything about Al Likchah in the Arabian Peninsula or what that group did or didn't do. Correct?"

"That's true. Not of my own personal knowledge. But I've learned about them from this case."

"As far as you know, Al Likchah in the Arabian Peninsula used this funding for traditional Red Cross activities, or Red Crescent activities, like helping people get over disasters?"

"I don't know. Someone else will testify about Al Likchah."

"I don't have any further questions for *this* witness." One of Jimmy's most serviceable skills was that he could look and sound disgusted better than anyone else, and he put that talent to use here.

31

Jimmy got to us," Tom said. "It was all a lot of baloney, the stuff he asked about. But I think he poked holes in Chipmunk's testimony, or at least the jury thinks so."

"Well, that's right, unfortunately." Robert was philosophical. "Any lawyer can do what Jimmy did, just by figuring out what the witness hasn't been asked to investigate, or facts outside what he's looked into, and concentrating the questions on what the witness won't know. Jimmy's just more effective at that trick than most lawyers."

"We'll have to answer it the best way we can. And our next witness is the professor who is the terrorism expert."

"Professor Andrew Edmonds. Our expert." Robert was looking forward to this witness. "And Professor Edmonds can tie it all together. Or at least . . . I *hope* he can tie it all together."

* * *

An hour later, Professor Edmonds was on the witness stand in Judge Domínguez's granite-backed courtroom, with the jury staring at him. The professor wore a dark blue suit. His gray hair contrasted with it, but he had an athletic, military bearing. He looked back at the jurors and smiled.

"Good morning, ladies and gentlemen of the jury." This was a witness who was familiar with the courtroom.

"Morning!" said the jurors back. So far so good, Robert thought. But then he realized that that wasn't saying much, because he hadn't begun the examination.

"Professor, please introduce yourself to the members of the jury."

"Andrew Edmonds, ladies and gentlemen. Or, just Andy Edmonds. I am the Lee Memorial Professor of Political Science at the University of Virginia."

"And please tell the jury your qualifications as an expert on the subject of terrorism."

"I am a former professor at the United States Military Academy at West Point, where our country trains its finest officers. There, I taught courses such as Terrorism, Weapons of Mass Destruction, and Terrorism Financing and Recruitment to future officers. I have a Ph.D., a doctorate, from Stanford University and a bachelor's degree, myself, from West Point. I served as an army officer in a number of overseas posts, the last one being Iraq. My overseas service was related to terrorism issues."

"Just to be clear, Professor Edmonds, is there really a school subject called Terrorism? We've gotten that far away from reading, writing, and arithmetic?"

The professor smiled at the comparison. "Yes, and let's be glad that there are universities studying terrorism, because there are fewer of those than there are universities that cover Elvis."

Several jurors were amused by that, but they nodded. They probably were thinking, Yes. . . . That's too bad, but it sounds like the way universities are today.

"Professor, have you testified in Congress or in trials?"

"I've testified many times before Congress, mostly to the Armed Services or Homeland Security Committees. I've testified in twelve court cases, but not all of them went to trial. Some of those, I gave deposition testimony."

"Now, have I furnished you with information about this case? Depositions and other documents?"

"I have read all of the depositions in this case. And the Complaint and defendant's Answer. And, of course, the events that created this trial are well known to the public, and I have studied the incident itself. Not merely as part of this case, but to keep up with my profession, because the Holy Faith Foundation and Al Likchah are well known to terrorism scholars."

"Professor, do you have an opinion about the financing and recruitment that lay behind the Delmar Stadium terrorism incident? I note that you have taught courses in Terrorism Financing and Recruitment. Do you have an opinion about the chain of financing in this case?"

"I do."

"And what is that opinion?"

"The financing came originally from The Holy Faith Foundation. It was sent, however, in a roundabout pathway, which is what happens almost always, with terrorism financing. That way, a charity donor can stay clean, at least in public. The Holy Faith Foundation gave a grant to the International Red Crescent. The Red Crescent, in turn, gave a grant to an organization called Al Likchah in the Arabian Peninsula. And that group—ALAP, or Al Likchah—that's who provided the direct funding to the individuals who carried out the Delmar Stadium incident."

"Now, Professor, let's back up and explain how you arrived at these conclusions. . . ."

This was the standard technique for examining expert witnesses. The method is simple: have the expert tell his conclusions first, before explaining it. The expert will tell the jury how he reached his conclusions, of course, but that comes afterward. This way, members of the jury who can't or won't follow the explanation still get the opinion, before they tune out.

And also, the explanation makes more sense if the jury knows the conclusion the expert is driving toward. And then, the lawyer can ask about the conclusion again, afterward.

It took hours for Professor Edmonds to explain all of his reasons for concluding that Al Likchah had financed the individuals, Ibrahim, Mansouri and Hamadi. His testimony covered all of the signature methods of Al Likchah; the type of incendiary device, the path of the money, the financial institutions involved, the claim of responsibility, and the target. It took even longer to explain how the money trail connected to The Holy Faith Foundation. The Professor had a dozen charts to help explain it in numbers and pictures.

And, of course, the explanation was delayed by repeated objections from Jimmy Coleman. The judge ruled that several points that Robert wanted to make were prohibited by the Rules of Evidence.

After getting the witness to repeat the conclusions he had stated at the beginning, Robert said, "I have just one more question."

"Your honor," he asked, "may I approach the witness with an Exhibit?"

"You may."

The jury watched as Robert walked to Professor Edmonds's side. "Professor, this is one of the pages of Exhibit 16. There is a handwritten notation on the page. Professor, you can read Arabic, I believe?"

"Yes. I can."

"Please read the Arabic notation here in pencil on Exhibit 16 and tell us what it means in English. What does this pencil writing say?"

"It's not very good handwriting, but the meaning is clear. This handwritten note says, 'Personal, per Bedouin.' It's right beside the entry that shows the Red Crescent's grant to Al Likchah in the Arabian Peninsula.

And Bedouin is the name of the head of The Holy Faith Foundation, which had just given a similar amount of money to the Red Crescent. This hand-written note ties all of it together in one place."

"I pass the witness," said Robert finally.

As he sat down, a satisfied Tom Kennedy whispered in his ear. "Good job. You kicked Jimmy Coleman right in the nuts."

"Don't get too excited. Remember: Jimmy Coleman gets to cross-examine this witness, next."

32

So, now it was Jimmy Coleman's turn to question the professor, and he came out swinging.

"You've been paid for your testimony here, haven't you, Mister Edmonds?" It was *Mister*, not professor. Jimmy's tactic was to avoid showing respect.

"No." The professor wrinkled his nose. "I haven't been 'paid for my testimony' in the sense of getting compensation for any particular point of view. I've agreed to testify for my customary fee for the time, effort, and expertise that I have spent on the case."

"Aren't you just quibbling, by saying that? You've been paid, haven't you?"

"Yes, but not the way you put it."

"Well, let's look into that. Your overall fee will come to more than twenty-five thousand dollars, won't it?"

"Probably so."

"And on an hourly basis, you're getting $ 350 per hour for working on this case. Now, that's probably five or six times what you earn as a professor, right?"

"Yes, but that's based upon a lifetime of expertise that I have built up."

"So it's not really anything like a *customary* fee, if we compare it to your customary salary as a professor. Isn't that true?"

"Any professor would make more as a consultant to industry, or as an adviser to the government, or as an expert witness, than the salaries we earn from education, because education doesn't pay high salaries, even to those of us who have significant expertise."

"So the answer is, No, it's not customary. Now, let's talk about what you call your 'expertise.' In at least one of the few cases where you testified in front of a jury, a case called *Johnson v. Fakhouri S.A.*, the jurors didn't believe you, did they?"

"I can't say which witnesses the jurors believed or didn't believe, because that's not something that they report."

"Aren't you quibbling again? The jury decided the case against the side that hired you to testify. Isn't that correct?"

Robert was on his feet. "Objection, your honor. This is improper cross-examination."

"Sus-tained!" said the judge forcefully. "Members of the jury, you must disregard that last question and those last remarks from Mr. Coleman."

Jimmy was unfazed. His voice was just as coarse and just as brazen now, when he asked, "Now, Mister Edmonds, let's talk about this handwriting that's on exhibit 16. It's not very clear writing, even in Arabic. Isn't that right?"

"It's not very good handwriting."

"Isn't it possible that it says something else, something other than what you translated?"

"No . . . I don't think so."

"In fact, the pencil handwriting is so shaky and difficult to read, that would be possible for another translator to have a completely different translation of that handwriting, than what you gave this jury?"

"That's the way it always is with translations. You can always change the words around a little, but only a little."

The rest of Jimmy's cross examination was equally combative. It was accusatory, angry, and very effective. It consisted of more than two hours of unpleasant challenges to the professor's abilities, motives, and thought. And as usually happens when a person has been in the witness chair for the better part of a day, Professor Edmonds gradually became tired—and like most witnesses in that situation, he let his guard down as he became tired. Facing a long pressure-filled cross-examination after a long and difficult direct examination is like taking a day-long college exam. It's like a complicated and tricky test, in a technical course, for a full day. It precipitates mistakes. And that, of course, was what Jimmy intended.

"Well," Tom said at the end. "I don't think Jimmy shook the professor's conclusions or his real testimony. *But*—and it's a big 'but'—he's got a lot of ammunition that he can use in his final argument to knock the professor down and challenge his credibility. Even if none of it has much to do with the case we're trying."

* * *

The next day was going to involve three or four different witnesses. They would be assistant medical examiners, testifying about the autopsies performed on the deceased loved ones of the plaintiffs. The testimony was going to be disturbing, and it might be seen as ghoulish, no matter how it was done. The challenge, for Robert and Tom, was to get across to the jury that the dead, in this case, were worthwhile and living human beings, active and healthy, and not just corpses to be cut open. The point was obvious, but these lawyers knew that it tends to get lost.

At ten o'clock at night, a call came to Robert from Jimmy. "Hello, Jimmy," he said. "I'm tired and about to go home, but I want to listen to whatever you're calling about. So tell me, but bear with me, please."

"I just talked to my client in Qatar, or actually, to their Qatari lawyers," Jimmy growled. "It's early morning there. They're nine hours ahead of us. Anyway, they know about the witness today. I thought he was extraordinarily weak. The entire case is lacking in direct evidence. But my client wants to get out of the business of litigating, which isn't their business since they're a charity, and get back to the business of making grants to help the world become a better place."

Robert's eyes closed. But he just waited, instead of saying something disagreeable.

Jimmy cleared his throat. A long and vibrating sound. "The Foundation believes, truly believes, that it is offering a grant to your clients for their loss, whatever you may think of that point of view. And they want to settle the case. They have authorized me to increase the settlement offer."

"Well, good. But let me ask, Jimmy; what is it, that they want to increase it to? What amount?"

"They've offered you fifty million. For settlement of the whole case. As I understand it, more than half of your clients would accept such a settlement. The Foundation wants to buy its peace and to buy it completely. It is no good to the Foundation to settle with some of the plaintiffs but have a substantial number of them keep on with the lawsuit, so that they put the Foundation through an entire trial and through all of the appeals, anyway. The fifty million was a generous offer, I think. The plaintiffs might get nothing. In fact, that is what I firmly believe they'd get."

"All right. But we need specifics. Jimmy, you said you wanted to increase it. So, to what? What amount?"

"Sixty million. And if you don't think that's enough, make a counteroffer."

"As always, Jimmy, I appreciate any settlement offer. I can't just accept it by myself, of course. I'll have to present it to all of my clients and explain it to all of them. You know what the law is: the *Burrows* case. That case says I can't lump the clients all together. I have to treat each one as if he or she were the only client. But I'll certainly present it. And Jimmy, I think you are doing the lawyerly thing, the professional thing, by attempting to settle the case."

"Bear in mind, I'd rather try it to the end, myself. I think you've got nothing. But let me know."

"It will take some time, with more than a hundred clients. But I will. I'll get back to you."

33

T his looks like a boiler-room operation," said Robert, as he stepped into the big workroom that was part of his law firm.

The area was set up with a battery of seven telephones, all set on individual desks. At each desk, a legal assistant sat, ready to talk to a client about the proposed settlement that Jimmy had offered. A group of three attorneys stood at the ready, waiting to back up any legal assistant who had finished talking to a client about the basics of Jimmy's offer.

One of the attorneys smiled while waiting to be called upon. "A boiler room operation is just a telephone bank with a mission, whether it's in a conference room or an actual boiler room. And this looks like a boiler room operation because . . . well, that's what it is!"

Robert laughed. "Well, that's right. It's our way of complying with the rules, by making sure every client group is well informed. And we've taken all of you away from your other work at this law firm, and pressed all of you into service, because we really need you for a day or two."

The room hummed with voices discussing the details of the settlement. "What would happen in your case is that your family group would be paid three quarters of a million dollars. . . . Yes, you'd have to release the defendant. You'd have to give up your claim. Otherwise, the defendant, the Foundation, has no reason to settle. . . ."

"The proposal is that most living plaintiffs would receive either $ 400,000—just under half a million dollars—if injuries are no longer life-threatening; and more if they are life-threatening. . . ."

"The total settlement offer is sixty million dollars, you see. But there are more than a hundred family groups. . . ."

"No, ma'am, we aren't telling you that you have to settle. We recommend it, though, because it's a difficult claim and you're likely to get nothing if you don't settle. . . ."

"Yes, sir, but please don't get mad at me. The rules say that we have to tell you about this settlement offer. And no, you don't have to take it, but we recommend it, because the claim can easily be lost at trial, and then you wouldn't get anything. . . ."

Robert shook his head. Sometimes clients become angry at their own lawyers because their lawyers give them honest advice. The advice that they, as lawyers, believe is accurate, and therefore, they are required to tell their clients, as a matter of legal duty. The clients, though, have read John Grisham books, and they don't believe that they can possibly lose. That's not what's supposed to happen, they think; and it won't, because the client doesn't lose in those books.

"You folks seem to be doing a good job," Robert said to the lawyers who weren't immediately occupied. "Keep me posted at the end of the day, when we come back from the courtroom."

* * *

When the first pathologist testified, Tom Kennedy did the direct examination. He took the assistant medical examiner through a shortened version of the autopsy, from beginning to end. The following autopsies might not require so much detail.

"The body was that of a 33-year old male named Daniel Swindell," Dr. Alma Rodriguez told the jury. "He had no external signs of anything but good health. But it was difficult to tell, because the entire corpus was macerated, distorted, from burns, beyond recognition."

"Doctor, did you open the abdomen of Mr. Swindell with the usual Y-shaped incision?"

"I did."

"Were you able to examine Mr. Swindell's intestines, the liver, pancreas, heart, lungs, and major arteries, and to weigh the organs?" Tom was particular about using the deceased man's name, rather than referring to "the body" or "the heart."

"I was. All were normal, except the lungs, which were desiccated and burned. The findings are in my report."

"Is this document, Plaintiff's Exhibit 33, a copy of your report of examination of Mr. Daniel Swindell?"

"Yes, it is."

Tom went through the formalities of offering the autopsy report and having it received into evidence.

"Doctor, please tell us about the condition of Mr. Swindell's heart and lungs."

"His lungs were burned internally. That happens in this kind of incident. The blood in the heart was congealed. There was post-mortem lividity in the body generally, including the organs. That means that the blood had stopped circulating and was pooled toward the person's back from the effect of gravity."

"Doctor, what is your opinion of the cause of Mr. Daniel Swindell's death?"

"Asphyxiation and cardiac arrest resulting from severe burns and desiccation of the lungs."

"Are these the kind of injuries that would be painful to Mr. Swindell, for the amount of time from when they began until death?"

"Extremely so, yes."

Tom omitted the part of the autopsy that involved opening the skull, called "reflecting the head," during which the pathologist saws off the top and examines the brain. Usually, listeners find this description dehumanizing, and it was not essential in this case. It was part of these lawyers' effort to tell the jury what was important, while keeping the focus upon the fact that the body was, after all, that of a person: Daniel Swindell.

"Doctor, did you follow the customary procedures for repairing Mr. Swindell's body? And if you did, tell us why did you do so, although it may seem obvious."

"Of course. We always sew up the body with fine stitches after the autopsy, even though that was difficult for Mr. Swindell's burned anatomy. The reason is to preserve the appearance of the body in a condition as close to life as we can. After all, this is the body of someone's loved one: someone's father, brother, or son. It was valuable during his life and it still is valuable to his family."

Robert noticed that the eyes of several of the jurors were glistening. Shining. It was painful for everyone in the courtroom, but that was to be expected. Tom had covered what needed to be covered about the autopsy, while keeping Mr. Daniel Swindell human.

* * *

The rest of the day was composed of many more autopsies. But Tom's questioning was different. He was able to avoid so much detail, while calling each person by his or her name. The cause of death was remarkably similar in most cases, although there were some differences, such as those for victims who attempted to run, to leave the conflagration, and who fell and were injured.

Several times, Tom felt the need to apologize for the length and nature of the day's evidence. "So that the jury can know, doctor, can you please tell us: is this kind of testimony disturbing to people who must listen to it?" . . . "And so, while we are sorry to have to subject anyone to this information, do we have to have it, to understand how she died?"

Finally, Tom passed the last witness. "This has been a long and difficult day. Thank you, doctor."

One disturbing factor that had been present throughout the trial was absent today. Jimmy Coleman asked only a few questions of any of the witnesses, and those that he did ask were not like his usual cross-examinations. "Thank goodness for pleasant aspects of this," Robert thought to himself, "even the small things."

34

brahim was restless again. "Bedouin, we've got to do something. Now. This lawyer's pursuing this lawsuit just as hard as if I'd never even gone to visit him. He should have listened, or at least, he should have respected the Glock that I pointed at him. We've got to do something. I've got to do something."

"Ibrahim, my son, you must be patient." Bedouin's own voice was very, very patient-sounding, but there was an edge of exasperation behind it. "Remember, my Warrior Ibrahim, the words of the Prophet (peace be upon him). 'The strong man is the one who is able to control his anger.'"

"But Bedouin, I told him, this foolish lawyer, that I would 'visit' again. I need to do something. If I don't, our promises will seem empty."

"Ibrahim, my son, the lawyer has tried to settle the case. Exactly what you told him to do. In fact, most of his clients have accepted the settlement offer our lawyer has made. There are only a dozen or so plaintiffs in the lawsuit, still wanting to try their claims in court."

"But this lawyer is stupid. He is still pursuing the lawsuit."

"Ibrahim, my son, the settlement may still resolve itself. It is foolish to resort to violence when another solution is possible. I know you have heard this saying, even though it was not the words of the Prophet (peace be upon him). 'You can catch more bears with honey than with a club.'"

There was an awkward silence. Bedouin spoke again. "Ibrahim, my son, your duty is to wait."

Ibrahim blustered, without words, and then he said, "Yes. I will follow your lead, my Bedouin."

* * *

In the courtroom, it was another difficult day.

"I hugged Brett, my only son, and said goodbye to him," said an attractive middle-aged woman. Obviously a mother. A mom. "My Brett walked out the door to go to the football game, and . . . that was the last time . . . I saw him."

This was the day to present testimony from family members about their damages. Their pain from the loss of their loved ones. On the transcript, the testimony would seem overwrought. Artificial. Dead, and at the same time, too emotional. But in the stark atmosphere of the courtroom, the testimony was gut-wrenching. With each witness, Robert asked a variation of the question, "When did you last see your son?" or "daughter?" or "husband?" And he followed by taking the witness back to the lost child's birth, babyhood, preschool, and teenage years.

"What was Brett like as a baby?"

"He smiled early. He loved what he called the flashy thing that was one of his toys. He had a little siren in his crib and that was his favorite thing to sound off. One time, when he was just starting to talk, he said, 'Got two books in my crib.' But he said 'cwib,' because he couldn't pronounce his r's at that age. He said, 'Want five books. Got two. Need three more.' My husband and I thought we were raising a math genius; not yet two years old, and he knew how to add two and three to get five. Looking back, it was probably just a coincidence that he got the numbers right. But we loved it."

And there were exhibits. There were crayon drawings, pictures of the baby with his Daddy in the pool, and first-grade writing on tablet paper. Then, Robert would ask: "He became a Cub Scout? With how many arrowheads?"

The child's development as a baseball player, swimmer, photographer, woodworker, or Eagle Scout came next. With smiling pictures. Then, boyfriends or girlfriends. With smiling pictures.

There were moments of raw emotion. "I miss him. My Lord! I miss him so, so much. . . . I expect to see him when I go by his room, to see what a mess the room is with posters and pictures over each other, a familiar jumble . . . but he's . . . never there, and the room is neat, and I hate . . . the neatness. . . ." Robert had prepared these witnesses to express their real emotions, and he knew how to ask questions that would show the jury their genuine pain.

Tom's job was to watch the jury. People hearing these kinds of stories are deeply sympathetic. There is no phoniness to them in a courtroom, however exaggerated and overdone they seem in print. But a curious condition sets in. People sitting and listening, people such as jurors, experience a kind of compassion fatigue. Sooner or later, the stories suddenly become too much; and Tom was charged with watching the jurors for signs that their eyes were starting to glaze over.

In a way, it was impossible to calibrate the moment at which to stop piling on the families' stories, because every dead relative had to be described at least to some degree. But Tom gave Robert a distant early warning in the second day.

And the stories of loss from the families occupied just more than a day and a half.

* * *

That evening, there was another call from Jimmy Coleman. "Herrick, I've pumped my client to add another chunk to the settlement offer. More money. They've authorized me to go up to seventy-five million."

"I will convey that to my plaintiffs with my recommendation." Robert was exhausted.

Jimmy's voice made him sound like a Doberman chasing a mailman. "But Herrick, listen. You will need to convey to them that this is the limit. There is no more money in the bank. I'll send you a letter that makes it clear. And this is not merely the settlement of a lawsuit. It is a charitable contribution to these plaintiffs to compensate for their losses."

"Send me your letter. By all means. I will convey that, too, to each client. It may help to convince them."

"And I have to remind you—my client insists, and I would say it anyway—this offer is not out of fear of this lawsuit. My client is confident of its position. The offer is purely a matter of getting back to the Foundation's charitable purpose so that it won't spend more of its time and treasure in the trial of this lawsuit. Actually, if I were to say it, I'd put it even stronger. I'd say it this way: 'Herrick, you've got no case. You've got nothing.'"

"Jimmy, that goes without saying." Or at least, Robert wished Jimmy could leave it without saying.

They said their goodbyes. Jimmy was very different in his attitude when negotiating to settle. He sounded almost polite.

"Tom, we're going to have to start up that boiler-room operation again. We've got the job of informing every client group. And this time, it's seventy-five million. I think we would do best to strongly recommend this to our plaintiffs. In the first place, much as I hate to say it, Jimmy Coleman is right. I'm not confident at all of getting a plaintiff's verdict. Our evidence is circumstantial, hard to follow, and tarnished by cross-examination. And there's something else to think about. Solvency."

"How's that?" Tom asked.

"Solvency of the defendant. That's frequently a problem, and Dun and Bradstreet's reports show that it's a problem here. The Holy Faith Foundation is big, but it's not infinite in size. Bigger charities exist, but no charity is as big as the big industrial companies that can pay damages in the hundred millions. And with this seventy-five million, we are approaching the limit of what the Foundation can pay. If we get a judgment that is multiples of this settlement offer, it may be uncollectable."

"That's always a sobering thought." Tom shook his head. "A sad thought. Realistic, but sad, painful, and most unfortunate, to think that we might dismember the defendant and still not collect."

"And talk about dismembering the defendant is premature, because we, ourselves—the plaintiffs—may end up being the ones who get dismembered."

35

We're nearing the end," Tom said. "Now, we're about to find out how good our strategy is."

"We tried to start strong," Robert mused. "I'm not sure we did, but we tried—the usual advice, start strong and end strong. We may be making a mistake with the ending we're about to supply."

"By making this guy Hamadi our last witness? The co-terrorist, the inside guy? Yes. We may have made a mistake. It may turn out to be a really smart move, if Hamadi turns out to be a good witness. Or, it may lose the case for us, if our last witness looks dishonest and offends the jury."

"Well, if we had a stronger case overall, we wouldn't take this chance. As it is, if we try to play it safe, and we try to be *too* safe, we may lose it anyway."

"We're about to find out."

* * *

The courtroom was crowded but oddly quiet. The spectators knew that the end of the plaintiffs' evidence was near. The excitement that had gripped the audience in the beginning was dissipated by day-after-day witnesses.

"Mr. Herrick, call your next." Judge Elsa Domínguez's voice broke the strained silence.

"Plaintiffs call . . . Hamadi Attah."

The witness entered the courtroom, escorted by two uniformed sheriff's deputies. In a criminal trial, as the defendant, he would have had the option of wearing a business suit, and if he didn't have one, the county would be responsible for getting him one. But in this civil trial, where protecting him from adverse jury prejudice was not the issue, he wore a white jail jumpsuit. Robert was content with that. A prisoner's outfit would decrease the impression of favoritism toward the witness, which was going to be a real problem.

"Tell the jury your name, please."

"Hamadi Attah."

"And how old are you?"

"Twenty-one. I was eighteen when the . . . when I went to the stadium."

"So that the jury can know, let's tell everyone what you did at the stadium. And in the events leading up to it."

"I was one of those guys who sent the balloon into the stadium. I helped to set it up and I got away with the other two guys."

The jury was staring at the witness with disgusted fascination.

"Tell the jury your background, please."

"I was raised in New Jersey. My parents were first-generation from Pakistan. They died when I was eight. I lived in a series of foster homes after that. But I had been raised with Islam, and my foster homes respected that. My parents were what Americans would call 'good Muslims.' They worked hard and were proud when they became Americans. After they died, my life was not so good."

"And you left home?"

"I coasted through the internet, and I learned about the struggle. The oppression that Muslims faced. The religious persecution. There were parts of the Quran and the Book of the Prophet that I didn't know, before that. It sounded right, when I finally read it and studied it. Doing something to help the struggle sounded like doing something right. If I helped, it would mean something, which I wasn't doing in my life, for sure; and I was miserable. I was also foolish. I stole enough money to fly to Saudi Arabia and from there to go to Yemen."

"And in Yemen, you met Mr. al Ibrahim."

"He was like the father I had never known. My Arabic improved under him, and my study of the Holy Books improved too."

"And so, what happened that brought you back to America?"

"It was simple. Ibrahim just announced that we were going. I went with him. Everything was paid for."

Robert led the witness through the events. Assembling the parts for the balloon and its cargo. Stealing the big truck. "It was easy." The flight of the balloon. The explosion. "Like a whole bunch of cannon shots, and it lit up the sky with red and white fire." And the escape of the three terrorists, and then, getting caught near the Mexican border.

"Now, let me ask you about something different. Did you, on one occasion, answer a telephone call for Ibrahim? And did it involve a short conversation with someone who knew about the stadium plan?"

"Ibrahim was temporarily away. I don't remember; maybe he was taking a shower or something. The voice on the phone identified himself as 'Bedouin.'"

Jimmy was on his feet. The jury was as riveted to this testimony as Jimmy was upset by it. "Objection, your honor, because no proper predicate has been laid to authenticate this telephone conversation or to show who was really on the other side of the line. It could have been a prankster, for all this witness knows."

The judge hesitated for a moment. She sat back and looked at the ceiling. Finally: "That's overruled. There has been enough background evidence about Bedouin and his connection to the defendant and to this situation, so that the jury could, if it decided to, believe that the voice was Bedouin. Ladies and gentlemen of the jury"—she turned toward them—"it will be up to you to decide whether this testimony is credible. You are the exclusive judges of the evidence."

So . . . Robert continued. "What was your conversation with the man identified as Bedouin?"

"He just called himself Bedouin and asked for Ibrahim. I told him it would take a minute. And so I talked to him, or mainly, I listened. He told me he was part of the Holy Faith Foundation, which I had heard of. He told me that he was proud of what we were doing, and he mentioned the bombing in the stadium, and he quoted from the Quran."

"Now, Hamadi, I need to ask you about why you're here today. Have you offered to plead guilty to murder and to testify about what you and the others did?"

"Yes."

"Tell us about the arrangements for that." It's best, Robert and Tom had agreed, to bring this out now, rather than leave it to Jimmy's cross examination.

"I will plead guilty and if I testify truthfully in trials of other people for these murders, I will be sentenced to life imprisonment."

"With the possibility of parole?"

"That's . . . correct."

"And you understand that you may never get out, even with the possibility of parole, because parole for convicted murderers is not guaranteed?"

"Yes." The witness had tears in his eyes. "I was surrounded by a bunch of bad influences!" He blurted. "I don't want a trial. I don't want a jury trial. The idea of a trial, of a whole case against me, scares me more than the sentence does."

"I pass the witness." The outburst surprised Robert. But then, he reflected: many defendants plead guilty because they are petrified of being tried before a jury. It is something that beginner defense attorneys struggle to become accustomed to and to handle properly.

Tom was more pragmatic. "So far, so good," he whispered. But immediately, he added: "I know. I know. Jimmy's turn is next."

* * *

The judge turned to the other side of the courtroom. "Mr. Coleman, cross-examination?"

Jimmy wasted no time. "Hamadi Attah, you were charged with capital murder at first, not just murder. That's a death penalty crime. You know that?"

"Yes."

"And the fact is, you're testifying here, and you've agreed to testify in criminal cases, to save yourself from the death penalty by being convicted only of murder, not capital murder."

"Yes."

"And also, to save yourself from life in prison *without* parole."

"Yes, I guess so."

"To save your own worthless skin."

Robert started to object. But then—I'd do better to limit my objections to the ones I need, he thought.

"I—I don't understand why you would say that," answered the witness quietly.

"Anyway, this idea that you were just wanting to avoid a jury is baloney, isn't it? Since what you wanted was to bargain against a more severe penalty. Like being put to death."

"You can put it that way. If you want to."

"In your confession, you said that someone gave you the money to go to Yemen, and you thought the money came from the middle east. Today, you've said you stole the money. You've contradicted yourself, haven't you?"

"I don't remember."

"You're not a credible witness, are you?"

"I don't know."

"Fact is, you've put together a whole string of false statements in your testimony, haven't you?"

"I don't know."

"Well, let's see. In your confession, you said that during that famous phone call you claim happened, you asked the caller on the phone his name, and you couldn't remember it, then, at the time you confessed. But here, you remembered it without hesitating. Didn't you contradict yourself again?"

"I don't know."

Jimmy's cross examination brought out more contradictions. The way Hamadi had said the parts for the balloon were put together didn't match his confession. Neither did the way the truck was stolen. And on, and on.

Robert slumped down in his seat. He had expected a vigorous cross examination, but not so many contradictions. "The jury will blame us for calling this witness," he said to Tom when it was over.

"He's a criminal." Tom was philosophical. "And a kid. The jury will understand. . . . I hope."

36

called this meeting," Jimmy Coleman announced in his inimitable throaty voice, "to study how we should present our defense evidence. Or whether we should present any evidence at all."

The big conference room at Booker and Bayne was huge. The walls were white birch, to match the rest of the office. From perches high on every side, portraits of long-dead partners kept an unseeing vigil. An elaborate gold sign identified the likeness of Colonel Henry Anderson Booker, the firm's Founder, with his striped suspenders and long white mustache.

"This trial involves a particular kind of case," Jimmy went on. "The only issue is about the plaintiffs' evidence. It's thin. The only direct evidence they have, unfortunately for them, comes from an admitted terrorist who has bargained with his testimony and who contradicted himself over and over. And in this kind of case, it's usually best to do nothing as a defense, other than cross-examining the plaintiffs' witnesses and reducing their credibility. In other words, the conventional wisdom would be: we put on no evidence at all."

Jimmy waved his hand toward the seat beside him. "This gentleman is Abu Al Temani. He's a Qatari lawyer who also represents our client, The Holy Faith Foundation, but usually in Qatar. I wanted him here because it's a big decision and we need the client's input. I know what I think, which is that we shouldn't present any witnesses, but it depends on the circumstances. And that's what this meeting is about."

Bill Watson spoke up. "Shouldn't we consider the possibility that we could call at least somebody from the Foundation itself, to deny that it participated in terrorism?" Bill was a securities lawyer, but Jimmy wanted him here because his litigation experience included proof of illegal financing, and he was a veteran trial lawyer. "I mean, I know it has risks to call any witnesses, but the jurors may expect us to deny it."

"I've discussed that with Mr. Al Temani, here." Jimmy shook his head. "The only credible witness who knows that sort of thing would be the head of the Foundation, the man known as Bedouin. But if we brought Bedouin to the United States, there could be all kinds of problems. He could be served with process personally, in a lawsuit against him, if he came here. He is independently a billionaire, with more net worth than the Foundation. It's not been possible for anyone to serve suit papers on him in Qatar, under Qatari law. It is even conceivable that he could be arrested for crimes based on the testimony in this case, even though we don't consider that this testimony means much."

Jimmy looked around the table, and then he went on. "And even if Bedouin testified here, it might end up hurting us. Don't forget: he'd have to be cross-examined. Robert Herrick would have a field day asking him questions. You never know what's going to happen on cross-examination. There would be a lot of stuff that he'd have to admit. Such as that the grant was made by the Foundation to the International Red Crescent, and within days, the money went to Al Likchah in the Arabian Peninsula, which he'd have to admit, has been involved in some bad stuff."

The Qatari lawyer, Abu Al Temani, spoke up. "I agree. Getting testimony from inside the Foundation is not a good idea. I'm convinced."

"Another idea," Jennifer Lowenstein suggested, "would be to call our own expert witness. We engaged this Professor Nowlin from New York University a long time ago. He's got some opinions that differ from that expert the plaintiffs used, that Professor Edmonds."

"But that would be risky too." Jimmy sounded like a wire brush scraping a plaster wall. "He'd end up agreeing with the plaintiff's expert on too many things. Such as that this Yemen connection, Al Likchah, is a terrorist organization. He could undermine some things, yes; but the fact is, we'd end up with an overall negative. Now, don't get me wrong. We were right to get our own expert. He's been very useful in helping us cross-examine the plaintiff's expert. But to call him to testify and be cross-examined, that's a bad idea."

There was silence throughout the room.

"You see what I mean," Jimmy said after a moment. "There's a negative side to every possibility. To every witness we might think of calling. But if we just sit back and argue to the jury that the plaintiffs don't have any credible evidence, we can point out the failings of every witness. And there are plenty of those flaws, and there's not much that proves anything. We would be likely to lose some of the force in that attack if we called our own witnesses. Robert Herrick's best arguments would come from points that our witnesses would have to admit."

Again, there was silence.

"Mr. Al Temani, you're here from Qatar." Jimmy waved toward him again. "I asked the Foundation to bring someone to speak for it. Do you agree that our best course is not to present witnesses?"

"It sounds strange, when you hear it, at first. But yes. You've convinced me."

"Then that's what we'll do. No witnesses. I think it's a winning strategy."

* * *

Robert and Tom sat across from each other at Robert's big desk. Outside, the day was cloudy and gray, but there was enough light to see the sparkling greensward that lined Buffalo Bayou and stretched toward the horizon. The sun illuminated the reds, blues, greens, and yellows of the big Oriental carpet and brightened the banks of flowers that lined the huge windows.

"We don't have many plaintiffs still in trial," Tom said. "Most of our clients have agreed to settle. These eight families still trying the case, they balked mostly at the document they'd have had to sign, that Jimmy's client insisted on, that said that by settling, all parties agreed that the payment would be a 'charitable grant.'"

"I can understand. They firmly believe that the Foundation killed their loved ones."

"Well, as I count it, we have only these eight families still in the trial. The number keeps changing. More than ninety percent have taken the settlement deal."

"Well, eight families, or eight groups, is a big case for trial, by itself."

"Here's the problem, of course. Will Jimmy's client still fund the settlement, if we still continue to try the case? It's in their interest to say, 'We won't do this unless we get a hundred percent to settle.' And they've reserved that right in the settlement agreement."

"As the end comes near, more of the plaintiffs will settle. I doubt we'll get a hundred percent. But yes, I think it'll be in the defendant's interest— the Foundation's—to settle even with a handful of trial cases remaining. For one thing, if we win, it will be a fraction of the damages that could be awarded if everyone's in the trial. And that's the amount, a lower amount, that the newspapers would report."

"Well, yes. But we have to keep driving forward. As if there were no settlement at all."

"Oh, yes. We'll end up with a trial case, I predict. And at this point, I'd be disappointed if we didn't get to try it to the end."

* * *

"Jimmy," said Jennifer Lowenstein when the meeting ended, "do you really think it's best to present no witnesses? No defense evidence?"

"Absolutely. The fact that we don't call defense witnesses doesn't mean we don't have a defense. We do. Our defense is: the plaintiff's haven't proved it and our client is a fine charity."

"But our expert would make a good witness, for example."

"It's not that anyone would make a good witness or a bad witness. The problem is, anybody we called would be cross-examined. And they'd give up some evidence against us." Jimmy's voice dropped its volume, now, as he said, "You see, Jennifer, The Holy Faith Foundation does have some expo-o-o-sure. A lot of expo-o-o-sure."

Jennifer knew what that meant, in Jimmy-Coleman language. Saying that a client had "only a little bit of expo-o-o-sure" meant that it had done something wrong but still was likely to get off scot free. But a defendant that had "a lot of expo-o-o-sure" was guilty. Really guilty. Guilty as sin. Jennifer was disappointed. She still hadn't gotten over what Jimmy would call a bad habit: believing in her client's righteousness, or at least hoping for it.

"I don't care about exposure except in terms of strategy," Jimmy added. "There's nothing like the thrill of getting a client off when you know they're guilty. It's really fun if your client skates out of the courtroom with a win, after they've done something horribly awful. And that's what I'm doing here. It's our best strategy not to present defense witnesses. To remain silent."

Jimmy shook his head. "I never judge my clients. Unless, of course, they don't pay their attorney's fees."

37

Robert Herrick stood and looked toward the judge. "Plaintiffs rest, your honor."

Quickly, Jimmy Coleman also stood. "Your honor, The Holy Faith Foundation has prepared numerous witnesses to call in response to the plaintiffs' charges. We're confident. But we have decided that the plaintiffs haven't even come close to proving their case. Every witness has either had nothing to say about the Foundation or has given contradictory and unbelievable testimony. . . ."

"Objection, your honor!" Robert realized, too late, that Jimmy was breaking the rules by giving a speech instead of just resting his case. "Your honor, Mr. Coleman is giving an improper final argument instead of calling witnesses. Because it's obviously improper, we ask that your honor instruct the jury to disregard."

"Sus-tained!" Judge Domínguez sounded angry. "Yes, that's improper, Mr. Coleman. The jury is instructed to disregard those improper remarks. Mr. Coleman, are you saying that the defense rests?"

"We don't think we need to call any witnesses in this case."

"Do you speak English, Mr. Coleman? Does the defense rest, then?"

"Your honor, the defense rests."

Jimmy sat back down, heavily. He smiled amiably, just to show that the judge's remarks did not trouble him. The four other black-suited Booker and Bayne lawyers smiled too, along with Jimmy.

"Ladies and gentlemen of the jury," the judge said in measured tones, "the evidence in this case is concluded. I will need to meet with the lawyers to write the instructions and verdict forms for you. Mr. Bailiff, the jurors are excused for the time being."

* * *

"In this conference, which is about the charge to the jury," the judge said to the lawyers, "I will need your help in putting together an unusual set of instructions and questions. The measure of damages is clear. The fact of the damages is clear. The fact that they were caused intentionally by three on-scene actors is clear. The main issue in instructing the jury will be how to ask whether the Holy Faith Foundation acted in a way that will make it liable for what was done at the stadium. The jury will have to decide about damages, too, but those instructions will be more or less standard."

Robert nodded. "Yes. That's the way we see it, your honor. We've submitted a proposed charge like that."

Jimmy shook his head. "Those are all issues, your honor, but we disagree with Mr. Herrick's vision of the charge. We've submitted a contrary proposal."

"All right." The judge sighed. "How is it possible for the Foundation to be potentially liable? Let me count the ways. And I see at least four. I know that you think it's not liable at all, Mr. Coleman, but we have to ask the jury. First, the Foundation possibly aided or encouraged the on-scene actors to commit the acts in the stadium. Second, they possibly engaged in a conspiracy. Third, they may have acted together, or in other words, in concert. Fourth, the Foundation approved the actions during or after the fact, or as the law would put it, they 'ratified' what the three on-scene actors did."

"I don't think there's any evidence to support any of those issues, and I move for a judgment as a matter of law on all four," Jimmy said tonelessly.

"That's overruled," said Elsa Domínguez immediately.

"Our proposal is for a set of four verdict questions, one after the other, asking about each of those four kinds of fault by the Foundation," said Robert.

Jimmy growled at that. "No, that's not the right way to do it. It should all be in one question. Like the proposal we have submitted to the court, along with a supporting brief. Otherwise, the defendant has to run the gantlet through four different questions. And it's really all the same issue, so it ought to be asked in one question. 'Did the defendant do this, or this, or this?' all in one question."

The lawyers proceeded to argue for a half hour about whether the four kinds of liability should be four questions, or combined into one question. And about where the commas should go.

"All right." The judge was exasperated. "I think Mr. Herrick is right. They are not all the same question. And it will be useful, in granting judgment, to know which ones the jury has decided on. That wouldn't be knowable if it were all one question. I'm going to submit the issues as four different verdict questions."

She sighed again. "Usually charge conferences are polite and simple. Sometimes they are contentious and unpleasant. This has been one of those."

* * *

"Members of the jury," said the judge, "you are excused for the week-end. Remember my instructions. Most importantly, do not discuss this case with anyone, including your wife or husband. And do not read or listen to any news reports about this case."

As they left the courtroom, Tom said, "It's good that we got four different questions."

"Sure." Robert felt upbeat about that. "We'll have final arguments to the jury on Monday. If there were only one question, Jimmy would be able to just argue, 'The Foundation didn't do anything wrong,' over and over, and say, 'The answer to this one big question is No.' But with four different questions, he'll have to get down into all four, and we'll be able to base it on each of the four legal reasons why the Foundation is liable."

He smiled. "The charge conference was about fine points. And technicalities. But technicalities matter."

* * *

Mohammed al Ibrahim felt himself pulsing with anger, still. The lawyer he had visited, the lawyer he had forcefully told to settle the case against the Foundation he so respected, hadn't listened to him at all. Now, he forced his voice to remain level while he talked to Bedouin, the great leader. But it wasn't easy. His hatred for that disrespectful, heretical lawyer was like a living thing inside him.

"If we don't act now, the lawsuit against the Foundation will go all the way through, Bedouin," he breathed into the telephone. "You know how I look up to you. You know how I love the Holy Faith Foundation. You know how I love Islam. I'm not trying to act against your wishes. But I think that it will be a disaster if we don't get this infidel lawyer, this Robert Herrick, out of the way."

"What makes you so sure, Ibrahim, my son?"

"I have followed this court case day by day, intensely. I have no other obligation. One thing is clear to me. If this cursed Robert Herrick were not in charge, there would be no one else who could carry it forward. The case would collapse, and it would get settled quickly. But if we don't get him out of the way, he will keep pursuing this case. And I'm convinced he will fool this crazy American jury if we let him. He will command the judgment of this bunch of simpletons, because he is a magician with persuasion. Robert Herrick is a sugar-voiced dissembler, like Machiavelli or Svengali."

"The American legal system is ludicrous, for sure. Lots of mouthpiece lawyers like that."

"My praiseworthy Bedouin, I can feel it. It is time to act."

"I too have been thinking about it, Ibrahim, my son. You are the most faithful of the faithful. You are the most beautiful fruit of the divine flower. If anyone should be able to get this task finally completed, it would be you. I believe you are right."

"My thanks, my leader Bedouin. You do me great honor, even as I struggle mightily to make myself fit for your faith in me. Please know that I am here to serve you and the Foundation."

"You do *me* great honor, Ibrahim, my son. Here is what I ask you to do."

38

What the lawyers say to you is not evidence," Judge Domínguez intoned. Unnecessarily, because she had already said it several times. "But now, ladies and gentlemen of the jury, the lawyers will have plenty to say. It is time for the attorneys' closing arguments. Remember, ladies and gentlemen of the jury, that you are the sole judges of the evidence." This was also unnecessary, but repeated frequently. "And so, we now have final jury arguments from the lawyers. First, the plaintiff's opening argument. Mr. Herrick?"

"Thank you, your honor." Robert stood and faced the jury. "And I want to thank you, ladies and gentlemen. In America, we have the privilege of serving on a jury. But it is a privilege that sometimes is painfully time-consuming, and it involves sacrifice. My clients and I are grateful. We've seen you during the trial, ladies and gentlemen, and you've obviously paid attention. I've seen jurors go to sleep, occasionally. But this jury was the opposite from that. In totalitarian countries, they don't have juries, and they're part of the exquisite rights we have as Americans. Thank you for doing a good job of it."

It was a standard beginning, he thought to himself. A well-worn beginning, maybe even tired, trite, and hackneyed. But it always seemed to work. Psychologists call it the "audience-reward" factor, as Robert knew. People tend to like people who like them back. Who knows?, he thought. If it works, the jury will like me and my case a little better, even if all the lawyers have heard it before.

"The judge has read instructions and questions to you." He held up a written copy of the court's charge to the jury. "These are the judge's words, not mine. You are bound by law to follow these instructions from the judge, and so am I."

This was also a matter of psychology. The appeal to authority is an age-old persuasion technique. In this instance, the authority of the judge, announcing the law.

Next, Robert was ready to read the beginning parts of the judge's instructions. These portions of the charge defined the legal terms in each of the first four questions that the judge had decided upon: questions about different ways that the Foundation could either be liable, or not. And then, Robert would proceed to read the four questions, restate them in simple terms, and hammer home the evidence that supported answers of "Yes, the Foundation is liable" to each one. Jury arguments tend to follow a well-established pattern.

"On television," he added, "we often see shows where the judge just asks the jury, '*Who wins?*' But that's not the way it is in real life. Instead, in a trial like this, the judge asks you specific questions about the events in the case. It's like the old saying: '*Just the facts, Ma'am.*' You're asked to answer particular questions about the facts."

And now, Robert held up the judge's charge, ready to concentrate on the jury questions. "The first question the judge asks you is, '*Did the Defendant, The Holy Faith Foundation, aid or encourage the acts that caused the incident in question?*' And all that means, ladies and gentlemen, is, '*Did the Defendant do something that helped the three individuals who sent that incendiary device into Delmar Stadium?*' And respectfully, I beg to tell you, the overwhelming evidence shows that the answer is Yes. There's really no question that the Defendant, the Foundation, financed the entire operation. They did it through a series of handoffs, and they passed it through several hands to get the money there, but that's just because they wanted the money trail to be invisible."

Now, Robert went through all of the evidence that showed it. There was Chipmunk's testimony, and there was the Exhibit that showed that "Bedouin" had ordered the Red Crescent to give the money to Al Likchah in the Arabian Peninsula. There was Professor Edmonds' expert testimony that tied the Foundation, the Red Crescent, and the Al Likchah together. And there was Hamadi's testimony from inside the terrorism conspiracy that directly involved the head of the Foundation.

Next, Robert stepped to the other end of the jury bar, to signify a change of subject. "The next questions the judge asks you are about damages," he said. "There are eight sets of questions, about eight different people. The eight deceased loved ones. All dead, now. Human beings, accomplished and intelligent human beings, some of them high school students, some of them parents. All of them went to a football game, as alive as you and I are now, but suddenly, too soon, they were dead. Burned alive. Reduced to ashes, cinders, and soot."

He asked the jury to award ten million dollars for each one. "The law says that we compensate the survivors," he added. "Not with the lowest coin of the realm; not with reduced or play money, but with real compensation. There may be a temptation to say, 'No amount of money could compensate for this,' and to throw up your hands. But under the law, I can't, and most importantly, the law tells you not to. The law says you should find amounts of damages for each family of survivors that will compensate them, actually compensate them, for their lost loved ones, however difficult that may be."

And unemotionally, Robert sat down, then.

Many plaintiffs are surprised by this kind of argument, he knew. It was a bloodless and restrained speech, in circumstances that begged for tears and shouting. But the plaintiff's lawyer always gets another chance to speak to the jurors, *after* the defendant's argument. The defense is sandwiched in between. The emotional, value-laden argument, the one that speaks to the horror of the defendant's conduct and the overwhelming magnitude of the plaintiffs' loss—that comes last. In the plaintiff's rebuttal argument. Otherwise, the defendant's best arguments would be criticism of the plaintiff's lawyer's emotions. This way, the defendant cannot answer the plaintiff's final, final argument.

And that was why Robert sat down, now, quietly and unemotionally.

* * *

Eight time zones to the east, the man called Bedouin, whose real name was Sharif al Shaikh, sat near the top of the Aspire Tower. The building that looked like a torch, nearly a quarter mile tall, shaped like a cylinder but with a curvy, pinched waist. From here, in the beginning darkness, Bedouin could see the blinking colors of the 4,000-lamp grid that circled the building and was programmed to show different dancing patterns. Beyond that, he could look out at a magnificent view of the downtown area in Doha.

"We have a decision to make," Bedouin said to the men who surrounded him at the conference table. "We are in the middle of that awful trial, in America, as all of you know. We have our lawyer telling us that we could win, or we could lose. If we lose, we will face international harassment from hordes of Americans who will try to collect hundreds of millions of dollars from us. Or, we can offer to pay hundreds of millions. Or we can take drastic action."

The Vice President of the Foundation spoke up. "And, my Bedouin, the drastic action is . . . what?"

"The drastic action is to activate our man Ibrahim." Bedouin's beard and mustache were bulky and black, and now they bent down at the corners of his mouth, showing his distaste for this lawsuit. The anomalous bump in the center of his forehead, which gave him a permanent appearance of anger, reddened and flared now. It made him look even more disturbed, above his too-big nose. As usual, he wore a white burnoose with a gold band and a robe with an arabesque pattern down its middle. He had dozens of different arabesque garments. Today, the pattern was red and black, and it suggested even more anger.

"Well . . . but correct me if I am wrong," said the Vice President hesitantly. "Even a drastic action of this kind. . . . Even from a very competent, loyal follower like Ibrahim . . . will not assure a solution to the problem we face with this lawsuit."

"That is right. The courts in America are farcical, and they presume powers that Allah never gave to judges. They think they have the power to reach all the way to our country and bankrupt our charitable foundation. And the trouble is, they may turn out to have that power. There are no guarantees that taking action through Ibrahim will solve the problem completely."

"I am with you, my Bedouin." The Vice President was somber. "I am sure everyone is with you. It is better to take action, even against an unsure problem, and even if action is not a sure solution. We depend upon Allah, of course; but sometimes, Allah depends on us to depend on ourselves."

* * *

Now that Robert had completed the plaintiffs' opening argument, it was time for the jury to hear from the defense. "Mr. Coleman?" said the judge.

"Ladies and gentlemen, I too thank you for your wonderful service as jurors." Jimmy's voice grated as usual, but when he talked to the jurors, it sounded like coarse honey. "You have sacrificed to be here, and the defendant appreciates it.

"I want to disagree with Mr. Herrick. You know that he is doing everything he's doing, just to try to win for the plaintiffs. And I think he's distorted the law. It's not enough that the defendant, this generous, civic-minded Foundation, somehow 'helped' this terrible incident to happen. It had to be intentional, as the judge tells you. 'The defendant must have acted with intent or knowledge of the consequences to be liable for aiding and encouraging,' says the judge's instruction. Those are the judge's words, not mine."

Now, Jimmy sounded like grating thunder. "Mr. Herrick is trying to pull the wool over your eyes! To distort the law and fool you. He'd like you to think that just because it happened, and just because the Foundation made a grant to the Red Crescent, which is perfectly normal since it's like the Red Cross—even without *knowing* that these three criminals were going to bomb Delmar Stadium, even without that—the Foundation is guilty, he'd like to say. But that's wrong."

Jimmy frowned. "That's ... not ... the law!"

Robert sat in pain while Jimmy went over the verdict questions and answered each of them, his way, using the evidence. The aiding and encouraging question had to be answered No, because there was no proof at all that the Foundation knew or intended what actually happened. "The witnesses just are not credible, about that! This guy Chipmunk is a direct employee of Mr. Herrick. He's paid to testify the way he did. The so-called expert, Mister Edmonds, is the same thing. A hired gun, even if he uses a professor's words for bullets. And then, there's this *criminal* ... this ... Hamadi. He's testifying and lying to save his own contemptible, murdering hide. And he contradicted himself a dozen times, right here in this courtroom, in front of you."

And what about the plaintiffs' claims for damages, Jimmy asked? "Your answer should be zero!" His voice gyrated and shook. "Zero, to each of those questions. The Foundation is not responsible for what happened. The correct number for damages, every time, is zero."

Robert's pain reached its height when Jimmy neared the end of his argument. "Picture yourself. Picture yourself. You're involved in a charitable organization, one that does good works all over the world. Along comes a lawyer like Mr. Herrick. He picks out a tragedy and blames *you* for it. He has no credible evidence, but he claims that at the end of a long line of funding that started with your contribution to the Red Cross, there was a crime that he blames you for. And he wants to take away all that the Red Cross does and get the money for himself. He uses hired mercenaries as witnesses and distorts the law to do it."

Jimmy was practically shouting as he said, "Have you yourself ever given to the Red Cross? Mr. Herrick might just as well say that you're guilty of this act of terrorism. Ladies and gentlemen, no charity can exist in that kind of atmosphere! No citizen can live freely with that kind of injustice waiting to happen."

The jurors watched, spellbound, as Jimmy bowed and sat down, heavily, for the last time.

39

The evening developed into a night as dark as the blackest corner in a cypress swamp at midnight, with no moon and no stars. Where the flares of Orion ought to have been, with its starry belt and nebular sword, there was only black mist, as thick as moss. Driving a stolen car, which was customary for him whenever he needed to avoid leaving a trail, the tall, tall man named Ibrahim drove toward Inwood Drive in River Oaks. He was on a mission.

He slowed as he reached the address. There were a few parked cars on the curbsides, and a block behind him, there were two neighbors in their front yards, talking over a magnificent iron fence. Ibrahim watched them all. No problem.

He had also stolen a panel truck. And filled it with chemical fertilizer soaked in motor oil. A serviceable bomb, made from untraceable supplies, powerful enough to take down a building and kill anyone inside. The driver of the panel truck was an unsuspecting unemployed Guatemalan, chosen because of his need for a little money, as well as a cold calculus that would allow Ibrahim to sacrifice this man for the Faith. For Allah.

Ibrahim knew Robert Herrick's home well. The large curtilage; the heavy Southern columns. The high roof.

The Guatemalan driver steered the panel truck into the driveway. And up to the corner of the house. Ibrahim called the driver and told him, "Now, get out and run. Get out! Run! If you don't run, you will die, because the truck is about to explode."

That way, he gave the Guatemalan a sporting chance. In the rear view mirror, he saw the man get out and move. Would he get far enough away? It was an idle question, a matter of indifference to Ibrahim.

Ibrahim drove on. As he turned the corner, he fingered another cell phone, one that dialed a number imbedded in a trigger mechanism.

Outside the Herrick home and down the block, a private detective watched. As soon as Ibrahim went by, he was suspicious—and before the truck entered the driveway, he had called the patrol officers who drove about nearby. Detectives Slaughter and Cashdollar had told Robert, "We can't dedicate five shifts of officers to provide so-called 'protection,' because that's just in the movies."

But, they said, they could make sure that Robert's own security guard could call a patrol car on speed dial, and that a car would continuously roam nearby.

Now, Ibrahim pushed the button on his cell phone to trigger his bomb. The panel truck erupted in yellow flames and steel automobile parts, flying like shrapnel.

Ibrahim fleetingly wondered whether the Guatemalan driver had escaped. But he didn't have much time to wonder, because there were flashing blue-and-red lights behind him, a siren, and words spoken over a loudspeaker: "Pull over, right now, and get on the ground! With your hands behind your back!"

Taken by surprise, Ibrahim drove into the curb and bounced backward. The patrol officers blocked his stolen car. Ibrahim got out by the passenger's side. Off balance, and trying to run and shoot at the same time, he sprayed automatic fire across the front of the patrol car.

The officers already had their shotgun unlocked. Two immediate bursts caught Ibrahim squarely in the chest.

* * *

The President of the United States was humbled. "We dodged a bullet with that one. I mean, we were lucky that guy Ibrahim wasn't able to pull off another disaster."

The Chief of Staff sat across from him. "Yes, sir. It was good police work, bagging that outlaw."

"And also, no deaths from the latest terrorism exercise by that same Ibrahim."

"We certainly were lucky, Mr. President. This lawyer—this Robert Herrick, the one who's taken the lead in tracing that Delmar Stadium bombing—now, who on earth would have known how prepared he would be, with his house reinforced against this kind of event?"

"That house of his sounds like Fort Knox. That lawyer's had trouble before, where he's been shot at. More than once. No wonder he hardened his home. He wanted himself and his wife and family to be just a little bit safe."

"Right. And the good news is, Mr. President, I don't think we need to transfer anyone to Guantanamo now, or anywhere else. The state authorities have that case well in hand. The District Attorney's office will start trial against that terrorist Mansouri next week. He's eligible for the death penalty and has a good chance of getting it. That guy Hamadi will testify against him. So, that problem looks like it's wrapped up."

"And speaking of Fort Knox, not to change the subject . . . or actually, I do want to change the subject; . . . what's happened to that silly Federal Reserve Board?" The President frowned. "It looks like they're going to tighten the screws on interest rates again. The economy is fragile enough already. What do we do about that?"

"Well, Mr. President," the Chief of Staff grinned, "now you've suddenly transitioned from a problem that we have under control, to a problem that has no solution at all."

* * *

"Take a day off, Robert." Judge Domínguez was sympathetic. Sitting at the huge walnut conference table in her chambers, she added, "I'm grateful to the good Lord that you and yours are all right, but you've got to be . . . well . . . a little bit discombobulated after that truck exploded against your home."

Jimmy Coleman understood it too. "That's right, Robert. Take a day. Or two, if you need it."

"All right," Robert agreed. "You're right. I'm shook. But I don't want us to lose our place. We're in the middle of final jury arguments. We need to get back to it before the jury forgets."

The judge smiled. "Spoken like a lawyer. You're right, but the jury will remember it, whether you take a day or two. Robert, only you know how long you need."

40

Tom sat, once again, across from Robert at his big mahogany desk. "Boss, are you still turned upside down about what happened at your house? Well . . . of course you are."

The sun shone in from a beautiful day. The huge Oriental carpet sparkled, and under the floor-to-ceiling windows, a hundred flowers bloomed. As always, paintings by Mondrian, Wyeth, and Picasso brightened the walls. But Robert looked as despondent as Tom had ever seen him.

"It's two days later," he said. "And I'm still pretty wiggly. I think I'll be shook up about it for the rest of my life. The house can be repaired, and insurance will do it, but my wife isn't sure she wants to live there anymore. And I'm not sure either."

"Of course."

"But what spooks me the most is the situation in our lawsuit. Jimmy Coleman's got us, once again, by the short hairs. What he said in his final argument is probably what the jury believes. Namely, that the plaintiffs, or in other words we, don't have any credible evidence."

"Well, but we have one more shot at a final argument. Thank goodness for our system, where the plaintiff goes first, the defendant goes second, and then the plaintiff gives a rebuttal argument. A true closing argument. Let's get you ready to do a barnburner of a closing argument tomorrow, something that will get the point to the jury."

"All . . . right." Robert stared out the window at the horizon, where the green of Memorial Park, beyond the banks of Buffalo Bayou, melted into the blue sky. "I don't feel up to it, to tell you the truth. But let's do it, so I can go home to my fortified but burned-on-the-outside home."

* * *

"Robert, you think you're ready to give your closing?"

He stood. "Yes, your honor," he answered, with more confidence than he felt.

"Bailiff, bring in the jury."

And everyone stood as the citizens took their places in the jury box. These are the architects of my future, Robert thought. The guardians of the prize my clients hope to win. And they don't look sympathetic.

"Ladies and gentlemen." The judge turned to the jury. "We have had two days of absence from the trial. I had to meet with the lawyers and decided that events outside the courtroom required us to have a short delay. Do not speculate on the reasons for our two days off. Those reasons have nothing to do with our trial. But now we are back at work, and soon, this case will be in your hands. Only one event remains to be done, and that is the plaintiffs' closing argument. Mr. Herrick will address you now."

"Thank you, your honor. Ladies and gentlemen, we are late in the trial, and I will not take an excessively long time, in relation to the importance of these questions. Let me begin by answering just a couple of points made by Mr. Coleman."

Robert shook his head. "Mr. Coleman tells you that there's no evidence. He didn't mention the handwritten note in the records of the Red Crescent, saying that Bedouin, the head of the Foundation, ordered them to send money to a notorious terrorist organization: Al Likchah. And Mr. Coleman tells you that Professor Edmonds wasn't a credible witness. He didn't mention Professor Edmonds's service as a professor at West Point, where the finest anti-terrorism force in the world is educated."

His voice rose. "And Mr. Coleman criticizes me for the witness named Hamadi who was inside the conspiracy ring that included this Foundation. What Mr. Coleman doesn't tell you about that is, I didn't choose Hamadi. Instead, the man named Bedouin, at the top of the Foundation, is the one who chose to deal with Hamadi. *It was Mr. Coleman's client, who chose Hamadi.*"

This part of the argument carried out the conventional strategy: if you rebut your opponent's argument, pick out two points, or three at the most. And choose issues that you can answer in one sentence. Don't let your opponent define your argument. Get in and out quickly.

Robert stepped to the end of the jury rail, to signify a change of subject. "Now," he said firmly, "I want to tell you what this case is really about."

He held in his hand a number of blown-up photographs. "This case is about people who were alive, who are speaking to you now from beyond the grave. It is a kind of Roll Call of the Dead."

He held up the first picture. It showed a young boy, a teenager. "This was Daniel Yarbrough. He played the clarinet. Was a magnificent soccer player, too. On his way to becoming an Eagle Scout." And with that, Robert put the picture on an easel, and held up a second picture. It showed a face and chest blackened into the appearance of coal. "This, too, is Daniel Yarbrough. This is what the conspiracy did, financed by this defendant, this Holy Faith Foundation. Daniel Yarbrough. The first person in our Roll Call of the Dead." The death picture went onto the easel, too.

A murmur sounded from the audience. And from the jurors, too. It was hard to look at. The contrast between death and life was shocking, even though the photographs came from the admitted evidence.

Robert held up another picture. "The Roll Call goes on. This is Sylvia Painter. When she was alive, she was in the National Honor Society. She was a member of the swimming team. She died because she went to a football game with her boyfriend, Daniel Yarbrough." The photograph went onto a second easel. "And this is also Sylvia Painter," Robert said, holding a death mask of black captured in another picture. That likeness also went onto the second easel.

The Roll Call of the Dead went on for nearly an hour. Part of the way through, Robert cautioned the jurors, "Please don't tune out or think this is too long. This is the handiwork of the defendant in this case, the Foundation. Each one of these people is worthy of your most careful consideration. There are many of them, and that is because the acts financed by the Foundation killed a lot of people."

Finally, it ended. "That is the Roll Call of the Dead. Living, breathing people, who only went to a football game. And this Foundation saw fit to have them all killed, at random."

Once again, Robert changed his position to the other end of the jury rail.

"But I don't want you to think that that's all the evidence," he said firmly. "In a conspiracy, like this one, it's hard to get on the inside. But we have. We've got a witness from inside, and hard evidence from inside. First, there are the records that show that the Foundation made a grant to the International Red Crescent. And what was that grant for? The Red Crescent's own books show that the head of the Foundation told them to pass it on, in nearly the same amount, to Al Likchah in the Arabian Peninsula. Why? Because that organization is a well-known fountain of Islamic terror. Bedouin and the Holy Faith Foundation knew they were a bunch of killers. There it is in black and white, in handwriting. I almost said, 'in plain English,' but actually, it's more credible than that, because it's 'in plain Arabic.'"

Robert held up two fingers. "But there's a second insider witness. And that's Professor Andrew Edmonds. Extremely well qualified. With dozens of professional publications, teaching courses at West Point and at the University of Virginia about terrorism. He traced the money path for you.

"And there's one more thing, because Mr. Coleman has told you throughout this trial that the defendant, this Foundation, is a *charity* that does *good works* around the world. Professor Edmonds tells you that the financing of terrorism often involves so-called charities. It's a good way to hide the bad works that this Foundation does. And that's not just Professor Edmonds's opinion; he's quoted the Council on Foreign Relations, which also says so."

And now, he held up three fingers. "Then, there's a third kind of insider proof. You heard from one of the conspirators themselves. Hamadi. How often do you imagine that a trial includes one of the conspirators, who testifies in a court of law like this? Well, Bedouin communicated directly with the on-the-spot actors. He actually talked to Hamadi, praised his actions, and asked for Ibrahim."

The last part of a closing argument is sometimes called "the plea for law enforcement." It is where the plaintiff's lawyer pounds the table, or if he does not literally strike his fist on something, it is where the plaintiff's lawyer uncorks the most emotion.

"You know," Robert said slowly, "you were ordinary citizens before you came to this courtroom, but now, you are the last link in the law. And I wish that the courtroom had glass walls, so that all of the other citizens could look in and see how everything happens. You have a chance to stand up and represent all of them: to represent every citizen out there. Do not let this chance pass you by. Do not let the Foundation say to you, 'Wash my dirty linen for me.' Tell them, No, sir!"

Robert's voice was urgent, now. "I can do my job by trying this case. The judge can do her job. The witnesses can come in here and risk their lives to tell the truth. But it doesn't matter, without you. Jurors. You have a chance to make it right and to do it as representatives of every citizen of this country. And now, I must ask you, on behalf of the dead whose roll I have called, for a verdict saying that the Foundation has done exactly what it is accused of doing. I ask you"—Robert's voice caught, here, and he bent, slightly, in supplication—"I *beg* you . . . for a verdict that compensates the plaintiffs for their full damages. A verdict that speaks to the world about what this Foundation has done."

After a pause, he added, quietly: "Thank you." And there was silence, dead silence, as he sat down.

41

The jury was out deliberating for the entire first day. Then for a second day.

On the third day, the jurors sent out a note containing a question. The bailiff delivered it to the judge, who summoned the lawyers. It took three hours for Jimmy Coleman to arrive, and during that time, Robert and Tom waited. And worried.

Sitting on the bench, looking down at the lawyers, the judge read the jurors' note. *"If we decide to answer 'No' to all of the questions about whether the defendant is guilty, can we skip all the other questions, about the amount of damages?"*

Judge Elsa Domínguez stared at the note. "Well, that's a type of note a plaintiff's lawyer never wants to see. Counsel, do you have thoughts about whether and how I should answer?"

Jimmy Coleman was on his feet. "That's a perfectly acceptable verdict, your honor. If they say 'No,' the Foundation is not liable, and they don't have to answer the other questions, because that's a complete enough verdict."

The judge gave him a skeptical look. "Why does it not surprise me, Mr. Coleman, that you'd say that? . . . But I also need to hear an answer from you, Mr. Herrick."

"Your . . . honor, I . . . disagree with Mr. Coleman." Robert's head was spinning. The note obviously suggested that the jurors were about to return a losing verdict for him. A verdict saying that the Holy Faith Foundation was not guilty. "No," he said. "I think your honor needs to tell the jurors that all of the questions have to be answered."

"I tend to agree. Mr. Coleman, sometimes it happens that a court of appeals, or for that matter even a trial court, decides that the liability questions are so solidly proved that the court has to answer them in the

183

plaintiff's favor, and find the defendant guilty. Even if the jury has decided the opposite. I'm not expressing any opinion on what the answer should be at this time, if that comes up. But it happens in some cases."

Jimmy Coleman had the answer. "Your honor, in that case, you can declare a mistrial on the damages questions."

The judge's eyes bugged out. "But that would mean we'd have to try this entire case over again, if the court decided in the plaintiffs' favor and if we didn't have any damage findings! No, thank you."

"We certainly don't want that, your honor." Robert's disappointment was eating a hole in his stomach.

"I'm going to send back an instruction saying, 'You are instructed to answer all of the questions.'" And with that, the judge stepped down from the bench.

* * *

A few minutes later, out in the hallway, Tom Kennedy was shaking all over. "Is there anything we can do at this point?"

"You know the answer to that." Robert was queasy inside but struggling to keep a calm appearance. "The jury is deliberating. Nothing we can do but wait."

"Well, so now we have the jury answering the damage questions, right after their answers to the liability questions, but the liability answers will throw us clean out of court with a 'not guilty' verdict. But Robert, this idea of yours, about the judge deciding that the defendant's guilty, against the verdict—well, that's virtually impossible in this case. The damage verdicts won't do us any good whatsoever."

"Maybe not. But here are a couple of thoughts. Sometimes the questions that a jury asks aren't really good predictions of what they're going to do. They may not have decided against us, in reality. And sometimes a question like this comes from just one or two jurors. The rest of them may be the majority, and maybe they're trying to persuade a couple of dissenters, and the majority may have agreed to ask this question for those dissenters, just to be nice."

Robert shook his head, not really believing what he was saying, but trying to think it through. "And there's even another possibility," he went on, "which is that when the jury focuses on the damage questions, they might consider the guilty-or-not-guilty questions differently. In other words, thinking about the damages might make them decide that, Yes, the Foundation is liable, after all."

"I . . . suppose."

"It's hard to wait. But that's all we can do."

Two days later, the jury was still out, with no end in sight. Jimmy Coleman couldn't stop smiling, and he had a spring to his step. Judge Domínguez, on the other hand, was as frustrated as Tom and Robert. And these two plaintiff's lawyers were not just frustrated, but also, solidly miserable.

"I'm going to give the jury an *Allen* Instruction," the judge said finally. "Also known as a 'Dynamite Charge.' To push them into deciding this case."

"I've heard of that," Tom whispered to Robert. "But I've never seen it, myself, and I'm not sure I know what it means. Robert, tell me."

"If it looks like the deliberations are heading toward a hung jury," Robert answered quietly, "the judge will sometimes tell the jurors that there's no reason to think another jury can decide the case better than this jury. And so, the judge will say, it's best if this jury makes a decision. The *Allen* Instruction was approved by the Supreme Court in a case where a man named Allen was one of the parties."

His voice was quiet as he went on. "And usually, the judge also tells the jury that no one should surrender a conscientiously held belief, but the minority should listen carefully to the majority and see whether the majority is persuasive, and the majority should listen to the minority. The instruction is also called the 'Dynamite Charge,' because it's intended to 'dynamite loose' a verdict from an indecisive jury."

"Well, I hope it helps our plaintiffs. Somehow."

"It can hurt us if the jurors decide in Jimmy Coleman's favor instead of being a hung jury and not deciding. Which is what I think they might do, after that note they sent out."

42

Two hours after the judge had given the Dynamite Charge, the clerk called. "The jurors say they've reached a verdict."

"Well, Tom, let's go see." Robert tried to look optimistic.

They arrived at the courtroom door just as Jimmy Coleman got there. He was uncharacteristically charming. "Well, gentlemen, good afternoon. You've given this case your best shot."

Everyone stood in the courtroom as Judge Domínguez ascended to the bench, and then, they stood again as the bailiff brought the jury in. It seemed to Robert that it took hours for the jurors to file into their seats.

"Ladies and gentlemen of the jury." The judge sounded upbeat, probably because she expected an end to this difficult case. "I understand that you've reached a verdict."

"Yes, your honor," said the presiding juror.

"Please hand the verdict to the bailiff." And the bailiff wordlessly gave it to the judge.

There was stone silence, next, while Judge Domínguez studied the verdict. Page by page. Looking at every word. To Robert, it seemed that the judge was studying even the edges of the paper. Come on, judge!

Finally, the judge said, "The verdict seems to be in order, and it's signed by the presiding juror. Let me read the questions and answers."

Robert held his breath. The judge paused to find the first question, and again, to Robert, this ordinary step seemed to take hours.

"The first question is, 'Did the Defendant, The Holy Faith Foundation, aid or encourage others to cause the event in question?'

"To which the jury answered . . . "

Robert was silent, but he wanted to scream, Come on, judge! Read it, please.

". . . Yes."

Tom reached over and grabbed Robert's shoulder. "We . . . won! The jury says Yes."

Robert just sat and stared. It dawned on him only gradually. In spite of the disappointing question the jurors had asked, in spite of all of the time he and Tom had spent lamenting the fact that the jury was going to decide against them, the jury had decided . . . in their favor?

Slowly, deliberately, the judge read the other three questions about the Foundation's liability: its guilt or innocence. Did the Foundation engage in a conspiracy? Yes. Did it act in concert with others? Yes. Did the Foundation ratify the acts, or in other words, approve it during or after the fact? Yes.

Half of the courtroom emptied. News reporters were rushing to get the result of the trial into the papers and on the air. But some of the news reporters stayed, because they realized that these verdict answers were only part of the story.

"Next," said the judge. "The fifth question asks, 'What sum of money, if paid now in cash, do you find as damages for the wrongful death of Daniel Yarbrough?' To which the jury answered . . . 'Five million dollars.'"

Elsa Domínguez looked up. And she said, slowly: "Wow."

* * *

"These few plaintiffs may think they've come out better by trying the case," said Tom, as they left the courtroom. "The damages add up to more than what Jimmy would have settled the case for. They could have avoided the risk and received less, but still significant amounts. But now, will they ever get what they've won?"

Robert laughed in spite of himself. "I guess you're right. The jury did what juries so often do. They took the numbers we gave them in final argument and cut them in half. They gave us half the damages we asked for."

He thought for a moment. "Well, I bet the plaintiff families think they're better off after the trial. If they had settled, they'd have had to sign a release saying that the Foundation denied that it was guilty of anything. And the plaintiffs would have had to acknowledge that this was the Foundation's position. As it is, the plaintiffs now have a finding of guilt. Fault. Liability. A finding by a jury."

"Well, yes, I guess so. . . ."

"But the trouble is, now, we'll have Jimmy filing motions to overturn the verdict. A Motion for Judgment as a Matter of Law, asking the judge to give judgment to the defendant in spite of the verdict. A Motion for New Trial, and Jimmy will plaster that motion with claims about all kinds of trial errors. And then, Jimmy will appeal. And after that's over, if we're still winning, he'll file a petition to the United States Supreme Court."

"It's going to be years before anything happens, is what you're saying. And that's right."

"And I'll tell you what else will happen. The Holy Faith Foundation doesn't have any assets in the United States. Nothing that can be used to satisfy a judgment. You realize, Tom, what that means? We may have to go back to the courts in Qatar to enforce this judgment, assuming it makes it through all the motions and appeals. The State Department will get involved and try to make things work out diplomatically between the United States and Qatar. And that will take forever, and it will mean that the State Department will try to reduce the amount we'll get."

"The plaintiffs who went to trial probably didn't factor all of this into their decisions."

"No," said Robert ruefully. "Usually, the plaintiffs think the defendant will have to write a check to them right after the jury has a verdict."

He thought for a minute. "You know, Tom, I talked the other day to one of the plaintiffs who settled. He explained to me why he didn't want a trial. He said, 'I miss my brother, and I'm glad I was part of the lawsuit against that Foundation in Qatar. But I can't bring my brother back, and I don't want this trial. My life is good now. I don't want to give more depositions and remember my case number and receive updates and technical advice about skirmishes that don't have anything to do with my brother, just courtroom battles. I'm at peace. And I feel, down deep, that my brother is at peace too. He and I are both moving on.'"

* * *

Shortly after the verdict was reported, Donna DeCarlo buzzed Robert in his office. "It's someone named Woody. He says you know him from law school."

"Woody? Oh, it's Elwood R. Musgrove again." He picked up the receiver. "Hello, Woody. How's my friend who's at the bottom of the class and always proud to brag about it?"

"Great! And you're great too, Robert. Congratulations, of course. Now, listen, and put your generous hat on. What do you think is a fair referral fee to pay to me? I'm the one who talked you into this case, at Andy's funeral. Remember?"

"Ahhh ... what? Woody. A referral fee? ... It's a non-starter, Woody. Number one, you didn't refer the case to me. The Governor of Texas did. And second, to get paid a referral fee, you have to stay in the case and work on it. But you didn't. It would be illegal to pay you a referral fee."

"So, then, the usual referral fee would be one third of your fee. But don't pay me that. Just pay a fee of whatever you think it's worth. It would be appreciated by the bottom of the class, from the bottom of my heart."

"Woody, . . . I can't. It would be unethical, because you weren't involved in working on the case, even if you somehow had referred the case. Which you didn't."

"Oh, well, it was worth a try." Elwood R. Musgrove was cheerful, as always.

"Woody, you haven't changed much. I can't help liking you. But sometimes, you blur the lines."

Woody just laughed at that. "You know me too well, I guess."

* * *

"The trial for Mansouri—you know, the second terrorist—has been reset again." Maria Melendes looked disgusted. "Something about how his lawyers need even more time to prepare, after all these years. But he'll be tried, sooner or later."

Robert nodded. "And it's a strong case."

"Especially with testimony from the third terrorist, Hamadi. Juries don't like deals with witnesses, of course, but it's pretty clear that Hamadi is the least responsible of those three criminals, and the biggest one, al Ibrahim, is dead."

"Hamadi is an oddball witness. He can't tell a coherent story. He's just got to contradict himself. We've all had witnesses like that. And I think the jurors in my case believed Hamadi and sort of liked him. The prosecutor who tries Mansouri will have to tell the jurors in his opening statement, 'Jurors, just listen, because Hamadi is credible about the major points.' And then, when Hamadi testifies, the prosecutor will have to wink at the jury every time he deviates, as if saying, 'There he goes, again.'"

"Did you ever find out what the jurors in your case had in mind, when they sent out that question? The question asking, if we decide that the Foundation isn't guilty at all, do we need to answer the damage questions?"

Robert shook his head and laughed. "As best I can tell, there was one juror who wanted to ask that question. Nobody else knows why. But he refused to deliberate until the question got asked. The rest of the jurors finally agreed to ask it, if he would start deliberating with them again. It was just one juror, being nuts, and driving us batty as a result. It happens."

"Definitely, it happens." Maria smiled. "And now, Robert . . . I have one piece of information that you'll like."

"What's that?"

"The Justice Department is finally moving on this case. They're going to seek the extradition of—get this—the man named Sharif al Shaikh."

"Sharif . . . al . . . who? Who's that?"

"He's also known as Bedouin."

". . . Well, . . . I'll be. They're going to ask to extradite . . . Bedouin? The head of the Foundation?" Robert was beginning to get a warm, satisfied feeling.

"There's even a chance, I understand, of the Qataris agreeing to it," Maria said. "The publicity has been very bad for that Holy Faith Foundation. And this guy Bedouin, the whole country knows he's a criminal now. The Qatari Minister of Justice has made a statement in a speech—a vague statement, but still, a statement—about respecting the laws of other countries. Bedouin may find that he's out on a limb that doesn't have the support he's been used to."

"You know what, Maria?" Robert smiled. "I feel good about this case, even though we've got a long fight ahead, with Jimmy Coleman filing motions and appeals. But most of my clients have already received solid compensation because they settled, and I've certainly made enough money myself, in my life. The plaintiffs who went to trial have a verdict condemning the Foundation, which they wanted above all, and now they may get Bedouin into a jail cell. And after a few years, they may get their money too. More than the settling plaintiffs. It's certainly true that I've made enough money. More than enough money. In the second half of my career, maybe I can concentrate more on getting justice done."

"Well, yes. You can. And that's certainly what your wife—that's me—has struggled to do all along in the District Attorney's office. To make some justice happen."

She laughed. "Remember the movie *Casablanca*? At the end, Paul Henried says to Humphrey Bogart, 'Welcome back to the fight. This time I know our side will win.' Robert, with you on the team, the side called Justice will win, maybe."

" . . . Mayyy-be." And Robert laughed too.

Postscript

I wanted to keep this story real, even when the legal happenings were complicated. Not because I needed to struggle to get the lawyering right, but because it's difficult to get all the technical details correct while telling a page-turning story at the same time.

In a novel, the action should create more excitement than real life does. It's supposed to involve the reader. But real cases have a lot of boring jobs and monotonous moments that require lawyers to fight their way through them. That won't do, in a novel. Still, I wanted this novel to be a realistic description of what happens in big lawsuits. And I think it is.

The story follows some of my own experiences. The difficulties created by the Rules of Evidence have plunged me into inconsistencies and circular reasoning like the ones shown here. The Rules are supposed to bring out the truth, but too often, they do the opposite. The way that an expert witness is questioned in a trial is shown here with typical strategies. The methods shown here of taking depositions, doing cross-examinations, picking juries, and giving final arguments, all are consistent with the ways in which experienced lawyers might perform these tasks. The problems that Robert and Tom have in preparing the Complaint to begin the lawsuit are very real—it's more difficult than it should be—and the Supreme Court decisions that they cite are the real ones.

But there are some instances in which the conventions of storytelling have pushed me to vary from what I think would really happen. This Postscript is included so that I can describe how truth and fiction are different in this story, and how they are the same.

* * *

First of all, is the case itself realistic? Could an act of terrorism produce a lawsuit that would result in a judgment against someone in another country? The answer is yes. Last year, on September 22, a federal jury in Brooklyn found the biggest lender in Jordan, The Arab Bank Plc, liable for damages for financing two dozen deadly suicide bombings carried out by Hamas, a listed terrorist entity. The attacks took place in crowded restaurants and buses in Tel Aviv and Jerusalem. The damages are undetermined, as yet; they will be decided in a separate trial. A defense lawyer promised an appeal because, he said, the judge's instructions to the jury were erroneous, and there were mistakes in the evidence rulings. "The Second Circuit [Court of Appeals] is going to reverse this," he predicted. He sounded just the way Jimmy Coleman might have.

One interesting aspect of the Arab Bank case was that the plaintiffs only received limited responses from the Arab Bank to their requests for discovery. That is what happened in the story in this novel, too. The judge in the Arab Bank case gave what is called a "spoliation instruction" to the jurors, telling them that they could infer that the Bank financed terrorists from the failure to answer completely, so that the plaintiffs started that case with an advantage. This kind of instruction could have been given in the case against The Holy Faith Foundation in my story, but I didn't put that into this novel, because I thought the plot was complicated enough.

More recently, an American jury rendered a whopping verdict against the Palestinian Authority. The damages were fixed at $218.5 million, which under applicable laws, would be trebled to make a $655.5 judgment. The lawsuit was based on the financing of terror, just as the lawsuit was in my novel. "Money is the oxygen of terrorism," said one of the plaintiff's lawyers. The size of the award, it was predicted, might be more than the Palestinian Organization could pay.

But those were governmental and commercial organizations. Jimmy Coleman repeatedly pointed out that The Holy Faith Foundation, instead, was a charity that did good works all over the world. Would a charity be involved in terrorism? Well . . . , yes, unfortunately. The Council on Foreign Relations says so in its report, which is quoted in this story. Robert O. Collins, author of the book *Alms for Jihad*, writes that "In the Islamic world, there are tens of thousands of charities," and although only a few sponsor terrorism, "these are some of the wealthiest charities."

Would a financier of terrorism ever settle a lawsuit against it? Yes. In 2005, the Arab Bank agreed to pay a $24 million penalty to regulators in the United States, although it expressly denied any wrongdoing. A former executive of the Bank testified that the penalty was "a great disappointment" and said that the Bank had paid it "in order to get the matter behind us." Defendants often take that approach, just as Jimmy Coleman's client did in this novel.

Would victims of terrorism and their relatives settle a bloody case like this? Again, yes. Some are like the plaintiffs who went to trial in this story.

They value the fight and the verdict. But some would settle, and they may be like the plaintiff Robert quotes, here, to explain why he settled. Consider the trial of Dzhokhar Tsarnaev, one of the Boston Marathon bombers. Some bombing survivors planned to attend. But others said they had no desire to. One survivor, who suffered burns and shrapnel wounds, told the Associated Press, "It's not something I feel I need to do[, attending the trial]. I have closure in my life. I'm happy. I have a second chance at life, and I'm living it." This attitude would depend, of course, on the victim, the case, and the survivor.

* * *

Most of the pretrial and trial events depicted here are realistic, I think. The writing of a Complaint has become complicated after the Supreme Court's decision in a case called *Twombly*. The Supreme Court said that the Complaint has to contain actual "facts" sufficient to show that the claim is plausible. But sometimes the facts aren't completely known because they're known only to the defendant, and yet, those facts are needed for a "plausible" Complaint. The Supreme Court didn't provide an answer to that problem, except to say that it knew it was making some claims impossible. In my story, Robert and Tom discuss the Supreme Court cases, and as one would expect in a money laundering lawsuit, they have real trouble writing the Complaint even though they've got a proper claim. Their way around it, relying on a lesser-known provision in the Federal Rules of Civil Procedure, is also realistic. It might succeed, depending on the judge, but I can't say with certainty whether it would or not.

The depositions that are taken in this story are as true to life as I think fiction can be. So are the arguments and strategies about evidence rules, particularly the hearsay rule. The claim of responsibility by Al Likchah was hearsay when taken by itself, and it was excludable by the hearsay rule if directly offered. The result in this story, then, sounds like double-speak, but it's not. The expert witness was permitted to consider the hearsay document in forming his opinion. This result follows under Rules of Evidence 702 and 703. The expert can then describe a conspiracy linking Al Likchah to the defendant. And that—the conspiracy—means that the claim of responsibility becomes admissible under Rule 801, because magically, now it's not hearsay. The law is convoluted, sometimes.

The autopsies are described accurately, I think. Every murder case I handled as an assistant district attorney involved an autopsy report, and I handled a bunch of them. The medical examiner, who would be called a "coroner" in some places, is based on my friend, the late Dr. Joe Jachimczyk, the medical examiner that I worked with. Just as the fictional pathologist in this story was known as Dr. Bill, he was Dr. Joe. He had unorthodox dress (not quite as bright as the doctor in this story) and an always-cheerful demeanor. He also had an M.D. degree, and a J.D. degree, and a position in his church as a deacon, in addition to plenty of expertise.

There are some features of the case that are shortened. The judge, in my jurisdiction, would almost certainly have required the parties to spend a day with a mediator, trying to settle the case completely. This process is fascinating in itself: how mediators try to push, persuade, and sometimes harass parties into settling. I've described it in another novel. Also, the plaintiffs would undoubtedly have presented an accountant as a witness to trace the money trail. I've included that feature in another novel. But life is too short to shoehorn absolutely everything into a story.

The controversy about the court's instructions to the jury is realistic. (Consider what's in another paragraph, above, in which the defense lawyer predicted appellate reversal because of allegedly erroneous instructions.) The arguments about the instructions and questions are realistic, but the questions themselves, the ones that the judge issues here, are simplified a little. There would be multiple questions about damages for each lost loved one, and I've simplified them into one each. The lawsuit takes years in this story, and that's realistic too, unfortunately. Plaintiffs who are genuinely injured often are taken by surprise when their attorney warns them that "This case may resolve promptly, or it may take five years." The wheels of justice grind slowly.

The "boiler-room operation" that Robert's associates and legal assistants set up is a realistic solution to a serious problem for plaintiff's lawyers. The ethical rules, in my state, disallow aggregate settlements of the claims of large groups of individual clients. Instead, the lawyer owes a separate duty to each client, to handle the issue of settlement-or-not as if that client were the *only* client. The trouble is, you can't settle a case with a hundred plaintiffs that way, most of the time. The defendant is trying to buy peace, and an end to litigation, and that can't be done with the plaintiffs going in all different directions. The defendant needs the whole case settled. Otherwise, a settlement doesn't help as much.

But the ethical rules make it difficult for the plaintiff's lawyer to achieve complete participation by a hundred plaintiffs in a settlement. The boiler room operation described in this story is one way to get it done, although it's likely not to work. There will always be holdout plaintiffs who won't settle, as is their right. The question then becomes, are the settling plaintiffs a big enough percentage of the total so that it's worth it to the defendant to settle? Incidentally, the boiler room operation is necessary even if the settlement doesn't work, because the plaintiff's lawyer has a duty to pass on every settlement offer and explain it reasonably to the client. The ethical rules that Tom quotes in this story are the reasons.

There is one aspect of this story that I think is sharply inconsistent with reality, and that is the depiction of the big-firm defense lawyer as unusually sleazy. In my experience, big-firm lawyers are not more unethical or discourteous than smaller-firm lawyers. If anything, my experience is the opposite; the sleaziest lawyers are solos or in small firms. Jimmy Coleman is a caricature—he's a grandiose version of some lawyers I've known, but not particularly in big firms.

Maybe large organizations automatically create pressures on big-firm lawyers to maintain minimum standards about everything, including morals. These lawyers are generally chosen because they are the best performers in law school, and so they have the abilities to become very good lawyers. And they tend to do well against their adversaries, and maybe the fact that they frequently beat other lawyers in lawsuits gives rise to an erroneous perception that they must be doing something underhanded.

* * *

The terrorism scenario that I describe in the first chapter is frighteningly real, and it could happen—possibly. Let me add that I have no desire to write a manual or give any encouragement to terrorists. I once was a lawyer in a case where a hired murderer read a book about how to commit a murder, and then he went out and committed a real murder with the techniques he had read about. I want this story to be realistic, but I don't want it to plant ideas in impressionable people, and I've set it up so that they'd be ill advised to try the method that I've invented here.

First of all, butadiene probably would not be the best incendiary. It would burn when exposed to air, particularly with a spark, because it has a chemical composition that invites combustion. A butadiene molecule has two carbon double bonds, which make it more susceptible to explosion when combined with oxygen. Every stable carbon atom forms four bonds with other atoms. In butadiene, besides the carbon atoms (four of them) there are hydrogen atoms (six of them). And so a crude diagram of the butadiene atom might look like this:

$$H_2C=CH-CH=CH_2$$

The double bonds, signified by the = sign, are tight, and the resulting ions will bond with oxygen explosively. But there are better incendiaries, and I chose this one precisely because although it could explode, it probably wouldn't work very well. Also, the use of a weather balloon as a delivery device would be complicated. But even bumbling terrorists are dangerous, and they don't need encouragement.

Otherwise, the scenario is real. I wrote to Dick Hudak, the president of Resort Security International, who has been in the security business for decades. As a former FBI agent, he had access to contingency planning for large events and worked counter-terrorism cases. "Dick . . . ," I asked, "please read this and tell me whether the scenario is possible." Dick studied the chapter and graciously pronounced it both "plausible" and "scary." He figured (and I agree) that terrorists wouldn't target a high school football game—they'd go for an NFL game instead, maybe—and they'd probably use a different delivery mechanism, but the story is possible. And yes, the likelihood of terrorists targeting so-called soft targets like malls, schools, or stadiums is frightening. Who knows? Maybe they'd go to a simpler place like a high school stadium and use an unorthodox delivery system, because they'd face less security. Our civilization just has got to solve this problem.

The explosive used to bomb Robert's home is familiar to a wide spectrum of people, unfortunately. Still, I've made the description vague here.

* * *

I think the nation of Qatar is accurately described in this story, although the obvious must be emphasized. It's not based on any Qatari Foundation that has ever committed or financed terrorist acts like the one in this story.

But Qatar is a conundrum. It's difficult to understand. It loves Americans and it hates them. There is a huge American presence in the country, because the biggest United States airbase in the middle east is there and Americans figure prominently in the oil and gas production that furnishes the nation's wealth. Numerous hotels, expensive retailers, and other businesses in the capital city of Doha are American or European. Qatar is indeed one of the wealthiest countries in the world on a per-capita basis. But the Qataris, including their government, have embraced terrorist organizations. And so this story depicts a kind of terrorism funding that *could* happen, but again, the Foundation in this story is not based on anything that in real life.

The description of the Qatari courts is based on research. These courts are organized generally as depicted in this story. There is a Minister of Justice, but the possibility of an influential Qatari citizen influencing the Minister is imaginary here.

The method of questioning people in foreign countries and obtaining documents from overseas is a procedure called "letters rogatory," as is depicted in this story. Letters rogatory are simple, in a way; they're just requests issued by American courts, directed to foreign courts, asking those foreign courts to allow questioning of persons in those faraway countries. But the discovery process in most countries is not as extensive as it is in America, and of course, another sovereign country is not bound to allow what is requested. I can't say that proceedings in a Qatari court would be exactly as I've imagined them here, but the result is realistic, according to my experience. With letters rogatory, you may—or may not—get some of what you've asked for.

It should be added that usually the plaintiffs can simply "notice" a defendant for deposition and expect the defendant to appear, even if the defendant is a foreigner. But that's limited to the defendant, and Bedouin, for example, was not a "defendant." He was only an employee of the defendant. There is a way to "question a corporation" (or foundation) in a deposition, and that might have made Robert and Tom's lives easier. But there's no guarantee of getting the right corporate employees to answer. The lawyers might well have been left to the letters rogatory method anyway.

* * *

The criminal process that I've described on the state level is, I think, realistic. The indictment would be like the one described in the book. Plea bargaining is always a tricky business when done with an inside defendant, who it is hoped will testify against other co-conspirators (and do it accurately). The trouble is, a prosecutor can't know everything that went on in the conspiracy, and there is always the danger of accidentally making a deal with one of the leaders to testify against one of the foot-soldiers. Figuratively, an assistant district attorney struggles to avoid agreeing with the mastermind to testify against a messenger for a lesser sentence. But it's hard to be sure, when everyone has a motive to point the finger at all of the others.

One thing that I think is not realistic is the attitude shown here of the Federal Government toward the criminal process. It's possible that this set of events could occur, but I think it's unlikely that they Feds would be this lackadaisical. They would have jurisdiction to prosecute because of the defendant's use of a weapon of mass destruction in interstate commerce, as well as other reasons, and it is to be hoped that these terrorists would be housed in Supermax—the Government's secure prison in Colorado—or even better, at Guantanamo, rather than a relatively insecure local jail.

Incidentally, I remember a successful escape by a prisoner using exactly the simple method that Ibrahim used in this story.

A few readers have asked me, wouldn't the CIA have been watching, monitoring, and scrutinizing a suspect like Ibrahim, already? And wouldn't investigators have found out what was going on in time to stop it? Unfortunately, the answer is, maybe not. It takes a huge expenditure of manpower to monitor a terrorism suspect: a team of a half-dozen people or more, day after day. There are thousands of individuals out there like Ibrahim, whom we'd like to watch, but it's impossible. And in a free society, nothing can be done but watching until the suspect breaks the law. Recent terrorism events in France, including the so-called "Charlie Hebdo" incident, raised the same questions, because the evildoers in those cases were well known to authorities but were not the subjects of monitoring. It cannot be done, unless we hire hundreds of thousands of watchers.

* * *

Islam is one of the world's great religions. I have no intention of criticizing Islam or its adherents in this novel. As is so often said, most Muslim people live normal lives and are peaceful. Arabic scholars have contributed enormously to our civilization in ways that are exemplified by Arabic numerals, without which we might still be using Roman numerals that make computation impossible, as well as algebra, which sounds like a word from Arabic, because it is. The mathematician al-Kwarizmi wrote a landmark book about "al-jabr."

On the other hand, there is such a thing as Islamic terrorism, contrary to what one particular President of the United States has seemed to think, and consistently with what a majority of Americans would say. Many people would qualify that statement, possibly correctly, by saying that these terrorists are not really Islamic, or that they have "hijacked" the religion, but unfortunately, most terrorists these days claim to be acting in the name of Islam. And many of them certainly are religious terrorists, wanting to wipe out "unbelievers" or "infidels." Unfortunately, they can easily find verses in the Quran to support their acts of violence, just as other Muslims can find verses to condemn those acts, and just as you can find violent and non-violent passages in the Bible.

Midway through this story, I imagine two public messages, one being a claim of responsibility by a financier of a terrorist act, and the other being a condemnation of that act by an Islamic Society in America. The condemnation follows the style of an actual message on a web site posted by Islamic scholars in Houston, eloquently condemning terrorism that took place in France. Both messages quote the Quran. Unfortunately, the terrorists can quote the Quran in support of the idea that infidels deserve death, or are "the people of the fire," and at the same time, other Islamists, from the more peaceful majority, can quote the Quran in support of the protection of life, the duty of helping other people, and the freedom of religion.

* * *

Some readers of this and other books have asked me about my depiction of Robert Herrick as scared—not just nervous, but scared—every time he tries a case. He's a professional, they say, and he seems good at his job; and so wouldn't he be calm and controlled when he started a trial? The answer is, some of the best trial lawyers have to suppress their nervousness, right before trial.

The problem lies in the prevalence of the unexpected, these days. There are too many "gotcha" rules. We as Americans believe in expeditious justice, but we also believe in processes that guarantee against miscarriages of justice, and you really can't have it both ways. Thanks to committees that include law professors, no one can be sure of knowing all of the rules that will govern the trial they start. For example, disclosure rules sometimes require pretrial notice to the other side of matters that you would never expect to be subject to requirements of disclosure. And then, a mistake can lead to the exclusion of an essential piece of evidence, or to a spoliation instruction, telling the jurors to infer that the client is at fault.

This kind of uncertainty is added to the fact that a jury of strangers will decide the outcome, and these strangers are not learned in the law. If you've seen television programs showing interview subjects as examples of how uneducated Americans are, remember: these people are eligible to become jurors. Then too, what's at stake is the client's money, or freedom, or safety. The lawyer has someone else's fate to protect. Finally, it's largely a no-holds-barred contest. There are rules, but if the opponent produces witnesses that you know are liars and the jury believes them, you lose. It isn't the same picture that is usually faced by a doctor, for whom catastrophic results are uncommon, or an architect, who usually does not see the building collapse.

And so, many of the best trial lawyers are scared. Scared of doing something dumb, or being surprised, or having overlooked a picky but crucial rule. They proceed to perform in a professional manner, but they do it not because they are unfazed by what they face, but instead because they confront their fears.

Just ask a trial lawyer!

Visit us at *www.qpbooks.com.*

CPSIA information can be obtained at www.ICGtesting.com
Printed in the USA
LVOW12s0226020715

444704LV00015B/139/P

9 781610 273039